The
Sweetest Taboo

One World · Ballantine Books · *New York*

Risqué

The Sweetest Taboo

a n o v e l

A One World Books Trade Paperback Original

Copyright © 2007 by Risqué

Published in the United States by One World Books,
an imprint of The Random House Publishing Group, a division of
Random House, Inc., New York.

ONE WORLD is a registered trademark and the One World
colophon is a trademark of Random House, Inc.

Library of Congress Cataloging-in-Publication Data
Risqué.
The sweetest taboo : a novel / Risqué.
p. cm.
ISBN: 978-0-345-49628-7 (pbk.)
1. African Americans—Fiction. I. Title.
PS3618.I736S94 2007
813'.6—dc22
2007028711

Printed in the United States of America

www.oneworldbooks.net

2 4 6 8 9 7 5 3

Text design by Laurie Jewell

Dedicated:

To my surprise who turned out to be a baby boy!

Zion, Mommy loves you!

And

To my mom and dad for being my number one fans!

Every day is Christmas
And every night is New Year's Eve . . .

— S A D E

The
Sweetest Taboo

Yuri

Sade's *Love Deluxe* played smoothly in the background as Yuri pressed the rim of her champagne-filled flute to her "Oh Baby" MAC-covered lips, leaving the imprint of a kiss behind. Caught in a daydream, she stroked the left side of her shoulder-length hair and toyed with the idea of making love to Britt. Hit it and quit it. Fulfill her big-dick-Rastafarian fantasy, then return to her fictitious role of the Christian Stepford wife. After all, she knew jonesin' for Britt's dick was on the losing end of the game.

Nevertheless, she still let Britt flirt and feel her ass in Port of Spain as they sang and winded onstage. She'd sung a soca duet with him, though she really didn't want to since she was American, but he convinced her that it was okay. Britt said that once people took in her thick thighs, voluptuous ass and the way heaven rang from her throat, they would be too caught up in the music to wonder which part of the world she was from. And she believed him, so she flew to Trinidad, got onstage, let her voice flow and the crowd went wild, confirming for her that no one would ever believe she was a Brooklyn-born "Yankee gurl" with a high-school diploma and a Medical Records degree.

"I told you not to take yo' fat ass, didn't I?" Jeff spat. "I don't know what the fuck is yo' problem, Yuri!" For a brief moment she'd forgotten her husband was on speakerphone singing his nightly praises into the intercom. "You just a fat fuckin' pain in the ass sometimes. I swear, what the hell are you really doing there? Huh? It ain't like you can sing that great, Yuri! If you wanna sing so bad, why don't you join the church choir instead of gyratin' yourself on some stage! Do something positive for once. I really don't understand how I survived tolerating you this long!"

Yuri could hear Jeff's son in the background. "Daddy," Jeff Jr. said, "can we call my mommy?"

"Wait one minute," Jeff responded in a much kinder tone. "I need to deal with your stepmother first." He turned his attention back to the phone. "Actually, we gon' skip all this ra-ra and you just gon' bring yo' fat fuckin' ass home. You hear me, Yuri?!"

"Uhmmm hmmm." She stood on the balcony, watching the fete down below.

"Well, then good, now what you gon' do?"

"I'ma take my fat ass downstairs and go handle some business." And she hung up. When the phone rang two seconds later, she didn't answer; instead she took off her tricolored gold wedding band and left it spinning on the hotel's nightstand, next to the complimentary Bible and the free notepad.

From the moment Yuri stepped onto the lanai the party was jumping. Flags were flying, music was blasting, drinks were floating and people were everywhere. Without hesitation Yuri began to dance. She could bet her last dollar that Jeff had called her back at least ten times to give her the same sappy-ass apology, which usually followed his tirades and consisted of "I love you" and "I miss you." All of which she'd grown tired of hearing around the same time she got sick of faking orgasms.

Unable to stop staring as Yuri danced, Britt sipped his beer and leaned against the bar. Two rows of neon lights, which hung over his shoulders, illuminated the perfect shape of her apple ass.

Yuri danced, spun around and then spotted Britt. Despite her best efforts, a wide smile spread across her face. Everything about Britt raised perfection to another level. His long and beautiful dreads, which usually hung midway down his back, were now wrapped in a sexy bun and covered with a traditional red-yellow-and-green Rastafarian mesh head wrap. The veins on the sides of his thick chocolate neck ran into his broad shoulders, leading directly to his well-defined six-pack, which Yuri could see the details of clearly through his knit wife-beater.

Britt stared at Yuri for as long as he could stand. He prayed that his hard dick would stay calm until just the right moment. Then the DJ played a live recording of the duet they'd sung earlier. And that's when it clicked. That was the moment.

Britt walked over to Yuri with a cold beer in one hand, and placed the other around her waist. "You know, I've been watching you," he whispered in her ear.

"I noticed that." She laughed, nervously running her fingers through the silky curls that framed her face. Her skin was the color of light and sweet coffee, her eyes were brown sugar, and her dimples sparkled like diamonds when she smiled. She bore a striking resemblance to Chilli from the group TLC, taking after her Native American father; however, her attitude, culture and brick-house hips came from her voluptuous black mother.

As Britt's cool breath hit against the side of her face, her erotic pearl swelled and her pussy ached. "Every time I turned to look at something," Yuri said as her stomach flipped into knots, "you were in my way."

"I was trying to be in your way," he said rubbing his cold beer against her right cheek. Drops of water ran down the side of her neck, finding refuge between her breasts.

Yuri bit hard on her bottom lip. She hadn't been this nervous since she accepted her husband's marriage proposal. Unsure if Britt was drunk or not, she took a deep breath and stuttered, "A-A-Are-you oh-kay?"

"I warned him . . ." Britt sang in a low tone in her ear, "not to sleep at night, 'cause a dirty ole Rasta like me . . . would take his wife. . . ."

"You've drunk a little too much," she laughed.

"I can handle my liquor," he said as he placed a series of soft bites down the side of her neck. "Now I need to know how to handle you. Would you be better on top or the bottom?"

"Depends," Yuri said nervously as she caressed the sides of

his face, leading him to kiss the palms of her hands, "on how you wanna start."

Licking between her fingers he said, "I'll start with my mouth." He rubbed the crease of her vagina through her flowing sundress.

Yuri closed her eyes and Britt ran his free hand across her hard nipples and then squeezed one between his thumb and index finger. "I don't know, Britt. . . ." She hesitated. "I wonder if we would be doing the right thing."

He pressed his hands on both sides of her ass, the sweat from the beer bottle soaking through her dress. "I don't wanna wonder, I wanna fuck and find out. I'm feeling the hell outta you, and I know you're married, but for real—no lie—I don't give a fuck. I considered caring once, but soon decided that was your husband's problem."

"How we gon' face each other in the morning?"

"Depends on how we lay down."

"I don't wanna lose our friendship."

"We're adding to it." Britt held Yuri around the waist and they rocked slowly from side to side. She could feel his hard dick pressed against her.

"You said that before and you left me. Besides, it's different now. Jeff and I are *married* this time."

"I know you're married, I was at the ceremony." He held her ring finger and kissed the imprint her wedding band had left behind. "And stop worrying about me leaving; just understand that I'm here now."

She placed her head against his chest, "How we gon' do this?"

"Quietly," he assured her. "Just come with me. Skip the hotel, let me take you in the Trace and make love to you under a Julie mango tree. Let the high grass blow in the night's wind while I lick your pussy dry. So, tell me, you comin' with me?"

"Yes . . . but just this once."

"Just once?" he whispered. "You gon' cum more than once."

Drae

Here's the fantasy: You got da bomb pussy. Here's the reality: There're a million bitches capable of takin' yo' man. So either you gon' bring it or be left at home wishing you had. And regret is not what Drae married Hassan for. She was in it to win it and she knew there could be no sexual limits or inhibitions if she didn't want another broad stealing her husband; especially since he was all she had.

She was a Brooklyn-born-Red-Hook-raised-around-da-way chick who didn't have shit when they first met except an inherited section-eight apartment, a few college credits, a headstone-marked MAMA and a pair of mashed bamboo earrings with *Tender* in one ear and *Roni* in the other.

Hassan had taken Drae from the piss-filled hallways of the gutter-most to the cathedral ceilings of the utmost, and there was no way she was gon' let some hungry bitch take the food out her mouth. They'd have to get up early in the morning to rock with Drae, because as far as she was concerned, in her pussy was where Hassan Shaw was gon' stay. Fuck all the shit that lay in between. It didn't matter that she was straight and didn't really wanna do this bitch spread out in her bed. What mattered was what Hassan had asked her to do. Besides she wasn't trying to beef, she was trying to eat. And seeing that producing and directing pornos is how her man got down, she knew she had to do what she had to do, and not let something like being the object of one of his auditions get in the way.

Drae could look at the bitch sprawled across the bed with diamonds draped around her neck and an open fox fur wrapped around her, revealing her naked body and giving sneak peeks of her clean-shaven pussy, and tell that she thought she was handling it. Lee-Lee Lickme was her name and, according to Hassan, she had the hottest pussy since before Apollonia was old and Vanity became Christian.

Even Drae had to admit that this chick was a bad bitch, with the prettiest titties she'd ever seen, the type that men always wanted to kiss and women went to plastic surgeons to get. She was the color of cognac and her eyes were black and hollow like a stray cat's.

Drae stood in the bedroom's double doorway with her left index finger suggestively in her mouth. She was dressed in a gold Frederick's of Hollywood leather, crotchless, one-piece corset and matching satin stilettos. Her nude thigh-highs, which were connected to her corset by suspenders, felt hot against her skin as she wondered what wet pussy would taste like. Would it be sweet like Hassan always said, or salty and sticky like it was when she tasted her own?

As she walked in she looked around their Westchester bedroom, catching glimpses of their imported Italian furniture, cherrywood floors, Waterford crystal chandelier, open French doors, the sprawling second-floor terrace and the flowing, well-manicured lawn that went on as far as the eye could see.

She psyched herself to believe that doing this would make her worth as a wife go through the roof, and would nail her ambition of never being left.

The heels of her shoes made music against the hardwood floor as she sauntered toward the bed.

"Sunshine"—Hassan licked his lips as he looked at Drae, calling her by a spontaneous nickname he'd just given her— "this is Lee-Lee; and Lee-Lee, this is Sunshine." He smiled and cupped Drae's chin as she walked by him. "You know I love you, right?"

Hassan walked across their master suite and sat on the other side of the room. His dick hadn't thumped like this in years and his hard-on made it somewhat difficult for him to walk and not jerk off. He poured himself a shot of Hennessy and lit a cocaine-laced cigar before taking his seat on the chaise and watching the two women.

"Don't be nervous." Lee-Lee stroked Drae's clit. "I know you been waitin' on it." She eased out of her fur.

"You know this?" Drae arched one of her eyebrows, climbing onto the bed. She climbed over Lee-Lee and, since they were the same height, they were pussy to pussy. Drae stroked Lee-Lee's hair back and kissed her, pulling her bottom lip in and out of her mouth. She did her best to pretend that Lee-Lee was a man and that she was preparing to ride the biggest dick in the world.

Lee-Lee massaged Drae's ass as both women gyrated their hips. Their breasts pressed against each other's as they kissed hungrily, like long-lost lovers. Breaking the kiss, Drae slipped one of Lee-Lee's nipples into her mouth. Unlike Hassan's nipples, which she always loved to suck, Lee-Lee had no hard chest that Drae could press her lips on; instead there was a cottony fullness that weighed heavily on Drae's tongue.

Taking the nipple from her mouth and rolling it between her fingers, Drae bent over and whispered in Lee-Lee's ear, "I thought you 'spose to be a star."

"I am," Lee-Lee said doing her best to stop trembling.

"Then, why am I doing all the work?" Drae rolled to the side and lay flat on the bed. She opened her legs. "I want you to tell me what's on your mind when your tongue enters the pussy."

Thinking that she'd met her match, Lee-Lee turned and looked at Hassan before she climbed on top of Drae.

"He's not joining us, baby." Drae turned her head back around. "I want you to focus on mama and live up to that name you got." Lee-Lee climbed between Drae's legs, opened the lips to her sweetness and began sucking her erotic sugar. "Tell me," Drae moaned. "I want you to tell me why you like pussy."

Instead of responding, Lee-Lee licked Drae like a cat lapping up spilled milk.

"Wait a minute, baby." Drae stopped her. "You gotta talk to me. You 'spose to be a hungry bitch—you better work for this nut your lips about to get."

"Such a good fuckin' pussy," Lee-Lee practically stuttered, her tongue tied by desire. She licked Drae from one side to the other, and the feel of Drae's clit rising and falling in her mouth drove both of them wild. The taste of Drae's pussy was so wicked that Lee-Lee shouted, "Sunshine!"

Lee-Lee couldn't believe that she thought she was coming here to turn Drae out, and here Drae's inexperienced pussy tasted so good she swore she was eating melting chocolate. Something had to be wrong. She was tempted to call Hassan over and ask him if he had ever licked this shit and, if so, what possessed him to stop. She knew if she had a pussy like this at home she would keep it on lock.

"What you thinkin', boo?" Drae asked, feeling her orgasm ready to pour from her throbbing middle like lava. "You thinkin' 'bout marriage? Give me one lick for no and two licks for yes."

Two licks.

"Uhmm, thought so."

"Always being able to eat this pussy?"

Two licks.

"Uhmmmm . . . I know." Drae moaned as she came, her candy sliding down Lee-Lee's throat. "That's it." Drae grabbed the back of her hair and pushed Lee-Lee's face in deeper. "Eat it up, baby, and show me your name is Lee-Lee Lickme for a reason."

Giving Drae's nah'nah one last kiss, tug, pull and pop, Lee-Lee reached for the nine-inch strap-on that lay on the end table.

"Oh you think you gon' work me with a fake dick? Oh, come on, baby." Drae pinched her clit, " 'Cause I'm ready for it."

Lee-Lee strapped the dildo on and as she lay back on top of

Drae, Drae opened her legs wide, giving her full access to the rawness of her pussy. "Let's see what the fuck else Lee-Lee Lickme came to do." Lee-Lee started thrusting the cocoa-brown hard plastic dick in and out of Drae's wetness and as Drae lifted slightly off the bed Lee-Lee slapped her on the ass. Drae's leather corset felt like butter in the palm of her hands. While pumping in and out Lee-Lee took her right hand, picked up one of Drae's breasts, removed it from the corset and sucked it as if Drae's nipple held a sensual secret.

Drae closed her eyes and pretended that the strap-on was Hassan's big black dick stirring the butterflies in her stomach. On the verge of calling Hassan's name, she opened her eyes and looked into Lee-Lee's face. Drae hated that she was enjoying the way she was being fucked. And although it felt good, there was something missing. Lee-Lee didn't have a hard back for Drae to scratch into. There was no thick neck or broad shoulders to wrap her arms around, and when it was all said and done there would be no line of pearls laced up her stomach.

"This ain't gon' work, boo-boo," Drae said. "I'm use' to that niggah over there"—she pointed to Hassan, who was jerking his shaft—"and his big black dick ramming the shit outta me and fucking up this punani. And you teasing me"—she flipped over and now Lee-Lee lay on her back—"so let me show you how to handle that."

Slowly Drae eased down on Lee-Lee's detachable dick and rode it. Drae placed one hand on Lee-Lee's right shoulder and the other hand on her left knee. "The next time you wanna fuck a pussy follow my lead."

Lee-Lee started screaming, "Ahhh! Yes! Oh my God, yes!"

"Why you screaming?" Drae asked her. "You feel the heat

of this hot, pink flesh? You feel that . . . or you simply wish you did?" Lee-Lee sat up and began sucking Drae's D-cups, biting them, pushing them together and simultaneously sucking them. If nothing else, this bitch appeared to be able to suck a tittie. So Drae grabbed the back of her head and let Lee-Lee's mouth fuck her nipples as if they were able to shoot cum.

Feeling her nut building, Drae started bucking the dildo faster. She began rubbing her clit and moaning. "Uhmm-mmm . . ."

After showering her juice over the strap-on, Drae rolled off Lee-Lee and fell onto her back. She could tell just by looking at Lee-Lee's face that she must've been in a trance and was experiencing the true essence of being pussy-whipped. And just to drive the point home, Drae thought about taking out the double-headed twelve-inch dildo that she and Hassan played with, so that she could show Lee-Lee how it truly felt to work a dick. But once she saw Hassan's nut was spilling onto his hands, she changed her mind and figured her point had been made.

Lee-Lee stared at Drae for a moment longer before biting her bottom lip and asking her, "Do you give private sessions?"

Drae felt like she could've smacked her. Hadn't she already proven to Lee-Lee that she wasn't working with shit? "Girl, beat it." Drae smirked. "That shit there was for my fuckin' man; chicks are not my thing." She climbed off the bed. "Give her the role and send her the fuck home," she said to Hassan. "I need a real dick to fuck with."

"Oh, you need a real dick?" Hassan smiled as he motioned for Drae to come near and Lee-Lee to leave the room.

Drae walked over to Hassan, who was working on

another hard-on, and kissed him. They could hear Lee-Lee slam the door behind her.

"She was better than me, baby?" Hassan asked Drae as he ran his hands up her thighs.

"Never, baby. You the best."

"You gon' ever leave me, Drae?"

"Never. Ever. Nothing and nobody could ever make me think about leaving you."

"I'm the best, baby?" he asked as she straddled his lap and eased onto his hard dick.

Gyrating her hips, she said, "You gon' always be the best."

six months later

Never as Good as
the First Time

Yuri

It was an honest mistake, her fucking Britt this long. This time she meant for it to be only once, maybe twice, but that was it. Take the nut and run with it; but she didn't. Instead she fell in love with his arrogance, and with his being six feet two and having seven tattoos etched into the protruding muscles on his chest, arms and one that lay seductively on the right side of his neck.

They'd been close since the eighth grade, when his family moved to Brooklyn from Trinidad. She would sit next to him in class, take notes for him, bring him lunch and act as if she could comprehend every word he said, when really she couldn't. Yet, despite how hard Yuri tried, Britt took her kindness for just that: kindness. And instead of kicking it to her, he used her to translate what she pretended to understand to all the chicks he really wanted to get with.

Which was why, years later, she never counted on his throwing salt in the game. Kicking it to her like he wanted more than just pussy. Like he had to have her heart too. Coming at her extra hard, knowing she'd never been treated this way: the late night phone calls, singing to her, rubbing her feet, cooking for her, buying her things, valuing her opinions, listening to her, loving her and fucking her like she'd *never . . . ever* been fucked before.

Yuri tried desperately to fight off her feelings and focus on the richness of Britt's Trinidadian dick. The length of it defied the twelve-inch ruler, the thickness and the uncircumcised tip made the myth of a big black dick exist. Even the ridges of his balls and the way they swirled across his skin and blended smoothly into one another exuded beauty.

Yuri glanced at the alarm clock flashing seven A.M. from the top of the maple nightstand while trying not to think about how quickly the last two hours had zoomed by, but she couldn't help it; like cheating, counting the time had become a habit she'd picked up.

She took a deep breath and wished Britt would resume seducing her again. He knew their time was limited, yet it seemed that getting zooted off ganja and practicing new scats for his out-of-town performance was all that occupied his mind.

Usually Yuri would just say whatever she had to and care about Britt's reaction later. But not this time; she was caught up. Caught up in too many fulfilled fantasies and tangible dreams. Life was sweeter with a shitload of woulda, coulda, shouldas and what-ifs, but now she had reality to deal with; and reality was kicking ass and fighting her like hell not to let go.

For a moment Yuri studied Britt to see if there was something about him that could make being in love with him feel better, but all she got was a confirmation that loving him had become a destructive mix of eating where you shit. "Look"—Yuri sucked her teeth—"we gon' fuck again, or what?"

Britt stopped singing and took a pull of his blunt. "What?" he said while releasing the smoke.

"I rushed out this morning so you could catch a flight this afternoon. Now either we gon' fuck or I got other shit to do."

"What?"

"*I said,*" Yuri stressed, "is this it for the dick? What, you need a pill and shit? Your hard on have a time limit?"

Britt raised one of his thick eyebrows and chuckled in disbelief. "Yo, my man," he said, calling her by the pet name he'd given her, "chill." He mashed his blunt in the ashtray and blew a cloud of smoke into the air. He grabbed one of the plush white towels that sat on the hotel's vanity and wrapped it around his waist, then took another and tossed it behind his neck.

"Chill?" Yuri spat, holding back tears, hating that her feelings were hurt by his saying something so simple. "Niggah, it's seven o'clock in the morning. I ran my black ass down here and all you've done besides give *me* a half-ass nut is get high and ignore the shit outta me. If I wanted to be ignored I would've stayed home."

"Yo, my man," Britt repeated himself, but with more base in his voice than before. "Trust me. Chill."

"Fuck 'chill,' and right about now fuck you. And by the way, I'm not a man, so stop calling me that!"

"What de muthascunt—" Britt quickly changed from his usual Brooklyn accent to a strong Trinidadian one.

"You called my mother a what?" Yuri cut him off. "Speak clearly."

"Oh, now you don't understand me?" Britt was pissed. "Gon' ask me what I say about your mother. You know damn well I ain't say nothin' about your mother." Britt sighed. "But what you don't know is I'ma 'bout to leave yo' ass alone and hit you off with some time to think."

Yuri tried desperately to control her tears. "I did not sign up for this!" She rose from the bed and started collecting her things. "I swear to God I'm too caught up in this shit. I don't even know why I'm still fucking with you. You don't give a damn about me, and I'm tired of playing myself for you!"

"Yo, my man—"

"My name is Yuri!"

"Yuri—"

"Don't fuckin' talk to me!"

"Why are you so pissed?" he asked, taken aback. "You never acted like this before; and we've said all kind of shit to each other."

"Why am I so pissed? What the fuck you think?!" Yuri's voice started to crack and her bottom lip trembled. She kicked the pillow they'd knocked on the floor earlier out of her way. "You so caught up in yourself and everything you doin' you don't even think about how somebody else feels. I swear to God I can't stand y'all foreign no-good, fig-boat motherfuckers. I'ma leave all y'all asses alone and stick with the American I got at home!"

"Yo." Britt walked toward Yuri and backed her into a corner. "Apparently your American husband ain't got yo' ass in check. Otherwise you wouldn't be standing in my face. But see, this West Indian right here will gank yo' fuckin' ass if you ever disrespect me again. Matter fact, peep this: It's over." He waved his hand as if he were slicing through the air.

"Over?" Yuri felt as if she'd been slashed across the throat. She couldn't believe he'd ended it. When did he get this kind of power to decide when and if they could be together? Who the hell was he? God? "Over? Did you say it was over?" she asked. "We'd have to be together in order for it to be over. And I'm already married. So as far as I'm concerned you can kiss . . . my . . . wide . . . black . . . ass, you no-good motherfucker." Tears raced from her eyes as she started collecting her clothes, which he'd so hastily strewn around the room earlier.

Britt pushed her back into the corner and pressed his forehead against hers. "I'ma 'bout two seconds off yo' ass, so just tell me you love me, 'cause all this extra shit is gon' get you killed."

"Move!" She wiped her eyes and pushed past him. She did her best to slip her blouse on.

Britt wasn't used to seeing Yuri act like this, so he stood back and watched her. Once he saw she was serious he said, "Man, calm yo' ass down."

"Oh, I'm calm. I'm calm enough to say 'fuck you' and not think twice about it."

Britt had to laugh.

"Now I'ma joke?"

"I didn't say that."

"Whatever."

"Where are you going, Yuri?"

"I'm going"—she rolled her eyes—"to fuck my husband."

"What?" Britt looked at her so intensely that she felt at any moment she would get her ass kicked. She watched his jaw twitch and his protruding pecks thump twice.

"Do what you gotta do, ma', you ain't my shittin' wife. Fuck it. You too goddamn bol'face anyway. Run so that niggah can think you nuttin' over his sterile-ass dick, but I know the real deal. Matter fact"—Britt waved his hands and his pecks thumped again—"I don't even know why I'm trippin' off this shit. I just said it was over. So fuck it. Bounce!"

Yuri felt her knees giving way. "You know what? I hate you!" she shouted through her tears.

Britt couldn't stand that she was crying like this, especially knowing that he was the cause. "Come here," he said as he motioned for Yuri to move next to him. "Why we arguing? This is ridiculous. Forgive me? I forgive you."

Yuri stood where she was and replied, "I wish I would. To hell with you."

Britt walked over to her and carefully unbuttoned her blouse; sliding it off, he said, "You in love with me?"

Yuri did her best to look away. She knew if she faced him she wouldn't have the nerve to lie.

"Your feelings about to run you crazy." Britt dropped the towel from around his waist. "I warned you I was a rude boy." He started kissing the side of her neck.

Instantly her nipples stood up. "Britt, just let me go."

"Now you tryin' to make the problem worse. . . ." He kissed around the sides of her neck and then moved to her nipples. "I love to suck these titties. Damn, they just melt in my mouth. This the shit that make me wanna suck the hell outta your pussy. You know this fat pussy taste like wet and sticky candy?" He slid two fingers in.

"Britt, please." She did her best not to open wide and gyrate on his fingertips. "Didn't you say this was over? Yes, I believe you did, so man up to your fuckin' word."

Forcefully but without much resistance Britt walked Yuri backward to the bed and laid her down. "You need to learn to shut up sometimes." He licked a rough, yet seductive trail from her neck, in between her breasts, and over her navel. Pausing at her pussy lips, he opened them up and sighed. "Damn, this shit stay wet. All this for me, baby?" He stuck his index finger into her melted candy, pulled it out and sucked off the drippings.

Yuri could feel Britt's wet tongue tickling her clit and flicking it up and down. "You still going home to fuck your husband? Knowing he don't fuck you like this?"

Instead of responding, Yuri grabbed the edge of the mattress and pulled up the fitted sheet. "Uhmmm lick it right there. . . ." she moaned.

"Answer me." He bit her pussy lips slightly.

"No . . . bite the clit, baby." She pushed his head in farther.

"He fuck you like me?" Britt gave her clit one last lick before moving his head from between her legs, turning her over and easing his dick in.

Yuri was silent. No matter how many times they'd been here, his dick always blindsided her and given the abundance of force he was now banging her with, she knew her pussy would be sore for days. "Britt," she managed to say, "your dick is too big to be fucking me like this. Slow down."

"Fuck all that." He stroked, while placing his hand at the back of her neck. "I asked you a question about my pussy."

"Britt!" Yuri couldn't help but scream as he flipped her over and her titties bounced in his face.

"Does he fuck you like this?"

"No."

"Are you going home to fuck him?"

Yuri cried tears of ecstasy and confusion. She hated that his freakiness clouded her thoughts with visions of crazy shit. Like how to leave her husband for Britt, and how to change Britt and convince him that she was all he ever needed. How to get him to see that if he had taken the time when they were teens he would've seen that she loved him. And maybe, just maybe, she wouldn't have been so desperate, fucked up her life and become the wrong man's wife.

"You gon' fuck him?" He stroked her as hard as he could.

Yuri tried not to answer and instead focused on the nut she felt building up. "Britt," she gasped, "do . . . what I like . . . baby."

"What?"

"Suck the nut out."

"You gon' fuck that niggah?"

"N-n-noooo . . . baby. . . ." she stuttered as he did what she requested. "No. . . ."

Drae

The extended version of Prince's song "Adore" tore through the surround sound in their master suite as Drae sipped on a chilled bottle of Hpnotiq and her husband, Hassan, unfolded a hundred dollar bill and snorted a white line of girl.

Nasty Naz, the aspiring porn star who Hassan brought home for an audition, immediately made eye contact with Drae as he slowly pulled his fitted V-neck tee over his head and unzipped his baggy jeans, revealing the waistband of his CK boxers. Bulging veins and rippling muscles traveled down his tattooed chest and flowed over his caramel skin like a Sugar Daddy. His beauty was unlike any other man's Drae had ever seen before. And although he was handsome, it wasn't his face that captivated her; it was his swagger, his confidence and his thugged-out presence.

As Prince's guitar took on a life of its own, Drae gently rubbed her clit and firmly pressed her lips against the sweaty neck of the Hpnotiq bottle.

Naz could tell he was nothing like she expected, as he blessed her with a sensual striptease. And his dance was nothing fancy, it never was. His perfect body spoke for itself.

Completely naked, Naz walked over to Drae. The muscles in his thick thighs showed off their magnificence as he stood between her legs. He grabbed a fistful of her shoulder-length hair and looked into her face. To most, Drae was the spitting image of Nia Long, her skin was smooth and the color of a new paper bag, her chocolate eyes Asian-inspired and her full lips were evidence she could blow a good dick.

"Don't play with me. Put the bottle down." His voice was raspy and sent chills through her. Fighting the urge to bask in his stare, Drae took her right leg and threw it in the crook of his arm. The strawberry face of her pussy was fully exposed. "Why should I?"

Instead of responding, Naz let her hair go, got on his knees and sucked the sticky folds of her pussy lips. The creamy juice from her G-spot ran down her thighs as he began to aggressively lick her clit. Instantly Drae started shaking and the bottle began to do a dance in her hands as she struggled to hold on to it. "Uhmmm . . . wait . . ." she moaned. "Let me . . . put it down."

"Nah, next time you'll do what I tell you." He looked up at her. "Now hold it."

Drae's eyes were closed tight. She'd never had this type of audition before. Hell, taking it to the head and simultaneously getting her pussy licked was her signature, but this niggah here was tongue-tying the game.

"In case you didn't know," he said in between sucks of her pussy, "Nasty Naz came to work."

Drae was speechless as she struggled like hell to hold on to the bottle. She held it so tight she was sure it would shatter in her hand. After all, she was used to getting her pussy eaten but never before had she had it spanked. This was one aspiring actor who beat all the others hands down. Even Hassan would have to put in some work to come behind this one. And it wasn't that Hassan had no back. Hell, he was six-two, two hundred and ten pounds and he had no problem putting pussy to sleep. It's just that Naz catered to the clit like he owned it.

Seeing that she was struggling to hold the bottle, Naz took it from her hand, poured what was left between her breasts and threw the bottle against the wall. Instantly it exploded, sending bits of glass soaring through the air. He gazed into her eyes, ran his hands from her ebony nipples to her cherry-colored clit. Drae tried her best not to respond, but his intense stare was putting her under a spell. "It's running all over me. . . ." she said nervously.

"Naz got you, ma'. Don't worry." His tongue took a bath in the generous amount of liquor that covered her fat nipples; tugging, pulling, biting . . . Afterward he ran his Hpnotiq-soaked hands over her flesh like a Swedish masseur, sucking her toes and reminding her clit of his presence. He flipped her over, kissed her ass and turned her back to face him again. Drae began to moan and shake like never before.

"Drae," Hassan said, as the high from his line started to take effect, "you like that shit, huh?" He started rubbing his dick as he watched another man pleasure his wife. For a moment Drae forgot he was in the room, but then she remembered he was usually quiet during the auditions. Besides, being able to watch was his favorite part. It reminded him of a sensual dance. The body moving to its own internal beat: jerking, making rhythmic motions and forcing the mouth to speak. "You's a fuckin' whore, huh?" he spat at Drae as he rubbed his shaft forcefully.

"Oh, daddy," she said, doing her best not to fumble over her words, especially since spitting out this line was one of Hassan's requirements. "You still the best. . . ."

"You lying, bitch?"

"He's making me, daddy." Drae held her head back as she took her hands and caressed the sides of Naz's face. He was back to tasting her pussy and feeling the motions of his mouth as his tongue flicked in and out drove her insane.

Hassan jerked his shaft and seduced his cum to the tip. Walking toward them he asked, "You lying to me, bitch?"

"No, baby."

"Yes, you are," Naz said as he pulled Drae to the floor a few inches from Hassan's feet, and bent her over doggy style. Drae lifted her eyes and looked Hassan in his face. His hazel eyes bore directly through her, while his sun-kissed skin looked to be frostbitten.

"Suck this dick," Hassan demanded.

Drae wrapped her hands around his dick and slid it in and out of her mouth. With her spit hanging off the tip she said, "You the best."

"Tell the truth," Naz said, causing Drae to look over her shoulder and get a full view of his beautiful dick. The color of it reminded her of Godiva dark chocolate. It looked to be more than ten inches. In fact, it was so big that it didn't look real. She could feel him rubbing the head between her legs. She closed her eyes and gasped as he pushed it in.

"Open your eyes," Naz demanded, "and tell ya man who's the best." Drae did all she could to catch her breath. Naz's dick was so big that she knew it didn't all fit, some of it had to be hanging out. "You the best, baby." Unable to fight it any longer, she screamed, "Yes . . . oh, yes . . . !" She bit her bottom lip and her round, melon-shaped titties bounced.

"He the best?" Hassan squeezed his dick.

"No, baby," she struggled to say. "No way."

"Tell the truth," Naz whispered in her ear before biting her on the shoulder.

Instead of responding, Drae took one of her arms, reached above her head and grabbed the back of Naz's neck, causing him to ram his entire dick into her, forcing the sugar walls holding up her pussy to collapse. All Drae could do was release the tears that filled her eyes. She knew for a fact the entire world heard the bottom of her punani fall out. Unable to grab on to a rug or the edge of a sheet, Drae pounded her fist on the floor.

Naz wrapped her hair around his hand, yanked it back and whispered, "Tell this niggah I just caught 'im slippin'."

Drae didn't know whether she was coming or going; she was lost in his dick, which was giving her the business. Naz thrust his pelvis and worked his groin muscles with everything he had. Initially his intentions were not to fuck her like this. He planned to knock it down and be on his way, but he got stuck. Stuck in the unexpected sweetness of her pussy. He did all he could not to call her Sunshine.

Drae knew she couldn't stand Naz beating up her twat

much longer; she could feel her erotic lips swelling with each stroke, and she knew cumming consistently was bound to be a bad habit. She looked up at Hassan and forced herself to say something. "You gon' join us, baby?"

"Naw . . . I don't think I'm needed."

"Let me suck you, baby." This was Drae's way of trying to make him feel better. And you would think Naz could pick up on the hint that Hassan needed to be in charge. After all, he was the porn director, this was his house and she was his wife. If Naz was gon' play him out, he could've waited until Drae invited him to a private session, not right here while Hassan was looking and, on top of that, paying for the shit. Didn't Naz get it? Hassan's threesomes were more about fucking his ego than anything else. Now Drae was shaky on whether Hassan would go through with his routine of waiting for the actor to leave so he could fuck her all night to prove he was the best. She knew this time he'd met his match and she wasn't so sure he could handle that.

"Oh, you getting your shit off?" Hassan asked, releasing his dick from his hand. "He killing that pussy, huh?"

Drae threw her entire ass into Naz's shaft, hoping to make him cum.

"Don't try and make me cum," he spoke into her ear. "I got this." Naz pumped as hard as he could, causing Drae to scream. As his dick slipped in and out of her wet canal, her mind traveled to space. He turned her over and now she lay in the missionary position. "How he trust you in the studio with me?" Naz whispered, running his hands through her hair. "Don't he know I'ma sex you continuously?"

Within seconds Drae was digging her fingernails into Naz's back, drawing blood. As she felt his pelvis start to contract, tears slipped from her eyes again. She hated that this had to end, and truthfully she wanted him to fuck her once more.

As Drae felt Naz pull his dick out, a surge of wind invaded her pussy, making his warm drippings feel cold as he led a string of pearls up her stomach and around her neck.

Judging by the look on Hassan's face Drae knew it was only a matter of time before he lost his mind.

Naz slapped Drae on the ass as he helped her from the floor. He looked at Hassan. "Cut." Reaching over to the chaise he grabbed a towel and threw it to Drae. Catching the towel she wiped the cum from her neck and her belly.

Drae stood up but felt stuck in her spot.

"Walk him to the door," Hassan spat. "What's the problem?"

She grabbed her robe and wrapped it around her body like a whirlwind. Naz was fully dressed and Hassan peeped him licking his lips and watching the material from Drae's robe ride her tight ass as she led him to the front entrance.

As Naz stepped outside the door, he turned around to face her. "You way too pretty to be pimped like this." He rubbed the side of her cheek.

"What?" Drae was stunned.

"Be easy, Sunshine." He kissed her forehead.

Drae watched him get into his silver Escalade and drive off. For a moment she was suspended in time, still feeling the softness of his touch and the weight of his dick. Never in all of her thirty-two years had she been fucked like this. This was the type of dick that made you stalk, trap and kidnap.

After realizing she'd been at the door for way too long, Drae took a quick shower and avoided facing Hassan right away. Afterward, she crept back into their bedroom. She hated that Hassan's ego was bruised, because she was sure there would be some shit. "Come on, baby," she said as she dropped her robe, doing her best to stick to what they usually did. She sat on the edge of the bed and spread her legs apart: her hot, pink pussy practically smiling at him. She dipped her fingers in. "You want some?"

Hassan stood still between her legs for a moment and instead of holding her by the neck and choking her, something new they'd started to try, he reached over her shoulder, yanked the telephone cord out of the wall and wrapped the end of it around his hand. The telephone made a lingering chime sound as it hit the hard wooden floor.

Drae's eyes darted across the room and back to Hassan. "What are you doing, Hassan?" she panicked. "What's up with the cord?"

"What, you don't like to be choked anymore?"

"With the cord?"

"A'ight." He threw the cord to the floor. So"—he grabbed her around the neck with his bare hands—"tell me this, you like that niggah's dick? His dick bigger than mine?"

"I thought this was about him getting a part—a movie role—not about how big his dick is."

"That big?"

"Hassan, why are you pressing this? It ain't like he Denzel Dick Down. Shit he just a lil' niggah—stop sweatin' that shit."

"You gon' answer me?"

"Shit, didn't you see it? Come on, don't beat me in the head with that. It's bad enough I'm even doing this shit."

"Why you bein' extra? I asked you a question."

Drae caught an attitude. "What you tryin' to prove? I'm startin' to get sick of this. I'm a fuckin' guidance counselor and I'm lettin' you and yo' aspiring-dick stars pimp me. It was bad enough I let Lee-Lee Lickme eat my pussy for a role, now I got to be harassed about dick size? What the fuck am I really doing here? Let's just chill. We freaky enough." She attempted to laugh. "Let's rock each other's world again."

"When I stop rocking your world? When your boyfriend left?"

"He's not my boyfriend," Drae snapped. "You picked him out."

"Why you being defensive? I'm cool wit' it. Tell me, and tell me the truth. You my wife, my best friend. So give it to me straight, that niggah's dick bigger than mine?"

"No," she tried to push his hand from her neck, as his grip tightened.

"Too tight? Oh, my fault." He loosened his grip. "Kick it wit' me. Now, you know we better than bullshit. Tell me 'bout his dick. It's bigger than mine?" He laughed. "And be for real wit' it."

"A'ight." Drae swallowed; although Hassan seemed slightly cool, she was still a little on edge. "It was a lil' bigger, not much. Yo' shit is thicker," she lied.

"True story? So a niggah was causin' it, huh? Bigger than me. He better than me?" Hassan gave Drae a devilish grin.

"He was okay, Hassan." She moved her hand from side to side.

"You lyin'. So now I know this niggah was killin' that pussy. You don't wanna fuck me no more, do you?"

"He was auditioning, Hassan."

Before Hassan could respond, he let Drae's neck go,

picked up the telephone cord and started whipping her with it. Drae was frozen in shock before she started to try to get away. "Hassan, what the hell are you doing?! Stop it!" She fell to the floor and started crawling toward the bedroom door.

"What the fuck you crawlin' around for? So he better than me?" The telephone cord sizzled across Drae's skin. As Hassan whipped it across her back she could feel her skin burst open.

"Get off me!" she screamed, trying to untangle her robe, which was somehow caught between her feet. Hassan took the telephone cord and whipped her again, this time slapping the cord across her thighs. "Get off me! Are you crazy! I'm not doing this shit no more! No fuckin' more!"

"You'll do what the fuck I say do!"

Drae pulled the extension cord running from the lamp, causing it to fall from the cherry nightstand to the floor. All but the burning bulb exploded. Drae grabbed the gold rod running through the lamp, stood, and pointed the naked bulb at Hassan. "I swear on my mother's grave that if you hit me again I'ma burn and bury yo' fuckin' ass!"

"Real talk?" Hassan walked closer to Drae and she swung the lamp, the hot bulb scorching a small portion of the skin on his chest. "You burned me, bitch?" Although Drae had the lamp in her hand Hassan slapped her so hard that it caused her to do a spin and fall to the floor. Instead of lying still Drae quickly crawled toward the door again. As she reached the doorway she felt Hassan grab her ankles, pulling her back into the room. Her hair flopped wildly while sweat caused some of it to plaster across her forehead. "Where the fuck you going?!" Hassan demanded to know. "I'ma beat yo' ass like never before! You lettin' this niggah fuck you better than me?!" Hassan lifted Drae from the floor and shoved his face into hers. "Look at me, bitch! And you do this to somebody who made you? Without me you ain't shit!"

"Hassan, please!"

"Don't 'Hassan, please' me. Say it. Say, 'Hassan, I ain't shit without you!' And say you're sorry while you at it. Sorry for fuckin' this niggah better than me! I hate that I sent yo' fuckin' ass to school; now you think you too good for this shit. You think 'cause you workin' in a school that you don't need a niggah no more. When I met you, you barely had a few measly-ass college credits and then here comes Hassan, Captain Save a Ho. You wanna go to college, Drae? Yes? You love me, Drae? Yes—"

"I do love you, Hassan."

"You more than love me, bitch, you owe me!"

"Don't call me a bitch anymore!"

"What you prefer, whore?!"

Drae swallowed. "What you want from me, Hassan?"

"I want you to apologize!"

"For what?" she cried.

"For sayin' that niggah's dick was bigger than mine."

"Then you need to stop bringing people into our bedroom!"

"Oh, now," Hassan said in disbelief, "you gon' leave me for this niggah?"

"What are you talking about? I would never leave you! But you my fuckin' man, not my father. Why you doing this? Naz is an actor; he's off auditioning for the next role, and you here beating on me. How that shit sound?"

Hassan had Drae by the back of her neck and let her go. He

stood quietly, watching her on the floor and thinking about what she'd just said to him. He looked around the room and saw the mess that they'd made. For a moment he thought it would be so much easier if she simply let him kick her ass and get it over with, but he knew she would never be that submissive.

Drae hated that Hassan loving her like this turned her on. She wished he had a better way to show how much he cared. Besides, where was she going? He was her dude, her dime piece, and she wasn't trading him in for shit. She just wished he would stop bringing his actors' dicks into their bedroom, and let her just settle with his again. She could accept the mountain of toys that he liked for her to play with; the only thing that turned her off was the loaded dildo he liked for her to strap on and stick in his ass. Other than that, she could deal with the balls, the beads and the bullets.

"Yo." She rose from the floor. "You be spazzin' too much. And another thing, you got to stop getting high. This is too damn much." She studied the welts popping up on her skin. She could see Hassan's apology in his eyes, but she wanted to run up and slap the shit out of him. "That was it for the auditions."

"Naw, baby." Hassan attempted to calm her down. "It's not the auditions; it's me. I know I started buggin', but I promise I won't do it anymore. Ever. But we can't stop."

"Why not?" Drae snapped, as Hassan started kissing the bruises he'd put on her body.

"Because." He kissed her and fondled her breast. "It's how I make my dough. Besides, I love to watch another niggah pounding that pussy and the way you scream when you cummin'; it drives me crazy."

"No, it sends you crazy."

He pulled her onto the bed. "Naw, I'm good. I won't spaz no more."

"You promise?" She rolled on top of him, his hard dick poking her clit.

"I promise, Drae." He caressed her waist. "Before I tear this pussy up, can I get some asshole?"

"Hassan . . ." she whined. She had really been looking forward to riding his dick. "Let me just ride it."

"Please, baby. You know I love that shit."

"All right." Drae took a deep breath and turned around. She held her ass in the air, giving full access to the baby pink inside her asshole. Hassan took his tongue and licked her ass.

"This all me?" he asked as he lubricated her anus with tongue.

"Yes." She suppressed a scream as he pushed his dick in.

"That niggah fucked you better than me?"

"Never, baby," she said flexing her ass muscles. "Can't nobody get with you."

"Say word?"

"Word." She turned her head to the side and smiled.

"You gon' leave me, Drae?"

"Never. Ever. Nothing and no one could ever make me leave you."

"That niggah dick really bigger than mine?"

"Baby."

"Yeah."

"Stop sweatin' that shit."

Yuri

They'd made plans to meet at IHOP in Brooklyn for brunch. It had been a few months since Yuri, Drae and Nae-Nae had gotten together. Although Yuri and Drae were cousins, they'd been best friends since Nae-Nae was "Nathan," Yuri was the fattest one in the class and Drae was a virgin.

They'd crossed their hearts and hoped to die at least a million times before they said they'd ever stop talking or telling one another everything. And they held true to their promise at first; so the lying didn't start out intentionally, life and bullshit just sort of took them there. But when the lying got to be too much, they just stopped talking. When they did speak again, it was only to make the others feel guilty about neglecting their friendship.

The most honest one was Nae-Nae, who didn't give a damn what anyone thought, because he didn't judge and he didn't want anyone judging what he did in his life. He was strictly dickly, wanted to rock patent-leather catsuits four days out the week, and wanted to spend time promoting his fashion line, Fierce, made especially for drag queens. That's how he met his boo, Raphael. Raphael was a part-time model, and full-time drag queen. He did shows all over New York, Vegas and San Francisco, and he loved him some Nae-Nae, especially since he and Nae-Nae both thought Nae-Nae was a homo thug. Needless to say it was a perfect combination.

About a month after Nae-Nae and Raphael became a couple, Raphael met Drae and Yuri. They all clicked instantly and Raphael became an extension of their clique.

Nae-Nae was the noncompetitive one between Yuri and Drae. He was also the one they never *really* lied to. Not that they told him everything, but he knew things about them that they would never breathe to another living soul. There were many nights they cried on his shoulder about shit in their lives. Drae told Nae-Nae about Lee-Lee Lickme, she just didn't tell him why she did it; and Yuri admitted to him about Britt. She just didn't tell him she'd become over the top with it.

As soon as Nae-Nae and Yuri walked into IHOP, Drae spotted them. "Look at you, bitch," Drae said as Yuri walked over to the booth where Drae was sitting. Yuri was wearing a pair of tight jeans and a fitted, tangerine hooded sweater. "You look fantastic!" Drae carried on.

"And you know this." Yuri smiled. "But look at you. What the hell you doing to be glowing? What's the secret?"

"Good dick."

Damn, Yuri thought. "Girl, don't I know." She smiled.

"So wassup with you, Nae-Nae?" Drae asked, as they kissed each other on the cheek.

"What, I don't look good, bitch?" Nae-Nae spat, sliding in the booth next to Yuri. "I see you all over this heifer 'cause she done lost a few pounds—"

"Seventy pounds," Yuri interrupted. "Seventy."

"Whew-whew," Nae-Nae snapped sarcastically. "Ring the alarm."

"Oh, you are such a hater."

"I don't hate, I state. Thank you. I'm tellin' you ya'll got this homo thug fucked up."

"I ain't never seen a homo thug rock a patent-leather cat-suit." Drae laughed.

"I ain't never seen pussies in my motherfuckin' business much as you. Back the fuck off me now. Been done stabbed you."

"Ill." Drae frowned as the waiter handed them their menus. "What's wrong with you?"

"Girl"—Nae-Nae wiped invisible sweat off his brow—"a bitch's ass is sore."

" 'Scuse me," the waiter said, but no one seemed to be paying him any attention.

"Shut up, Nae-Nae." Yuri shook her head in disgust. "Please, I do not wanna hear about your ass."

" 'Scuse me." The waiter tapped on the table, but still no response.

"Girl, I know what I meant to tell you," Drae said, excited.

"What?"

"Guess who's back in New York? Troi," she said answering her own question.

Without warning Yuri's heart dropped to the bottom of her feet and her mouth fell open.

The waiter cleared his throat.

"Britt's ex-fiancée?" Nae-Nae said as he lifted Yuri's bottom lip. "When that bitch come back around?"

" 'Scuse me?" The waiter pounded on the table, rattling the silverwear. "A ma'fuckin' 'scuse me!"

Immediately their conversation came to a halt and they all turned around.

"You know how long I been standin' here?!" the waiter yelled.

They each blinked their eyes at least a million times, especially since they just realized their waiter stood no more than three-and-a-half feet tall. His chest was puffed out and he was tapping his feet. He wore a white apron and underneath was a black ninja suit with a million zippers all over it, and instead of a hairnet he had a red tam cocked to the side.

"Shit! Can y'all shut the fuck up for a minute?" the waiter went on. "Yap-yap"—he clucked his arms like a chicken—"yap-yap-fuckin' yap. Big-ass mouths, that's what's wrong wit' niggahs now. They talk too much. Shut the fuck up sometime. What, y'all ain't never been to a restaurant befo'? Er'body know when I hand you the menu I'm 'spose to find out if you want somethin' to drink. Now, what the fuck is you drinkin'? Let's start with yo' big ass." He pointed to Yuri. "You look like you stay thirsty."

"What kinda shit?" Yuri said in disbelief. "Is this niggah a mad-ass guardian angel?"

" 'Scuse you 'scuse you . . . ah'scuse you. But you got somethin' to say to Squeak?" The waiter sucked his teeth and tapped his pen on his order pad.

"Who the fuck is Squeak?" Nae-Nae said, doing his best not to laugh. "You tryna flex on us, Squeak?"

"I don't go that way pot'nah and I'm tired of motherfuckers thinkin' I do."

"What?" Nae-Nae said in disbelief. "Squeak, wouldn't no fag want you. What they gon' do wit' yo' lil' ass!"

"You know I been in jail before."

"Whew," Yuri said. "I'm scared."

"And?" Nae-Nae spat. "What is that supposed to mean?"

"You asked me what a fag can do with my ass."

"Stop the visual please," Drae said, "and call the manager."

"Snitches get stitches." Squeak pounded his fist.

"You threatenin' me?" Drae asked in disbelief.

"Not unless you tryna do somethin'."

"Just call the manager," Yuri said.

"Fuck the manager," Nae-Nae spat. "I will beat the breaks off that—"

"Off what?" Squeak said. "In all that hot-ass patent leather what you gon' do but slide yo' slippery ass all across this floor. Lookin' like a big-ass ball of grease. Man, please, don't fuck with me. My woman left me, my dog done run away, child support lookin' for me and shit. For real, dawg, you want it wit' me, I will kick yo' fuckin' ass up in this here piece. Why you think they call this IHOP? 'Cause I will hop all over you." He placed his order pad on the table. "Now say I won't. Please, say it." He started skipping in place like a boxer. "I'll turn this motherfucker out."

Yuri, Drae and Nae-Nae sat there amazed. They couldn't figure out what was going on. Before they could call the manager to their table, she was already there. "Sorry y'all. I'm the manager, Freeda. . . . Whoool." She looked at Nae-Nae. "You is so sharp."

"Thank you," Nae-Nae said, caught off guard, as he realized the manager was puckering her lips and making kisses at him.

"Is you tryna flirt, Freeda?" Squeak asked.

She winked her eye. "It's . . . all . . . good."

"Freeda," Squeak said, "stop being a dumb dumb! Stevie Wonder can see that Super Freak ain't interested in nothing but dick and ass."

"Super Freak?!" Nae-Nae mumbled in disbelief.

"Y'all got to excuse him," Freeda said. "He on work release." She turned to Squeak. "Keep it up and you gon' be right back on the sidewalk sweepin' up shit."

"But they fuckin' wit' me, Freeda."

She looked at Yuri, Nae-Nae and Drae. "Sorry again, y'all, but I'ma talk to him. Here, I'm gon' call our best waitress over here. . . . Rafiquana!" she yelled. "Tamika-Shontell over here, and she gon' take your order."

"I'm tired of taking his customers, Freeda. He need to learn how to act." The new waitress walked over to their table. "Hur' up, what y'all want."

"Well, damn, should we eat here?" Drae asked.

The waitress sucked her teeth. "My bad. Y'all know what y'all wanna eat?" The new waitress wasn't the best, but she would do; besides, they were hungry. They each ordered a smorgasbord of meals so they could share their plates. Thankfully, the food arrived right away.

"So what?" Yuri asked nonchalantly, stuffing a piece of Drae's bacon into her mouth. "Did Troi call you?"

"No. I saw her at Negril, when Hassan and I went out the other night."

"She was by herself?"

"No. She was there with Britt."

"What?" Yuri did her best to control her attitude, but she felt like screaming.

"They were having dinner and I don't *really* know, but they seemed kinda cool. Don't you still talk to Britt? Didn't he tell you?"

"No," Yuri said, doing her all to look indifferent. "He didn't tell me anything."

"Well, why you look like that? And why you sound like that?" Drae looked at Nae-Nae; she knew if anybody knew, he did. "Yuri, you not feelin' some kinda way, are you? You not still feelin' this niggah, after all these years?"

"Girl, please." Yuri swallowed deeply and did her best to play off her feelings of being betrayed—and fuck all that she was married and knew what she was getting into—she'd loved Britt too many years to be going through this. And his being with Troi was worse than anything she'd ever felt, especially since there was nothing, at this moment, she could do about it but smile.

• • •

"For real, though," Britt had said to Yuri almost fifteen years ago. "She straight played me." He sniffed, doing his best to control his emotions, "Yo, am I stupid, or what? I had this ring and shit!" He threw it across her bedroom. "She was 'spose to marry me, and what did she tell me? She told me this niggah had a better job, that I was hung up on too many goddamn dreams!" Tears streamed from his eyes.

"Don't cry, Britt." Yuri said, unsure of what else to say. "There's nothing wrong with dreaming. . . ." She stood, nervously twisting the doorknob. Her short, peach cotton nightgown came midway down her thighs and the four buttons running down her cleavage were open.

"Yo." He tried to laugh, wiping his face. "I'm buggin', right?" He looked Yuri up and down, noticing her hard nipples.

"No, you're hurt."

"Fuck her ass. Sorry to bother you, I see you about to go to bed, let me roll."

"You can chill here . . . for a little while . . . if you want." She took her hand off the knob.

Hours later, Yuri awoke with the early-morning sun slipping into her room and Britt lying next to her in bed; his face resting in the crook of her arm, his mouth face-to-face with her nipple, and her right thigh thrown over his waist. She couldn't believe that fate had given her the opportunity to be this close to the man she'd loved all this time. For once she didn't have to pretend she was Troi. She didn't have to shut her eyes and have her pussy ache while she slid her fingers in and pretended that her tips were his dick.

"Britt . . ." She stroked his dreads and in between her words kissed his forehead. "Maybe . . . you should . . . wake up."

Britt could feel Yuri's soft lips and wet kisses. He didn't want them to stop; his heart needed soothing and being that he knew she was always open for him, he figured this was something they could do for each other. So instead of backing away he moved in closer and slipped his tongue into her mouth.

"What are we doing?" Yuri asked.

"You tell me," he said, running his tongue over her cleavage and kissing her breast through her gown. "You want me to stop?" he asked while kissing her stomach and working his way between her thighs.

"No, as long as you don't pretend I'm Troi."

"Yuri"—he looked up into her face—"I know exactly who you are." Britt pulled her panties off, causing Yuri to bite hard on her inner cheek. She couldn't think of how to respond fast enough, especially when he placed his tongue on her clit. This was ecstasy like she never imagined. Now she knew for sure Troi had gone mad. Slowly Britt sucked Yuri's pussy, her creamy jewel rising and falling in his mouth. After Britt was sure he'd pleased her more than twice, he started to work his dick in.

Yuri imagined her first time would be magical and she would hear the birds sing and see sparks fly through the air. Yet all she saw were silver stars as she squinted her eyes tight and winced from the pain shooting through her vagina.

"Whool," Britt said, feeling her pussy's extreme tightness. "Yo, this ya first time?"

"No." She opened her legs wider.

Slowly Britt pushed in deeper, but Yuri's tight inner walls clamped around his dick and shot pain through the tip, causing him to stop again. "Why you lyin'? You ain't never had no dick." He slid his dick out. "I'm not gon' play you like this."

"I don't want you to stop." She started kissing him, holding him and whispering in his ear. "Put your dick back in."

"Goddamn, Yuri." He looked at her. "For real." His dick felt so good and so warm sitting at the base of her cherry. "I wanna pop this shit so bad, but I don't want you to hate me."

"I'm not gon' hate you."

He took one of her legs, threw it over his shoulder and let the other rest on the bed. "Tell me if it hurts and I'll stop."

Yuri breathed deeply and as he slowly inched his dick in, she looked into his face. Thinking this would be their first and only time, she decided to keep the fact that she was in a lot of pain to herself. As she felt him push his dick in all the way, she winced again. "You want me to stop?" he asked.

"No."

"But I don't want you in pain. I want you to feel what I feel." He slipped his dick out and commenced sucking her creamy jewel. And just when she started pushing his head in and calling his name, he pulled his tongue out and slipped his dick completely into her pussy.

"Don't fall in love with me," he said, finding ecstasy in her virgin middle.

"I won't," she lied, knowing she already had. "I won't."

* * *

"Drae, please," Yuri said stuffing a bite of waffle into her mouth. "I don't give a damn what Britt does."

"Uhmm hmm." Drae twisted her lips and took a sip of her juice. "You know I don't believe that, right?"

"I don't know why not."

"Because I know you and right now it's obvious that you're lying to me. You cheating on Jeff?" Drae asked her.

"Why are you jumping to conclusions?!"

"Because I know you and I been there through all of the

shit. And you know Britt ain't nothin' but a fuckin' player, and he always has been."

"You just don't like him."

"No, I see right through him, and I don't want you gettin' caught up in no shit. Jeff is all you need."

"Jeff is not perfect."

"Hell, I can't tell!"

"Let me inform you Jeff has cheated and had a baby on me! Now how's that for Mr. Wonderful?"

"What?" Drae looked at Nae-Nae, and she could tell by the look on his face that he already knew. "I know yo' ass fuckin' knew and nobody told me?! So what the hell am I, nothing? Does your mother know this? I can't believe nobody told me! Are you serious, Yuri? A baby?"

"Yes, I'm serious. Why would I lie?"

"Why didn't you tell me?"

"Because your life always seemed so perfect."

"What does that have to do with you?"

"Well, everybody can't marry Mr. Wonderful, Drae."

"You don't know what or who the fuck I married, so don't even go there. Are you serious Jeff had a baby on you?"

"For the last time, he has a son."

Drae felt like crying for her cousin. "How old is this child?"

"He's five, and I've known since the day the child support papers came to the house."

"I can't understand why you didn't tell me?"

"Why would I do that and make myself look like a fool? Here I loved the man who's been with me since I was two-hundred-and-sixty pounds and he was out loving somebody else. Not to mention she's white—"

"He cheated on you with a white bitch? Oh, hell no."

"And you have a problem," Nae-Nae interrupted, "with her being white because . . . ?"

"Because," Drae snapped, "don't no black woman want to be cheated on with no white girl."

"What's the difference? Her pussy is pink. Please, how about he shouldn't have done the shit period."

"Whatever," Yuri said. "Her being white just makes the shit worse. And she was eighteen."

"What?!" Drae screeched. "So what you gon' do now? I know you ain't leaving him, so that bitch can try and step in. Fuck that."

"I may leave."

"Why?" Drae paused. "Women get cheated on every day; I wouldn't give my damn man away."

"She can have him."

"Why, because you back to fuckin' with Britt?"

"Why are you on Britt?"

"Because somethin' funny seems like it's going on— Nae-Nae?"

"Why you calling my name?" Nae-Nae asked.

"All I'm saying," Drae carried on, "is that if you even think about fucking Britt, you better remember that this is the same niggah who wouldn't even look at you twice when you wore more sizes than the average plus. And now that you're workin' the hell outta a fierce sixteen . . . all of a sudden this niggah can hollar and wanna spend some time? Spare me."

Yuri felt like she'd been gut-punched. "Well, don't you worry about Britt. You need to be worried about Hassan and his down-low ass!"

"Excuse you?!"

"Whoool, you way out there, Yuri," Nae-Nae said. "Bring it back."

"You the one said 'ring the alarm' that your gay-dar goes off when he's around."

Nae-Nae gave a fake smile. "I was hatin'." He looked at Drae. "I was. You know me, I wanted to fuck him. I'm sorry. I am." He looked at Yuri. "I'ma see you, bitch."

"Whatever."

Drae sat quiet for a moment. "Usually, I'da checked yo' fuckin' chin, but now that I see you goin' through some shit, I'ma let that slide. But if you ever come out your face like that at me again, I'ma see you myself!" Drae spat.

Yuri felt bad about what she'd just said. "I'm sorry Drae. I was out of line."

"Whatever." Drae resumed eating her food. "Whatever."

Yuri

Anthony Hamilton's "Where Did It Go Wrong?" made love to the deafening silence that danced through Yuri and Jeff's Central Park West apartment. Clouds of thick smoke from Jeff's Cuban cigar hustled their way through the air and floated to the ceiling, while streams of light, smuggled in between the eyes of the mini blinds, left their reflection on the bamboo floor.

While reminiscing and listening to music, it had crossed Jeff's mind to buy some weed and get high, but then he thought being high would defeat the purpose of reflecting on the months' worth of bullshit he'd been dealing with. He knew Yuri was lying about leaving at five o'clock in the morning to go to work. He just didn't know why, which made their whole situation seem even more fucked up, especially when he was giving his all to be a good husband. And he knew he messed up when he cheated and his mistress had his child, but that was five years ago, and this time he was trying desperately to get it right. But Yuri wasn't cooperating, and in a minute she was gon' push him to cheat again. Especially since she didn't seem to appreciate the wonderful husband he'd become.

Now he sat at home alone, entertaining every thought that popped in his head as being the truth. He couldn't stop the visions of Yuri freely giving pussy away: riding, spooning, letting some niggah—any niggah—hit it from the back.

He absolutely hated that he tolerated her losing weight. He had a good mind to kick Whoopi Goldberg's ass for acting like L. A. Weight Loss was the key to success. He was happier with his size-twenty-four wife, who looked in the mirror and complained every day about being fat. That he could deal with. But all this flying to Trinidad, shaking her ass and showing off cleavage he never knew she had, irked him. He was used to being king and now he'd been dethroned by a tight waist and a new shape.

All of which led him to think of standing tall on his five-eleven athletically built, masculine frame, rearing his shoulders back and kicking Yuri's natural ass when she walked in the door. But then again, he didn't want to bring himself to the point of no return. He knew if he hit her, he would kill her. And there was no way he wanted her dead without answers to the questions running around in his head like *What the fuck is yo' problem? And where the fuck you been all day? You lost yo' fuckin' mind walking into this motherfuckin' co-op I pay the mortgage for, with a scent that I swear is another niggah's dick! Have you gone stupid leaving me here all alone with nobody, when I'm the only man that loved you when yo' fat ass could catch nothing but a fuckin' fish to eat, and now you don't wanna give me no pussy? Ain't this some shit . . .*

As soon as Yuri closed the front door behind her, she could tell Jeff had been waiting all day with something to say. And since she'd just walked in from work and it had been a week since she'd last heard from Britt, she wasn't in the mood to discuss any *Where has the love gone?* bullshit. And she didn't feel like staring Jeff in the face while flashbacks of sucking Britt's dick invaded her mind; so her plan was to help him get straight to the point, so she could cuss his ass out and have all the unnecessary bullshit over with.

"I take it you ready to rumble." She sighed and sucked her teeth. "So let me just get this poppin'. I already know I'm still fat." She held her right hand out and counted on her fingers. "I may have lost weight, but I'm no fuckin' Oprah, and Halle Berry is putting my biracial ass to sleep. Let's see what else: Oh, you sick of me coming in here thinking I'm cute when you're the one who made me. And Drae is the only one in my family who's ever been close to being skinny, and I need to stop thinking I'm her 'cause I'm not. And if it wasn't for Hassan, her gold-diggin' ass wouldn't be shit either. We just a coupla sad-ass bitches, using niggahs like you and your weird-ass boy Hassan to make it through life 'cause if it wasn't for you I'd still be a lonely-ass, waiting on a dick to swing my way. So I better check myself before I wreck myself. Does that about sum it up? Or you got some new fucked-up shit you invented? Hit me with it now, so I can recite it tomorrow when I walk in the door." She paused. "Oh, you have nothing to say? Then good, you can kiss my ass for even thinking that shit." She slammed her Chloé bag and keys on the glass sofa table, causing a screeching sound. She took a deep breath and pulled her purple scrub top out of her matching uniform pants.

Jeff leaned against the couch, contemplating if now was the time to kick her ass.

"What," she said, exasperated, "the fuck are you staring at?" Before Jeff could answer she went on, "Paleeze, just say what the fuck you gotta say." She lit a long brown cigarette, and the thin smoke released from her lips mixed in with his. Yuri was even more disgusted that she felt forced to light a cigarette, especially when she'd lied and told Britt she'd stopped smoking, but smoking was the only relief she got from tolerating Jeff. " 'Cause, I'm not gon' stand here and figure out what the hell's boggling yo' mind, and my knees are too sore to be beggin' you to speak—"

"Where are you trying to take me, Yuri? You want me to cuss you out like the ho you are? Ever since you lost weight you like a whole 'nother person. Are you fucking somebody over there at L. A. Weight Loss? Or this some bum niggah you passed on the street?"

"Whatever, Jefferson."

"Yeah, I know." He wiggled his neck. " 'Whatever.' "

Just the sight of a grown man wiggling his neck like a fag-ass around-the-way girl made Yuri laugh.

"Oh, you just jolly, huh?" Jeff said. "But tell me this: Is this new niggah fucking your mind? Because I never said you and Drae were sad-ass bitches. I said y'all was some unhappy-ass tramps. Get it straight." Jeff took a pull off his cigar.

"Go to hell!"

"I just came back!"

"Fuck you."

"And get infected?!" As soon as he said that, he hated he'd spat it out. Now he knew anything was bound to fly out of her mouth.

"You Uncle-Tom, low-self-esteem-havin' niggah. Have you forgotten that your rotten-ass dick is the reason I had gonorrhea and chlamydia? Have you slipped up and forgotten that you were off fucking some eighteen-year-old-white-trailer-park-nasty-trash bitch, when you flew her to Aspen and had a skiing accident, where your black-ass balls split completely open causing you to be sterile? Have you forgotten about that five-year-old kid you have with that white bitch? The one and only child you will ever be able to make, cause yo' stupid ass is sterile now?! Need I remind you that we were supposed to have a baby, but when it became my turn your nuts had been ravaged. You're useless, Jeff. Get the fuck over it. It was bad enough your dick game was whack but now all you shootin' is water. Go pay child support or some shit. Just leave me the fuck alone."

Jeff knew she would come back hard, but this had left him damn near speechless. "Yo' fat ass must be on drugs."

"Oh, please, yo' problem is you've kicked dirt on me and now all of a sudden you wanna be all in my chest, like a collapsed lung and shit. But if you know like I know, you'll stop clouding my airway like you Mr. Fuckin' Asthma."

Jeff slid his tie from around his neck. He thought about laughing in her fuckin' face and then slapping the shit out of her. Finally he knew he wasn't crazy and all the thoughts running around in his head were a revelation: This bitch had lost her fuckin' mind. Never, ever since they'd been together had she spoken to him like this, so he was convinced this new attitude was from fucking another niggah. Whispering freaky shit in her ear, playing in her hair, telling her how much he liked her and how bad he wanted to fuck her. Perhaps eating her pussy and sucking her titties like soft cream. Maybe, Jeff continued to think, the man was taller than he was, had broader shoulders, bigger feet, more money and most of all a bigger dick. Suddenly all Jeff could see was Yuri letting this new niggah have her spread-eagle.

Jeff jumped up and shook his head. Just as he decided to get to the root of this situation, Yuri shot him a snide look, headed toward the bathroom and left him standing there with lingering smoke rising from the tip of her cigarette in the ashtray.

Yuri strolled into the master bathroom, took her clothes off, stepped into the shower and closed the glass door behind her. She was sick of Jeff's harassing her about what used to be. Couldn't he see that yesterday had packed its shit and left?

Yuri turned on the shower radio and to her surprise Davaad Levy, the station's DJ, was playing an evening mix of Britt's reggae. Britt had been singing since they were in high school and had had a record deal for close to five years, but only in recent times did his music career take off and get prime-time attention. Now he was on every metropolitan station, sharing airtime with the likes of Sean Paul, Beanie Sigel, Baby Cham and Beenie Man. And no, he wasn't exactly rich—the fame always came before the fortune—but Yuri didn't care. At this moment, if she couldn't have the man she wanted with her, at least she had his music.

As she lathered her body with sour-apple sugar scrub her nipples started to tingle; she wanted badly to rub her fingers across her clit and pretend that Britt was sucking it. Feeling as if someone was watching her she turned toward the glass door and saw Jeff standing in the middle of the bathroom floor. For a moment she felt her thoughts were fully exposed. "Jeff . . ." she said, but no words came behind speaking his name. She could see his eyes roaming all over her as he remembered how much he loved to stare at her naked body. How her breasts sat upon her chest like full moons with the blackest and prettiest nipples he'd ever seen. And the light covering of neatly trimmed hair on her pussy always turned him on.

As Jeff stared, he did his best not to lick his lips, but instead willed himself to remember the faceless new niggah he'd envisioned having his wife spread-eagle.

With Britt's music continuing to serenade them, Jeff swung the glass door open with such force that the wall it was connected to shook and the glass made a howling sound as it appeared to shiver. He stepped into the shower, and the water falling over his body reminded Yuri of a storm in the Trinidadian Trace.

"You think I'm stupid?!" Jeff asked as he grabbed Yuri's face. His fingers were pressed so deeply into her cheeks she could feel his tips against her teeth.

"Are you crazy?" she asked him, not knowing if this was the part where she should scream or ask him to leave. "This ain't no new version of *Psycho*. What are you doing?" She did her best to remove his hands from her face.

"What . . . the fuck . . . is yo' problem?" he asked her as the water drenched his clothes.

"Jeff, go away," Yuri said, beginning to feel frightened. Seeing that getting him to remove his hands was a losing battle, she said, "You're hurting me."

Jeff stared at her for a minute longer before he took his hands away from her face. The overhead shower, which was controlled by the motion of their bodies, followed their movement as Jeff pushed her into the corner of the stall. His starched-white shirt clung like a layer of skin to him as he placed his arms above her head.

"Oh, I know you ain't scared," he said as he studied her eyes. "You had more balls than me a few minutes ago! Yo' mouth was runnin' like a motherfucker when you walked in the door. Kick that shit while I'm breathing in your face. I'm listening. Now what you say?"

"Go 'head, Jeff."

"Naw, fuck '*Go 'head, Jeff.*' Say it now. Or are thoughts of this new niggah pressin' that hard on your mind?" he said, mushing his index finger into her forehead. Jeff took his left hand and grabbed Yuri by the back of her neck, causing her head to jerk back. Slowly he pressed behind her ears with his thumb and index finger and whispered, "How long this niggah been fuckin' you?"

Caught off guard, Yuri stood speechless. She started to get a painful crick in her neck as Jeff's grip became tighter. Tears filled her eyes, but she was determined not to cry.

"You know I been peeping this whole shit, right?" Jeff's deep voice seemed to echo as he took his free hand and ran his fingers through her hair. Her usually bouncy curls were now flat from the rising steam.

Yuri licked her plush lips and stared at him as if to say *Please*. Realizing fear was starting to enslave her, she screamed, "Jeff, stop it!" She pushed him. "Get off me!"

"No!" He pressed his chest farther into her breasts, pushing her deeper into the corner. "For the past six months you been switching yo' ass around here, ignoring me like I wasn't shit! You stopped talking to me, you stopped fucking me, and the next thing I know you playin' me. And the only thing I can see that would have you losing your fuckin' mind on me is a new niggah!"

"Jeff—"

"Don't fuckin' 'Jeff' me. See, Yuri, you got this Armani suit and tie fucked up. I will kill yo' ass before I let you cheat on me. So tell me, while you still got a chance, and don't lie, tell me now so I can think about what I wanna do with you. Are you fuckin' another niggah?"

"Jeff—" She did her best to twist her neck out of his grip. "Stop it! Let me go!"

"Why do you keep asking me the same shit? I said no. Now, are you giving this niggah my pussy?" He brushed his free hand across her pussy lips, parting them with his fingers. "Tell me, does he use one finger or two? Or, better yet, his whole fist?" He took four of his fingers and slid them into her slit, while having his thumb massage her clit.

Yuri was scared yet unable to stop the sensations running through her body. She didn't know if Jeff's fingers fucking her turned her on as much as his aggressiveness did.

Instead of fighting him and making him get off, she gave in to the feeling running through her pussy like a pulse. Her neck began to cramp, so she did her best to make her head comfortable in his hands. She could feel her abdomen begin to contract as the nut's rush greeted the anxious butterflies grooving in her stomach. She knew it was only a moment before the eyes of her pussy dripped tears on his hand.

"See the problem is," he whispered, as her cum began to thicken between his fingers, "that my dick is so hard I could fuck the shit outta you right now. But fucking you won't save your life. I could fuck you and wanna kill you all at the same time." Jeff rubbed his pasty hand in admiration across her hard nipples. He couldn't stand her naked body pressed against his any longer, so he released his grip on her neck and started kissing her from the sides of her face to her pussy lips. She loved the feeling of her clit being pulled between his teeth. If Jeff could do nothing else, he was a master at giving head. Once she came again, Jeff undid his pants, held his hard dick in his hand, and slid it in.

"Ohhhh . . ." she moaned as he stroked her. She wrapped her legs around his waist.

His strokes became more intense with every word he spoke, "Does he . . . fuck you . . . like this?"

Yuri did all she could not to say yes, so instead she wrapped her hands around Jeff's neck and moaned.

"What the fuck you moaning for?" Jeff asked her, as he pushed his dick in as far as it would go. "I wanna know, does that niggah fuck you like this?"

She didn't answer.

"What, you scared to say yes?" Unwrapping her legs from his waist, but never once letting his dick fall out, he placed her feet on the floor of the shower's stall. "Turn around. . . ." he demanded while doing his best to fight off her new man's face creeping into his mind.

He spread her ass cheeks and made her bend down. "You fuckin' that niggah in my position?!" Jeff slid his dick into the back wall of her pussy. The water sprayed their bodies like a waterfall as Jeff fucked her as hard as he could. "Is this what I gotta do"—he smacked her on the ass—"to make you fuckin' respect me?!"

Yuri closed her eyes and focused on the radio's master mix of Britt's music, which continued to fill the enclosed shower. Envisioning Britt's dick, Yuri worked her hips with as much muscle as she could. She felt as if she owed Jeff this nut; and if listening to Britt sing and imagining Britt was making love to her was the only way she could give it to him, then she had to do what she had to do. And that's when it clicked: She needed to make sure that it wasn't Britt's dick that made her forget how much she owed Jeff. And she owed him because he'd loved her all these years. And he took care of her, and like her mother and Drae always said, a good man was hard to come by. So, as she felt him begin to shudder, she opened her eyes and made herself realize he wasn't Britt. And when Britt returned from his trip she would lay all the shit on the line, so he could decide if he wanted them to be together or if she needed to return to her original position of being Mrs. Jefferson McMillan.

Drae

As Hassan held a burning candle above Drae's perfectly shaped D-cup breasts and dripped hot wax over her hard ebony nipples and between her cleavage, she did her best to push Yuri's comment out of her mind.

The triple-X pornos that played on the sixty-inch, high-definition projection screen illuminated the otherwise dark media room they were fucking in. For once, it was just the two of them. Drae was excited because she missed being exclusively with her husband. However, Hassan prayed he could get his nut off before the party. He knew achieving this nut would be extremely difficult because there was no one else in the room he could watch fuck and fondle Drae. After all, that was what he loved most about sex; more than the smell or the taste, was the look of somebody else's dick being smothered by vanilla cream.

Drae winced, even though she loved to feel the pain as she held her titties together and Hassan dripped wax on them; it sent unexplainable chills through her body and made her cunt stretch toward its pinnacle. She started to pant and hoped Hassan caught the hint: She needed his dick to start hittin' it. She couldn't remember the last time he'd fucked her in her pussy.

She let her titties go and opened her legs wide. Pinching her clit she said, "You're welcome to get up in this."

"After I put the dildo in." Hassan took Drae's finger off her clit and sucked it. Then he placed the candle down, grabbed the butterfly dildo from the end table and slowly pushed it into Drae's pussy. He loved the gasping sound she made every time a dildo or a dick opened her up. "You like that?"

"Yes."

"Now let me watch it." Hassan watched Drae fuck herself with the dildo while he continued to drip hot wax all over her. The mixture of pain and pleasure drove her insane and, although the feeling was better than she imagined, she still wanted to feel her husband's dick. As she went to inquire about his plans to officially fuck her, he blew out the candle.

Hassan walked over and stood behind Drae's head, which lay on the arm of the onyx lambskin sectional. He opened his legs, slid his hard dick into her mouth, and fixed his eyes on the porno, which had gone from two heterosexual couples to three gay men.

She couldn't believe it; and it wasn't the homosexual porno that bothered her as much as Hassan preferring brain over fucking her in her pussy. She couldn't remember the last time he'd unloaded inside her. Last she remembered he'd tossed her salad and shot off in her ass.

Suddenly Drae wanted Hassan's sweaty balls out of her mouth. She took her tongue and pushed his dick on the side of her teeth, hoping a good jawbreaker would get him to hurry and cum.

Hassan moaned as he continued to watch the porno, where the male couples lay circular on the floor and began to suck one another's dicks. As the porno seemed to get even more intense, Hassan grabbed Drae's titties and shot off down her throat.

Drae started to gag as most of his cum slid out the sides of her mouth.

"Damn, baby," Hassan snickered. "You can't handle that?" He helped her to sit up and looked at the clock located in the corner of the projection screen; it was six-thirty P.M. "We gotta get ready for my party." He flicked the porno off. "Honey, did you get my black dress pants out the cleaners?"

"And what goddamn soap opera do you think this is? *All My Pornos*? Niggah, please."

"Oh, you too good to pick up a pair of pants for me?"

Drae laughed. "Spare me."

"That's what I'm talking about, Drae. You can't never do shit for me! Think 'cause you teachin' them special-ed kids that you can talk to me crazy."

"I don't teach special ed, you crack fiend! I'm a high-school guidance counselor."

"Whew weee!" He flung his wrist. "I'm impressed. Guidance counselor, special-ed teacher, who gives a fuck? You just better be about them auditions."

"Whatever," she said as she walked out of the room.

"Check it." He followed behind her as she went into the bathroom. "Tomorrow morning you lined up for a gang rape."

Drae stopped dead in her tracks. "Excuse you?"

"I can see it now." He ran in front of her and waved his arms in slow motion. "Hassan presents *Run-a-Way Train*." He held his fist to his mouth, like he was giving his lips a pound, and started running in place. "That's some hot shit right there. Booyah! People gon' be like *Where he at? At the top, where he at!*" He carried on like a rap song. "At the top . . . I swear to God I'm 'bout to be on *Oprah*!"

"I think you've lost," Drae said slowly, "your fuckin' mind!" She turned on the water and stepped into the shower.

As the organic carrot oil ran all over her body, Drae started thinking about Yuri's comment and Hassan being on the down-low. She wanted to get over it, but something about it rang true in her mind. She couldn't figure out if it was the loaded dildo he liked her to fuck him with, the way he flung his wrist or the way he didn't fuck her in her pussy anymore. Or maybe she was making something out of nothing. Maybe Yuri was hatin', or maybe Drae was just sick of him walking around as if all that mattered was a big dick and a smile. There was more to life than a freaky fuck, yet it seemed sex was all their marriage consisted of. And sex was not what she married him for. She married him for security. He was rich, owned a mansion in Westchester, chartered private jets, flew all over the world at a moment's notice. So, she took her black knight and galloped into the sunset, setting her sights on being set for life.

Now Drae felt trapped, caught between X-rated love and

bullshit. And she was sick of being phony, desperately trying to fit into Larry Flynt's version of Barbie and Ken's cul-de-sac. As far as she was concerned, Hassan never gave a damn about who she really was anyway. For all he knew she was a Brooklyn-born pickaninny turned freak.

"Andrea!" Hassan called her name as if he'd just done some speed. "Hurry yo' ass up! The party's all set up downstairs. Now let's go! After all, it's my birthday."

Drae stood at the mirror, fluffing her hair, which was styled in an abundance of Shirley Temple curls. Afterward she walked out of the bathroom stark naked and looked at Hassan as if she dared him to touch.

"Why are you looking at me like that?" he asked her, as he stood fully dressed in cream Versace dress pants and a lavender shirt.

She didn't open her mouth; instead she kept a steady eye on him as she slipped on her gray pantsuit.

Hassan smiled at her. "You love me, don't you, Drae?" he said as the doorbell rang.

"Unfortunately"—she opened their bedroom door—"I do."

Yuri

Yuri sat in her living room, dressed in black dress pants, a black satin shirt that showed an abundance of cleavage, a black-and-white-polka-dot scarf wrapped around the front of her head, and a pair of Manolos. She was smoking a cigarette and looking into the kitchen, wondering when Jeff's son was going home. His mother was due to come and get him two hours ago and she hadn't showed. She knew that Jeff and Yuri had made plans to be at Drae and Hassan's for Hassan's birthday dinner and on the way there they were supposed to pick up Nae-Nae. But already Nae-Nae had called at least a million times asking what was going on, and Jeff sat in the kitchen looking stupid as he watched his son color the third picture of his mommy marrying his daddy.

"Yuri, baby." Jeff walked into the living room, sat beside her on the couch, and grabbed her hand. "Baby, I'm sorry."

"For what, Jeff? What could you possibly be sorry for? Sorry for not listening when I told you she was gon' do this shit because she always does?" She snatched her hand away.

"Look, Yuri." Jeff folded his arms across his chest. "What you want me to do? We can still go. We'll just take Jeff Jr. with us."

"This is a party for adults not kids! Believe me, he is grown enough."

"I'm tired of you not liking my son, Yuri."

"I don't have to like him!"

"What you want me to do, pay child support and that's it? Wash my hands of him?!"

"Now we're getting somewhere! How's that for a save-your-fuckin'-marriage idea!" Yuri jumped off the couch. What she'd just spat out rang in her ear like a bad tune. She looked at Jeff and thought maybe she'd cut him just a little too deep. After all, it wasn't the kid's fault, but it damn sure felt like it. Didn't Jeff have a right to take care of and spend time with his son? But did he have to keep him every other weekend? Did he have to attend every play, recital and parent-teacher conference? Was it a must that he join the PTA and come home to tell Yuri all about it? Did he have to hang his son's pictures all over their house? Was that how it was supposed to be? Was anybody sorry that this had happened to her? Or did Jeff's always wanting a son, and his now having one, make this all good?

"My fault, Jeff." Yuri walked over to him and placed her arms around his waist. "I know I shouldn't have said that."

"Who gives a fuck, Yuri?" He pushed her away. On his way into the kitchen the phone rang.

"Hello?" Yuri answered.

"Where's my son and his father?" Kathy, Jeff Jr.'s mother, spat.

"Lets clear this up." Yuri took a deep breath. "Don't call my house out the side of your mouth no fuckin' more, clean ya coochie up before you come talking shit to me, you trailer-park bitch! Jeff!" Yuri screamed. "Baby Mama Drama is on the phone. You better catch this skeezer!"

Jeff picked up the line and Yuri held the other end of the receiver to her ear. "You know, Jeff," Kathy said. "I'm getting really tired of her thinking she can say anything she wants to me. And I know you hear me, Boom'ki-ki, or whatever the hell your fat-ass name is."

"Unless that's some shit you plan on saying to my face, then you need to get to the point."

"I'm not coming to get him until tomorrow. I'm away for the weekend."

"What, you catching another disease, bitch?!" Yuri spat. "I told you this dizzy bitch was gon' do this, Jeff!"

"Oh, did I ruin your plans?" Kathy laughed.

Jeff shook his head; he looked at his son, who was still coloring, and patted him on the head. He knew his son's presence restricted what he could say. "Katherine," he said sternly, "tomorrow is Monday and we have to work."

"And so do I, Jeff! Send his stepmother to take him to school!" And she hung up.

"I hope," Yuri said into the phone, over the dial tone, "that this is worth every drop of that nut you brought to life! Now, I don't know what you gon' do, but I'm ready to go."

"I'ma let that shit you just said slide, 'cause if I think about it too long, I'ma hurt you." Jeff hung up the phone. "Jr., let's go, man. We're going out."

"What about my mommy, Daddy?"

"She'll be there to get you from school tomorrow."

"But I want my mommy." He began to cry.

"What did I say, Jefferson!" Jeff snapped. Realizing that he'd just taken his frustration out on his son, he turned to him. "Daddy's sorry, man. I am. Get your coat and let's go. You'll see your mommy tomorrow."

"Okay, Daddy." He sniffed.

As they headed for the front entrance to step outside, Yuri noticed that Jr.'s coat was hanging off his shoulders, his hat was still in his hands and his nose was running. She took a tissue from her purse and wiped his nose. "Sweetie," she said, making an effort to be kind to him, "let me fix you here." She squatted to her knees and pulled his coat onto his shoulders.

Instantly Jeff's face brightened up. "Thanks, Yuri." He stroked her back.

"Let me see your hat, baby." Yuri took Jr.'s hat from his hands.

Jr. squinted his eyes and snapped at Yuri, "My daddy can do it." He snatched his hat back. "My mommy said your fat hands were never to touch me."

Yuri squatted still on her knees for a few seconds before getting up; she had to talk herself out of slapping Jr. to the ground. Then she remembered he wasn't hers, he was Jeff's problem.

"He owes me an apology, Jeff." Yuri stood up.

"Apologize for snatching, Jr.," Jeff said.

"Snatching?" Yuri said in disbelief. "How about apologize for being disrespectful and not staying in a kid's place. He's just five years old."

"Yuri, please, you're being emotional again."

"Emotional?"

"Yes, because you and I both know he was simply repeating what his mother told him."

"Exactly, and it was disrespectful." They started walking to their SUV.

"He wasn't being disrespectful, Yuri," Jeff insisted as he clicked the remote entry to the Land Cruiser. "He was being a kid."

Yuri stopped in her tracks and stared at Jeff; he was two minutes away from being gut-punched. She hopped in the SUV and slammed the door. She opened her bag and pulled out her emergency chocolate bar. Whenever she felt like this, eating chocolate and smoking a cigarette somehow soothed her. As she placed a piece of candy in her mouth, Jeff snatched the bar out of her hands. "And you want my son to apologize for calling you fat."

"You know what, Jeff, fuck you and your whole motherfuckin' family."

"Watch your mouth around my child."

"Is he a child or is he grown? He seems to think he's my fuckin' equal."

"This is crazy, Yuri!"

"Finally we agree; this is crazy." Yuri had to laugh to keep from crying. After all, somewhere along the line this shit had to be funny.

"As a matter of fact," Jeff said, taking the candy bar and tossing it out the window and into the street, "you need to go back on your Philly, Boston, Dallas, L.A. or whatever kinda damn weight loss it was, and lose a few more pounds."

Yuri shot Jeff a nasty look and instead of cussing him out like she wanted to, she was quiet until they picked up Nae-Nae.

Nae-Nae stepped to the truck in a one-piece patent-leather catsuit, with a V dip in the front to showcase his chest hairs and a V dip in the back that stopped at the top of his ass. He wore three-inch-platform knee boots and as he walked his legs swayed from one side to the other. "Y'all niggahs is trippin'," he announced as soon as he opened the back door. "Here I am 'bout to turn Raphael out—"

"Nae-Nae," Yuri interrupted him, "please—"

"Ain't no please. I got needs. I swear I'm so sick of pussies hatin' on me!"

As Nae-Nae slid in the backseat he saw Jr. sitting there. He couldn't tell if Jr. was lit up with delight or embarrassment.

"Oh, I'm sorry y'all," Nae-Nae said as he closed his door. "Nae-Nae got a habit of showin' his ass."

"Nice apology, Nae-Nae," Yuri said sarcastically.

"Wheew, I see somebody in here has a soar ass besides me."

Yuri turned around. "Would you stop cussin'?"

"Oh yeah, excuse." Yuri could hear him mumbling, "Pussies is always hatin' on Nae-Nae."

After a few minutes of riding, they were all quiet, except for Jr. who kept singing the same verse from *The Suite Life of Zack & Cody.*

"This lil' niggah retarded?" Nae-Nae eased up from the backseat and whispered in Yuri's ear. Yuri, who sat in the front seat, looked at Nae-Nae's reflection in the flip-down visor's mirror. She gave him a look for him to cut it out.

Nae-Nae lay back against the seat and Jr. kept singing, this time even louder than before.

Nae-Nae looked at him. "What you singing, man?"

Jr. popped his lips. "I'm singing," he said with a slight twang that no one seemed to pick up on but Nae-Nae, "*The Suite Life*"—he clicked his tongue and wiggled his neck—"*of Zack & Cody*." As far as Nae-Nae was concerned all that was missing was a two-finger snap and a "How you doing?"

"Whoool, aren't you a lively lil' thing. Look at you." Nae-Nae tapped Yuri on the shoulder. "Ring the alarm!" He gave a snide laugh and batted his eyes at Jr. "I bet you be looking at Zack and Cody every chance you get."

"I love them!" Jr. said, excited.

"Nae-Nae can tell. Jeff—"

"Yes?"

"I don't think lil' daddy over here will be bringing Hannah Montana to your house."

Yuri whipped around in her seat and looked at Nae-Nae. She wanted to slap him upside the head. He already knew that Jeff didn't care for him and here he was saying some shit like this. She couldn't wait to tell Drae about this. "If you don't shut the fuck up!" she mouthed to Nae-Nae.

"Ewww, what?" he mouthed back. "What did I do?"

Yuri shook her head and turned back around. She peeked at Jeff from the corner of her eye and she could tell he was pissed. Yuri was sure she would be hearing about this later.

"Anybody wanna go to a Stacy Lattisaw concert?" Nae-

Nae said, cutting through the obvious tension. "Rick Ross is the host and Klymaxx and Johnny Gill gon' be there showin' they ass!"

"We been riding too long," Jeff said.

"What, y'all got something against Stacy Lattisaw?" Nae-Nae snapped. "I betchu lil' Sanjaya over here would go."

"Nae-Nae," Yuri said, "what kinda concert combination is that? Please be quiet."

"What, people can't have concerts the way they want to? They got to have them to suit you? Who would you like to sing at your concert, Yuri? Patti Austin and the Weather Girls? Just be quiet, Yuri. You have no sense of music."

As they pulled up, there were a ton of cars in the driveway. Yuri hated being late and she was pissed that it seemed they were the last ones to arrive.

They could hear the music pumping from the inside onto the steps. Once Drae opened the door, they could tell everyone had been having a good time. There was food everywhere, balloons all over, and everybody there was getting their party on.

"Hey!" Drae said as she greeted her friends. "What took you so long?"

Yuri quickly diverted her eyes to Jeff Jr., who was pouting and standing next to Jeff, and back again. "Oh," Drae said, knowing that now was not the time to ask what he was doing here.

"Hey, Jeff." Drae kissed him on the cheek.

"How are you, Drae?" Jeff kissed her back. "Where's Hassan?"

"Over there." She pointed to a crowd of some of their friends from high school and a mixture of new ones. Hassan was standing in the center with a drink in his hand and a cigar that she knew was probably laced with cocaine.

"Hassan," Drae called. "Jeff and Yuri are here."

Hassan and a few of their friends walked over to greet them. The men gave one another brotherly-love hugs and handshakes, while the women kissed one another on the cheeks. "Oh, wow," one of their friends, Lisa, said. "Jeff, Yuri, Drae and Hassan never told me you two had a son? Look at him." Lisa squatted to her knees. "He's adorable."

"Thank you," Yuri said, suddenly feeling like a fool. "Jeff," Yuri said, "why don't you take Jr. to the bathroom?"

"I don't have to go to the bathroom."

"You look exactly like your mommy, young man." Lisa pointed to Yuri and then pinched Jr.'s cheek as she rose from the floor.

"That's not my mommy," Jr. snapped. He turned around and looked at Jeff. "Daddy, I'm ready to go home!" He stomped his feet.

Everyone standing there, with the exception of Drae, Nae-Nae and Hassan, had a look of surprise on their faces. "I'm sorry, I thought he was your son. Well, who is he? Your godchild?"

"This is my son," Jeff said, squeezing Jr.'s hand in hopes that the pain would get him to behave.

"Wait." Lisa frowned. "But you two have been married for six years— Oh, I see— His mother is someone else— Is he adopted?"

"Goddamn, Lisa," Nae-Nae said. "That's why yo' ass couldn't keep no friends, you just nosey as shit."

"Lisa," Yuri said sternly, "this is Jeff's child. I am not his mother and he is not adopted. Can we please leave it at that?"

"Uhmm, we certainly can. . . . Well, what does everyone think of this weather? One minute it's hot and the next minute it's cold."

In an effort to knife the tension, everyone else joined the weather conversation, including Jeff. But as Yuri went to speak, she saw Britt walk in Drae's door with his arm around Troi, his ex-fiancée, stroking her hair and laughing while whispering in her ear.

Yuri did all she could to keep a smile on her face as Troi spotted them and waved. She could tell that Britt was in shock as his eyes scanned the room. They walked over and spoke to everyone.

"Hello!" Troi kissed everyone on the cheek.

"Hey, girl," Drae said. "I'm so glad you could make it. Britt, how are you?"

"I'm good," he said, nodding his head yet staring at Yuri. "I had no idea this was your spot, Drae. Nice, very nice."

Troi laughed. "I had to drag him out the studio. I swear I can never get any time with him because he's always recording."

"Excuse me." Yuri knew if she stood there any longer she was going to either burst into tears or come out swinging. And she didn't want to make any impulsive decisions she would regret. The only thing that this could do for her was make her face the fact that she couldn't have an affair and be married forever. Hell, didn't Jeff get caught? If anything, she owed Britt a thank you—thank you for making her face the inevitable. "This is my jam right here!"

The DJ was playing "One Night Love Affair." As Yuri took to the floor, she could feel Britt's eyes on her ass, so she threw it on extra thick. As far as she was concerned, this was the closest he'd ever get to her ass again, so, if anything, he needed to enjoy the view. Yuri was dancing so feverishly that she enticed most of the people to join her in the middle of the floor, and suddenly Hassan and Drae's dining room became a disco.

As Yuri turned to do a spin, she spotted Britt eye-fucking her. Since Jeff wasn't the dancing type she watched him stand against the wall and talk to Hassan, with his son falling out and crying at his feet.

Yuri motioned with her index finger for Britt to come near. She knew that Troi was staring at her, but she didn't give a damn.

Britt walked over to Yuri and started dancing with her. She threw her ass into his shaft as if they were the only two in the room. "Have you lost your fuckin' mind?" Britt asked her as his dick became hard. "You know you makin' my dick hard."

"So how long you been fucking Troi?" Yuri asked, oblivious to Britt's last statement.

"I'm not fucking her," he said, holding Yuri by the waist and imagining fucking her from behind.

"No need to lie, Britt."

"You fucking Jeff?" Before Yuri could answer, he continued, "And watch what you say, 'cause I will turn this motherfucker out."

"Oh, please."

"Answer my question."

"No," she lied. She'd just ridden Jeff's dick last night.

"Why would I play you like that, Yuri? Troi and I are business. As a matter of fact, I swear I didn't even know this was Drae's spot. She asked me to come with her to one of her friend's parties and I agreed. That's it."

"Why are you explaining anything to me? It's cool."

"What, you don't believe me?"

"No." She turned around to face him. "As a matter of fact, I don't."

"Why would I lie? You here with Jeff. What I got to make up an explanation to you for?"

"You don't." She did all she could to remain calm and not become emotional. She continued to dance her misery away.

"I hope you don't think I'm seeing her, because I'm not. She's an entertainment attorney for Sony and I'm an artist. That's it, nothing else."

"Look, stop explaining shit to me. It was fun while it lasted and now it's over." And, as if on cue, she stopped dancing. "I'll see you when I see you."

As she walked away she bumped directly into Drae.

"And you ain't fucking this niggah?" Drae twisted her lips. "Yeah, okay."

Drae

. . . All the chronic in the
world couldn't even mess with you . . .
You the ultimate high . . .

"Move over, Drae, I think I'm 'bout to cum. . . ." Nae-Nae squealed as he watched the male dancer gun his hard chocolate dick against the gleaming metal pole. Nae-Nae tossed a twenty-dollar bill toward the dancer's feet. "I don't know 'bout y'all, but I'm 'bout to give all my abortion money away."

Drae eyed both sides of Fantasy Island, an upscale nightclub in midtown, which featured exotic male dancers every Wednesday evening, better known as Hump Night. Seeing they'd gathered a few onlookers, Yuri spoke through clenched teeth, "If you don't sit yo' . . . punk ass . . . the fuck down . . . !" Yuri said to Nae-Nae.

"Drae, is there a fag-hag spewing hateraid?" Nae-

Nae tossed more money toward the stage. "I swear pussies is always hatin' on Nae-Nae."

Drae sat at the table smoking her Virginia Slims with ease. Although she heard Nae-Nae, she didn't respond. She was too busy staring at Hassan, who sat at the back of the club running his hands up a woman's skirt. Drae could tell by the way he was biting his bottom lip and squinting his eyes that he was getting off on the feel of her stockings. After all, stockings, stilettos and voyeurism were his fetishes. For a moment Drae thought perhaps this was the type of casting call he did for his pornos before he brought the aspiring stars home to her.

After a few minutes of watching Hassan feel-fuck a bitch, she hoped that Yuri and Nae-Nae hadn't spotted him. She wasn't in the mood to get funky, go off and pretend to care that he was checking for another woman; especially since she never told them he was an acclaimed underground porn director. As far as they knew, he created wildlife documentaries for *National Geographic.*

Drae sized up the six-foot-tall woman. She hated to admit it, but the chick was fly. And usually Hassan sizing up a chick didn't bother her, but something about this one was different.

"Snap, snap," Nae-Nae said to Drae, as he sipped on a Grey Goose martini. "Do you see the granddaddy of big dicks?" He pointed toward the stage, where the dancer generously massaged himself with motion lotion and baby oil.

Drae mashed her cigarette in the ashtray and looked. "Oh my God," she said, realizing that the dancer was Naz. Suddenly her heart started racing. She licked her lips as she stared at the muscles tumbling down his body like pouring rain, causing the beginnings of an orgasm to knot in her stomach. Her toes involuntarily curled up, she bit her bottom lip and imagined sucking his dick.

Flashbacks of fucking him made her clit swell as she felt the shudder of him ramming into her.

The flashing lights that illuminated his flawless body did him little justice as he gyrated his pelvis and jerked the muscles in his double-jointed dick. After a few seconds of popping his beautiful cock, he slowly wrapped his long fingers around his shaft and seduced his dick to release its personal liquid.

The crowd lost control and hundred-dollar bills floated through the air like a nor'easter. "I'm cumming, Elizabeth!" Nae-Nae stretched his arms out and fainted. The extremely tight, black patent-leather leggings and vest suit he wore caused him to slip to the floor, where he lay and looked to be having an epileptic seizure.

Naz spotted Drae in the crowd, gave her a half smile and winked.

"He lookin' at me, y'all," Nae-Nae growled as he came to and helped himself off the floor. "Drae, give this niggah a blank check. And, Yur'ray"—he exaggerated her name the way he always did—"look in yo' purse and give me one of your mornin'-after pills. I got a strange suspicion I might get pregnant tonight."

"I think I'ma throw up."

"I'll be right back," Drae said as she watched Naz leave the stage. She spoke as if she were in a trance, and for the moment she forgot about Hassan feel-fucking the chick in the back of the room.

"Where are you going?" Yuri asked as Drae disappeared from her sight.

Drae did her best to walk swiftly backstage and not get spotted by Hassan or stopped by the flashlight cop, who was eyeing her ass when she first came in. The club was so big that it felt like a maze. Moonlight and candlelit sconces lit up the glass ceiling, while the neon bars with "Red Light District" etched into the counter led the way to a swinging backstage door. There were naked dancers carrying their G-strings and half-naked dancers still sporting theirs. Most of them were holding someone's hand and leading them in and out of the swinging door.

With every step her heart pounded. As she walked through the swinging door she saw three more doors, all identical and painted black. She couldn't tell which was the right one, but she knew Naz had to be back here somewhere. After a few seconds of staring blankly at the doors, she pushed the middle one open, only to find the bouncer she was trying to avoid on his knees with his eyes closed and a dick in his mouth. Immediately Drae's heart stopped. As fast as she'd pushed the door open was as fast as she closed it. *What the hell am I doing?* She shook her head, feeling like a stripper's groupie on a dick-searching field trip.

This was ridiculous. She quickly came back to her senses and headed in the opposite direction to be seated with her friends. As she approached the exit, "Here I am" floated over her shoulder. She swallowed deeply realizing that Naz had been watching her this whole time.

"Who said I was looking for you?" Drae said as she looked up. If it weren't for his perfect smile she wouldn't have recognized him, especially since he was fully dressed: Prada jeans, white thermal, blue goose-down vest, and Timbs.

"There you go lying again," he said.

She stood silently.

"What are you doing back here?" Naz asked, using all of his will not to slam her against the wall and rape her pussy with his tongue, especially since, for the last three weeks, he had a craving for her cream. Instead he tucked his bottom lip into his mouth and pressed his top row of teeth into it.

He looked her up and down admiring the way she was dressed: nothing over the top, just a pair of tight-fitting Gucci jeans, pink V-neck satin wrap shirt that complemented the tattoo of cream-drizzled cherries on her left breast and a pair of water-colored Manolos. He pulled at one of her belt loops. "Look at you."

She searched his eyes for a reason to leave but couldn't find one. "I was looking . . . for the bathroom. . . ." She hated to lie but hated even more that he made her nervous. "I got . . . lost."

Naz let her belt loop go, turned her around and grabbed her by the waist. He pulled her back to his chest, inadvertently causing his hard dick to molest the crack of her ass. "Do you make a habit of lying?"

"What?" Drae prayed he couldn't feel her legs shaking.

"Let's cut to the chase." He kissed her on the side of the neck and massaged her waist. "You didn't come back here for the bathroom, 'cause you passed the shit on the way in here. You came looking for some dick. But let me school you real quick. You can't keep me, I don't want no cars, no jewelry, no tuition money, no gifts, don't give me access to your bank account and *don't* send me no sneakers. Now"—he turned her around and kissed her softly on the lips—"go sit yo' fine ass down."

Naz hated to play her, but what else was he going to do?

He'd been down the road of screwing the horny-ass married chick and he wasn't beat for it. He knew the only thing Drae could bring into his life was drama.

Drae could've choked on her own spit. She hadn't been this embarrassed since she was living with her mother, went to high school and a roach climbed out of her shoe. "You pornographic shakin'-yo'-ass motherfucker. Who you think you talkin' to?! Oh"—she laughed nervously—"hell no, I'll kick yo' ass 'fore you play me crazy; you got Drae Shaw fucked up. Don't stand up here and act like you got the biggest dick in the world, 'cause, truth be told, I was wondering where the rest of it was, *niggah*. Wit' yo' punk ass." Gathering her hurt feelings and doing her best to fight off embarrassment Drae threw her hips in motion as she hurried toward the door.

"Come here," Naz called.

"Kiss my ass," she threw over her shoulder.

"I've done that already. Now, I said 'come here.'" He walked in front of her and blocked her path.

"Didn't you tell me to leave? So move," she said, doing her best not to look him in the face.

"What's on your mind?" He caressed her cheeks.

"Nothing."

"There you go lying again." He kissed her from her forehead to her lips.

"I'm not." She hated that she was responding to his kisses, but his tongue was so warm and wet . . . and she loved the way it tossed and turned against hers. And to think she usually hated to kiss. It created too many emotions. She'd much rather him take his dick out and get right to the point, than to get her heart going, soup her up, and toss her away the next day. "Stop," she said, pulling away. She wanted more than anything to confess that he'd been riding her mind; not only his dick, but him. And she wanted to take his hand, sit Indian style with him and find out everything from his whole name to his favorite foods. "I . . . I . . . gotta go," she stuttered, pushing him off her. "Please, I need to leave."

Before he could say anything, she pushed past him and ran out the door, leaving it swinging behind her. She did her best to calm down before returning to her seat. As she approached the table where Nae-Nae and Yuri were throwing their hands in the air like whips, she noticed that Hassan and the woman he was feeling on were gone.

"What took you so long?" Yuri asked as Drae retook her seat.

"You just missed this Italian python-dick motherfucker!" Nae-Nae screamed. "Girl, that black-man-big-dick shit is a myth, 'cause that last mofo rocked a whole buncha niggahs to sleep."

"Get outta here," Drae said with no sincerity, doing her best not to feel how fast her heart was beating.

"And guess what else?" Nae-Nae asked, excited.

"What?"

"Yur'ray." Nae-Nae smiled. "Don't hate, ho. Tell this trick the deal, tell her the deal, Yur'ray."

"Chile, they called Nae-Nae onstage!"

"Uhmm hmm, yop." Nae-Nae was amped. "Sho' did. Don't hate, pussy, please don't hate."

"And you know Flamin' was acting ridiculous." Yuri rolled her eyes.

"Flamin'? Oh, you can slow the fuck down now, homegirl. I am anything but flamin'."

Drae attempted to show some interest. "I know he showed his ass."

"Chile"—Nae-Nae swept invisible sweat from his brow—"I was this close to showin' my ass, but security stopped me. Anywho, let me inform you." He pointed to his chest. "This homo thug still got his shit off."

"How?"

"I sang to that niggah." Nae-Nae stood up and started moving his midsection like a snake. "I said, 'Used to be scared of the dick, now I throw lips to shit. . . .'" He sat back down and popped his neck. "I'm so fierce I can't even stand myself."

"At least I ain't alone." Yuri laughed.

"See, what I mean. I swear on the Rainbow God that pussies is always hatin' on Nae-Nae."

"Why you so quiet?" Yuri asked Drae, as Yuri sipped on her drink. "You usually cussin' Nae-Nae out along with me. Who you thinking about?"

"Nobody . . ." she said agitated. "Y'all ready to go?" Drae fanned herself with a flyer.

"Hell, no." Nae-Nae twisted his neck. "You got this homo thug fucked up, I got one last nut to get."

"Would you stop calling yo'self a homo thug?" Yuri snapped. "Little Richard is mo' homo thug than you, spare me."

"Excuse you?" Nae-Nae couldn't believe it. "Little Richard? Lil Wayne maybe, but not Little Richard. . . ."

After listening to Nae-Nae and Yuri go on and watching two more dancers come and go, Drae reached for her purse. "Look, I'm leaving. And I don't give a fuck about who ain't rollin'." She stood up.

"Your period on?" Yuri frowned. "What, you suddenly got cramps or some shit?"

"I got some Midol if you need it," Nae-Nae volunteered.

"You going with me," Drae said, agitated, "or what?"

"Well, damn." Nae-Nae sucked his teeth. "What, you gon' stab us if we don't roll?"

"All right now." Yuri said, attempting to keep the peace. "Let's go."

Drae bolted out of the club, practically tripping over humiliation. She was pissed that confusion was fucking her up. The winter wind was sharp and cutting across her face. She didn't remember being this cold on the way in, but perhaps embarrassment had sucked all the heat from her body. "You might wanna go and get your coat," Yuri whispered in her ear.

"Damn," Drae said. "Wait right here." Drae ran back in and grabbed her coat. On the way to her car, she saw Naz talking to a unknown woman while leaning against his SUV. She could feel him watching her as she passed him by.

"Any time!" Nae-Nae yelled at Naz as he passed by Drae. "Any place!"

"Get yo' ass on in here!" Drae said as she pushed him in the car.

"Pussy, you better stop hatin'!"

"Yo' ma'," she heard Naz yell as she headed toward the driver's side of the car, "where you goin'?"

"Home wit' you!" Nae-Nae shouted. "Let me out Drae, I gotta ride."

"Shut up and stay in the car." Drae walked over to Naz. It was obvious that she had an attitude.

"Don't be like that, ma'." He tilted his head to the side as the light from the street lamp was reflected off the waves in his dark faded Caesar and his long side burns. He tucked his thumb behind his oversized silver belt buckle, showing the waistband of his boxers.

Drae stared at him and hated that she felt compelled to stand there. "What do you want?!" she practically screamed.

"Don't scream." He placed his hands under her coat and into her back jeans pockets. "It'll give me flashbacks."

Drae hated that she felt complimented. "Okay, so you called me over to talk about what?"

"To start over and apologize for some of the things I said earlier. My fault."

"What makes you think I wanna start over?"

"'Cause you standing here." Naz looked her dead in the eyes. "Check this: my fault. I talk too much sometimes. I just want you to know you should call me every now and then."

"How am I supposed to do that? I don't have your number."

"Check your back pocket."

"Oh, you a slick one." She smiled as she slid his number from her back jeans pocket. "Real slick."

He slapped her on the ass as she turned to go. "Don't forget me."

"Uhmm hmm, I won't." She got in her car and left.

Yuri

For the last two weeks Yuri survived at home by giving Jeff a few sessions of heartache-free and painless pussy. She was able to muster some lost emotion from the pit of her belly and act like the needy, sympathetic and doting wife, but now she was sick of the submissive bullshit. There'd been a few times she wanted to cuss Jeff out. Like when she came home to his son coloring on her kitchen wall and Jr.'s mother calling her house practically all night. Or when Jeff's insecurities reemerged and he started stalking her on the phone, calling her at least ten times a day to ask the same nagging shit about what she was doing and what time she was coming home. Not understanding that for the last two weeks she'd been in mourning. Mourning her decision to leave Britt alone, which was why she couldn't sleep, could barely eat and struggled like hell to say more than two words to Jeff without lighting his ass up.

It was nine o'clock on a Monday night and Yuri was extremely restless. She tossed and turned as Jeff lay back on his side of the bed with four king-sized pillows tucked behind his head, snacking on a bag of buttered popcorn and holding the remote control in one hand. He was watching old reruns of *American Idol* and falling out laughing at the contestants.

"This shit is ridiculous," Yuri huffed, looking at the TV while Simon cussed one of the people out by telling him he looked like a bush baby. "Why . . ." Yuri spoke slowly, "the fuck . . . we . . . watching this shit? Simon's ass is always cussin' people out; and God forbid if yo' ass is fat, that's a wrap; and you would think that Randy could understand and Paula Abdul with her drunk ass . . ."

Jeff continued to watch TV and toss popcorn in his mouth, never once looking Yuri's way.

"Oh, you just ignoring me, huh? Fuck it, then. But you better remember that shit."

Jeff didn't flinch; instead he reached in the nightstand, pulled out his box of Cuban cigars, lit one and blew smoke toward the TV. "The niggah playin' you, huh?" Jeff asked calmly. "What, he got another bitch or something?"

Yuri blinked her eyes and turned toward Jeff. "Excuse me?"

"Check this, it's some real disrespectful shit that you lyin' in the bed next to me and you going through a jump-off withdrawal." Jeff spoke matter-of-factly, never turning away from the TV. "You seriously fiending and shit—playin' ya'self like Superhead."

"Superhead, oh hell no you didn't, motherfucker—"

"Oh, this niggah got you flippin'?"

Instantly Yuri jumped up, waved her arms frantically in the air and yelled, "What . . . the . . . hell are you talkin' about?!"

"Goddamn!" Jeff yelled, giving Yuri a one-sided smirk. "What this niggah do? He fuckin' that bitch too?" He mashed his cigar in the ashtray.

"What?"

"Oh, well, fair exchange, no robberies." Jeff picked up the remote control and turned the volume up.

Yuri couldn't believe this. Who did Jeff think he was? Hell, she wasn't that transparent. Jeff was just trying to read her mind. Truth be told, he didn't know if she was unfaithful or not. Why couldn't he take the hassle-free pussy she'd given him and be quiet? Instead he had to be Dr. Phil and give unsolicited advice, as if she would actually admit he was right. "Kiss my ass!" Yuri snatched the pillows from under Jeff's head and grabbed her cell phone. "Crazy ass!!" she screamed, reaching for her cigarettes and slamming the door behind her.

* * *

Yuri paced back and forth in the guest room for over an hour, smoking one cigarette after the other. WBLS was playing The Quiet Storm and she couldn't stand the abundance of sad shit they kept hitting her with. And worse than that, Yuri was pissed she couldn't get the echo of Jeff's speech out of her mind; especially when all she could envision was Troi riding Britt's dick.

Yuri locked the guest-room door before she finally decided

to go through with calling Britt. She sat steady and prayed that Jeff didn't get paranoid and want to barge in. She pushed thoughts of hanging up out of her mind as she listened to Britt's phone ring. And finally, as if she were asthmatic and now able to take in fresh air, his phone stopped ringing, and between extremely loud music and background chatter she heard him say, "You done with having a fit?"

Yuri sighed. "Who said I was having a fit?"

"Yeah," Britt cut her off and starting speaking to someone else in the studio with him. "That shit is whack."

Judging by the amount of noise in the background Yuri could tell he was preoccupied, but she didn't care, she needed to hear his voice; and at this point she would take it any way she could get it. "I need to talk to you." She attempted to go on, doing her best to control her emotions. "Since I started giving you pussy you've pushed our friendship to the side."

When she didn't get a response, she snapped, "Britt, are you listening to me?"

"Yeah, I got you. . . ." he said distantly. "Hold on, baby. Sham, write this down for Lady Saw's part. . . ." Suddenly Britt started singing, "Me ride it like a rude boy doing his ting."

"You know what, Britt, I'm soooo sick of your selfish-ass shit! I need to leave you the fuck alone. Just go be with your ex-girl!"

"Who are you talking about?"

"You know who the fuck I'm talking about."

"Troi?"

"Funny how, out of all the ex-girlfriends you've had, the

first one you guess is Troi. So that just confirms it. Fuck you!" And she hung up.

Immediately after Yuri hung up she started psychoanalyzing herself. *I think I've lost my mind.* Two seconds later, her phone rang. "Yo, my man, you know what?" Britt said. "Why don't you act like an adult and have an affair for once?"

"Britt—"

"Shut up. All you do is fuckin' whine and complain and cry because you think I'm doing a buncha shit, and, for real, you gettin' on my last damn nerve. Now, unless you wanna be left alone, you'll cool out; you stressin' the fuck outta me. Please. I'm tryna do some things and I need somebody down for me and understanding, not somebody who's married one day and fucking me the next. So what you need to do is get all that worked out and let me know if you need to catch me later."

"Mighty funny you saying all of this after Troi comes back."

"I'm not fucking Troi, I'm fucking you. But if you keep it up—"

"So what you tryna say?"

"I'm not tryna say anything, I'm saying it: You slippin'."

"I'm slippin'," she said more to herself than to him.

"Yeah, but you're cute. You workin' my fuckin' nerves, but you fly. And right now that's what counts."

"You must want some pussy." She smiled.

"Come through real quick. I'm at the studio."

Yuri looked at the time. "I can't do that. It's going on twelve o'clock and this crazy ass here will flip his damn lid."

"So what you saying?"

Taking a deep breath, Yuri said, "I can't stay long."

. . .

Yuri couldn't think of exactly what to say to Jeff that would have him believe she had a good reason for leaving the house this time of night, especially when she had to be at work the next morning. And despite her cussing him out and his failed attempt at being cool, Yuri was certain if she stepped out the door all bets would be off and Jeff would do his damnedest to bust her ass. So instead of storming into their bedroom to instigate a weak argument that might or might not make way for her to fly out the door, she retreated to the shower, rubbed down in sour-apple sugar scrub, and packed her bag with a fly outfit she planned to change into. Desperately trying to think of a solid lie, Yuri set the ring-tone alarm on her cell phone, which dictated that she had at least twenty minutes to wing whatever she was going to tell Jeff.

"Jeff—" Yuri pushed open the frosted French doors to their bedroom.

"Don't come in here with no bullshit," he said as he calmly flicked the TV off. "Leave that in the other room."

Yuri stood still for a moment. A million lies ran through her mind. She thought about telling him that the constant arguing had her by the throat, which was why she needed some fresh air. But she quickly changed her mind, thinking he would see directly through that.

Unsure of what exactly she was going to do, Yuri walked over to the bed.

"I'm serious, Yuri," Jeff warned.

"Shhh, for tonight we're not gon' argue," Yuri said in a

seductive tone, dropping the towel wrapped around her body. Instantly Jeff's dick stood up and she could see the rise in his pajama pants. Slowly Yuri crawled on the bed and began kissing him on his stomach. "We gotta get ourselves together. . . . learn to make love again." She stroked his hard dick through his pants. "This a big dick, daddy."

Unable to speak, Jeff continued to bask in the feeling that Yuri was giving him. He watched her dip her hands in the slit of pants, take out his dick and kiss it.

"Yuri . . ." Jeff moaned; he couldn't remember the last time she'd kissed his dick.

She pulled his pajama pants off, slid between his legs and began licking the ridges of his balls. She could feel his hard veins rubbing against her tongue as she showered him with her mouth. Her tongue strokes alternated from head to base and back again. Knowing that Jeff loved it when she spat on his dick, Yuri spat all she could and then began sucking him as if she had a river between her cheeks.

"Damn, baby." Jeff ran his fingers through her hair. "Why can't it always be like this?" As he felt his nut ease toward the tip, his words slurred, "Please, baby, let's keep it like this. . . ."

Yuri knew that Jeff was reaching his climax, but she didn't want his nut rushing into her mouth, especially since she couldn't wait to kiss Britt. She'd much rather have Jeff splash off on her breasts. As soon as he started telling her how much he loved her, her cell phone alarm went off. *Bingo,* she thought. *Perfect timing.* "Shit," she said.

"Don't get that," Jeff insisted, pushing his shaft deeper into her mouth.

"Honey"—she lifted her head up—"it could be an emergency."

"If it is, they'll call the house phone."

"Let me answer it and see." Yuri eased off the bed and grabbed her cell phone. Before flipping it open she inadvertently cut off the alarm, then proceeded to act as if she was holding a conversation. "Hello . . ." She paused. "Oh my God, Nae-Nae, what's wrong?!" Another pause. "Oh no, please don't do anything until I get there. . . ." Pause. "Nae-Nae, what did you say? He's bleeding? No, you're bleeding?" Pause. "He did kung fu?! On you? No, don't call the police. Just calm down. I'm on my way!"

Yuri looked at Jeff, his hard dick standing straight up in the air. "Jeff— Nae-Nae and Raphael . . ."

"Fighting?"

"Yes." She did her best to suppress her smile. "And Raphael's a black belt, so you know he got Nae-Nae shook. . . ."

"I thought Nae-Nae was a homo thug."

"Don't be funny." She smiled.

"Yuri, why must you be Fag-Hag to the Rescue?" He pointed to his dick. "The nut is right at the tip, baby."

"When I come back." She kissed him on the lips. "We'll finish, I promise. I won't be long."

Jeff watched Yuri's naked ass switch as she pulled out a gray sweat suit and sneakers from their walk-in closet. Continuing to suppress her smile and making sure Jeff was unable to see, Yuri went in the closet's built-in drawer and slipped out a lace bra and edible thong. The thong was cherry-flavored the way Britt liked them. "I'm really getting tired of Nae-Nae's mess," she said as she hurried in the master bath to brush her teeth and throw the sweat suit on. She tucked the edible panties in her bra.

When Yuri stepped out of the bathroom she was fully

dressed. "Don't get hurt breaking up a kung-fu battle." Jeff laughed.

"Ha-ha-ha, Jeff." Yuri smiled, stepping out of the room. Before she left the house, Yuri ran in the guest room and grabbed the bag she'd packed.

When she entered the studio it was quite dark, and the only light came from the sophisticated engineering board with its thousand electric-blue knobs and buttons. Britt held a pair of headphones to his ears. His dreads swayed back and forth as he nodded his head. Yuri's heart skipped a thousand beats as she stared at the side of his face. She hated that she fell in love with him every time she saw him.

Yuri walked up behind him and bent down over his head. "So where ya crew at?"

Britt jumped. "Damn, girl, you scared me."

"You knew I was coming." She kissed him on the forehead.

"Yeah, but you usually give me a warning."

Yuri sat down on the small empty counter next to him. She looked around. "So where's everybody?"

"Gone. I told them I had something to do and would catch 'em later."

"Really? You had something to do?"

"Yeah . . . You look good, ma'." Before Yuri came into the studio she'd changed her clothes in the car. Now she wore a tight-fitting denim skirt, tailor-fitted suede shirt, blue lace camisole, and three-inch Marc Jacobs snakeskin boots. "I know I don't tell you that often, but I miss you." He stroked her cheek. Britt rose from his chair and stood between her legs.

"You miss me or you miss fucking me?"

"You want the truth?" He pulled her bottom lip between his teeth.

"Of course."

"Both. I be trippin' off you sometime and shit." He began to caress her breast. "Your smile." He kissed her. "Your laugh." He took off her blue lace cami. "Your touch." He lifted it above her head. "But I need you to stop flippin'." He pulled the straps of her bra down. "Stop being so emotional and let us just flow."

She opened her legs as she felt his hands ease to her pussy. "How long we 'spose to just flow?"

Britt moved the seat of her thong over and fingered her clit. "You looking for the magical answer that I can't give you. . . . Are these edible?"

"Yes." Yuri thought about pressing forward with more questions, but what good would it do? There was nothing they could do with their relationship at this moment other than ride it out, and either she was with it or she wasn't. "You know I love you, right?"

"Yeah," he said, biting a piece of her panties that covered her clit, "too much."

Yuri closed her eyes as her legs started to tremble and Britt's tongue smeared her clit with cherry-flavored juices. "Lay a track for me," he said as he rose from his knees.

"Later, Britt . . ." she moaned, unbuckling his pants.

"Naw." He kissed her lightly on the lips, feeling her palm his dick. "I wanna record you cummin'. But you gotta cum like you did that first night we fucked. Long, strong and in fuckin' tune." He laughed a little.

"You are so nasty." She lifted his shirt and kissed both of his nipples.

Britt briefly turned around and pressed the RECORD button on the engineering board. "Don't worry." He faced her again. "I'll edit and mix it later."

"What you want me to sing?" she spoke into his ear.

"Nothing," he whispered, "I just want you to cum. . . . I'll sing. . . . *It's 'spose to be a secret*," he began, "*you and me/but if I keep you cummin' like this,*"—Britt took his fingers, and circled her clit—"*one day you gon' forget the secret/and the next thing we know/ya man gon' wanna know, how long we been doin' him like this . . .*"

"*But I wanna keep cummin'. . . .*" Yuri sensually ad-libbed in a whispery Janet Jackson tone. "*So we can't let him know . . . 'cause then he gon' ruin what we worked so hard for. . . .*"

Britt got down on his knees and went to eating Yuri's thong completely off.

Slowly, Yuri's nut eased its way out and glazed Britt's lips, and still she kept her pitch, never once coming out of tune, yet cumming with all that she had, releasing herself like never before as they laid the track.

Letting the beat pump solo for a while, Britt roughly hiked Yuri's skirt up as far as it would go. Pushing her against the wall, he pounded his dick into her pulsating middle and started biting her neck.

Although Britt's biting was painful, Yuri enjoyed it. It was like being high, where pain and pleasure battled over the winning position. Yuri wrapped her legs around Britt's waist as he worked his dick in and out of her creamy canal. The rhythm of his dick singing to her pussy drove Yuri crazy, causing her to bury her fingernails into Britt's shoulders and scratch down his back.

"You think I'm playin' you?" Britt asked, doing his best

not to let the stinging of her scratches bother him. "Answer me."

"Yes. . . ." she panted, as he continued to bite her on the side of the neck. "Sometimes I do."

"Why would you think that?"

"I don't know." Yuri started to cum again.

"Don't lie."

"I'm not." She shivered.

"I would never play you. . . ."

"Sure?" Her chest heaved.

"I got you, baby. . . ." Britt said as his nut exploded into her pussy with some of its drippings sliding between her thighs. "For real, I do. . . ."

After sexing each other around the studio, making promises that neither one of them could keep, and recording their second duet together, Yuri headed home. It was three in the morning and she did her best to control the clapping of her heels as she walked across the bamboo floor. Slowly she pushed the French doors to the bedroom open, and prayed they didn't creak. She peeked into the dark room and tiptoed toward her side of the bed.

As she took one arm out of her blouse the room light flicked on. "Naah, keep that shit on." Jeff lit up his cigar as he sat on the edge of the bed. "Let me see this." He tugged at the hem of Yuri's skirt. "You look good." He twisted his mouth and released smoke from the side of his lips.

Yuri stood stunned, pissed at herself that she'd forgotten to put her sweats back on. She blinked several times and looked at Jeff. What the hell was he doing sitting on the edge of the bed and not *in* the bed sleeping? Why was he in her face preparing to argue about some ole bullshit and not asleep? Now, how could she even argue with him when it was obvious that whatever she said would be bullshit. So instead of snapping she sighed. "What are you talkin' about, Jeff?" Yuri turned her back to him. She looked at the ceiling and wondered how could she forget.

"At first"—Jeff walked around the bed and looked at Yuri—"I was like, naah, somebody need to whip Nae-Nae's ass, so fuck it. Yuri can handle that shit. But then, with you owing to suck my dick, I wanted to be sure you came back in one piece."

Yuri didn't say a word; instead she attempted to move out of Jeff's way, but he followed her. She did her best not to let the guilt show on her face.

"It's cool, you don't have to say nothing. But check this, Nae-Nae lives on Nostrand in Brooklyn. Why you head to midtown?"

He followed me? "Midtown?" She didn't know what else to say.

"Don't lie, Yuri."

"Jeff"—she resumed getting undressed—"go sit yo' paranoid ass down." She faced the dresser's mirror and started taking her jewelry off. She could see his reflection behind her.

"I saw you, Yuri."

"How, Jeff? Saw me where, doing what?"

"I followed you. We pulled off at the same damn time, you just didn't know it. So I saw you drive to midtown."

"So where'd I go, then, Jeff?"

"You tell me—"

Instantly Yuri realized that Jeff may have followed her to midtown, but he didn't know exactly where she went. "Oh,

I can't stand you! What the hell are you following me for? I didn't go to midtown, I went to Brooklyn!"

"I saw you, Yuri!" Jeff grabbed her by the left elbow and turned her around toward him.

She snatched away. "Well, if you saw me, then you should've tapped me on my shoulder and made your presence known. You ain't seen shit but a paranoid-ass vision. Driving around gettin' yo' Orange Juice jones on and all the time you wrong as ran-over shoes. You'se a damn clown!"

"Oh, you think I'ma clown?" He mushed her on the side of the head causing her neck to jerk. "Well, you must be a magician since your damn clothes are different!"

"I'm sooooo sick of you. And here I thought you were ready to work on this marriage!" Yuri pushed Jeff in the center of his chest and grabbed her housecoat. "I'm going in the other fuckin' room. Now follow me if you want to!"

Jeff walked behind Yuri as she sauntered into the guest room. She crawled into bed and did her best to act as if he wasn't standing there.

"You know what, Yuri?" Jeff said, deciding to end the argument, especially since his attempt to follow her was halted by a red light. "I'm doing all I can not to fuck you up, but I swear to God that yo' ass is reachin' like a motherfucker."

Drae

"What if," Drae said to Yuri as they browsed through the sale rack at Neiman Marcus, "I told you I'd thought about leaving Hassan?" Drae spoke casually, as if she just asked how the weather was.

"I'd say"—Yuri paused and held up a Norma Kamali blazer—"remember the piss-filled hallways, remember Red Hook, remember who put you through college, remember when we were seventeen and I asked you who was this niggah and instead of telling me who he was, you told me his pockets were laced?"

"That's exactly why," Drae snapped, putting the skirt she was holding back on the rack, "I don't tell you shit."

"Why? Because I give you the same shit you give me?"

"I'm honest with you."

"About what? You ain't honest with me about shit. All you do is sell me a buncha flighty life-is-so-wonderful nonsense and quite frankly I'm sick of it. All of my life that's all I heard, from my mother, from our grandmother, from everybody. Drae is trying so hard, why don't you do better, Yuri? You have a mother, she doesn't. Drae is a virgin, Yuri, how could you be pregnant at eighteen—"

"You being pregnant didn't have shit to do with me! It had to do with you giving up your virginity to Britt and allowin' him to nut all up in you, like he wasn't in love with Troi!"

"You act like it was a one-night stand. We were together for three months after that."

"No, he fucked you for three months after that. You were never his girl, and soon as you told him you were pregnant, he gave you the abortion money and he fuckin' stepped. Just like he gon' do again."

"Don't you worry about what he's gon' do again. Besides, I thought this was about Hassan."

"No, this seems to be about some shit you got on your chest that you wanna get off."

"Whatever."

"So are you fucking Britt? Again?"

"Goddamn, Drae. Yes, yes, I'm fucking him again."

"You so stupid!"

"Fuck you. I forgot, you're perfect."

"I told you before you don't know what the fuck I am!"

"What are you then, Drae?!"

"Miserable." Tears welled in her eyes. "The fuck miserable."

Yuri held the suit in her hand close to her chest. She knew the argument they just had had gathered some onlookers and eavesdroppers, but at this moment she was in too much shock to care. "What?"

"I'm just unhappy and I'm even more upset that you still holding some jealousy shit over my head from when we were kids. Yuri, you were the one who had it all. Not me. I inherited my mother's section-eight apartment and a buncha damn drama ever since."

"Drae, are you okay?" Yuri looked concerned. "You wanna tell me what's going on?" She hung the suit back on the rack and walked over to Drae. "What's the problem?"

Drae stared at Yuri and did her best to judge if she could tell her the real deal. When she couldn't decipher if she could be completely honest or not she lied and spat out, "Hassan wants to swing!"

For a quick second Yuri stood speechless, "Swing from what?"

"You know what I'm talking about!"

"He wants to see you ridin' another man's dick and he wants you to see him fuck another woman?" she said as she frowned. "What?"

"Damn, you can fix your face. Be honest, would you ever do that with your husband?"

"If I knew that bitch would keep him."

"You going to hell." Drae chuckled.

"So, you're serious, Drae?" Yuri asked.

"Not really. I think what's really bothering me," they

began walking out of the clothing department and over to the shoes, "is that I feel like I'm at a point in my life where I should be secure in who I am, what I want, and what I expect and I'm not there yet and the shit is eating me up. You understand where I'm coming from?"

"Do I? Please." Yuri picked up a snakeskin stiletto and looked at the price.

"So, what do you do?" Drae asked.

"I keep it moving. I avoid feeling the shit if I can. It's like okay, I'm not sure where I'm supposed to be in life, but I know I'm not supposed to be here, so what do I do about it?"

"And who has that answer?"

"No fuckin' body." Yuri put the shoe down.

"I think we have it, but we're just too scared to realize it."

"Gurl, please." Yuri waved her off. "You reachin' a little too deep for me. Just give me a man who loves me and the rest I'll deal with later."

"Hmph," Drae sighed. "That's the fuckin' problem."

For a few moments more they browsed the shoe section, picking up the floor samples and looking at the prices. After a while neither one of them had seen anything they liked.

"You hungry, Yuri?" Drae asked.

"Not really."

"My treat."

"Well hell," Yuri smiled, "you should've said that the first time. Then yeah I'm hungry."

"Cool, where you wanna go?"

"Mr. Chow's."

"Mr. Chow's." Drae smirked, "Bitch, no you not trying to spend all my money?"

"That's the price you pay for being rich bitch." Yuri smiled as they headed down the escalator to leave the store.

"Pussies is always hatin' on Drae!"

"Nae-Nae, gon' kick yo' ass!" Yuri said and they both laughed, heading down Fifth Avenue.

Yuri

"Take off your clothes and leave 'em at the door," Britt demanded.

As Yuri entered his loft the music immediately began to make love to her. She couldn't help but drip with wetness as Britt stroked the keys of his grand piano like a jazz musician. She wanted to sing, but couldn't think of what lyrics to contribute to such a melody; so instead she did as he said and began to undress as soon as she closed the front door.

The music traveled down the loft's hall and filled the air. The acoustics in his place were wonderful and besides his king-sized bed that sat on a second-story platform and his metallic kitchen area, his loft was designed like a top-notch recording studio—equipped with keyboards, congos, two copper pans, and more. And Yuri loved being here. Here, she felt famous and confident, like she was that bitch to be fucking a man like this . . . she just didn't want to be taken out of her element. After all, she and Britt shared a world built on Jeff's time and cheating him out of moments.

A heavy rain had started to fall, so the loft appeared dark despite the floor-to-ceiling windows that dressed every part of the room.

Yuri could clearly see Britt sitting on his piano bench, his defined back facing her, and his ecru silk boxers complementing the deep mahogany of his skin.

The heels of her Burberry stilettos clapped against his hardwood floor as she sauntered like a naked top model to greet him.

Doing her best not to be nervous, Yuri slid in between the piano and the bench, so she would be in front of Britt. As he placed his forehead on her belly, she began to massage his neck while he French-kissed her navel and rubbed her thighs. He loved every inch of her. From her French-manicured toes to the crown of her head. He especially loved how she wasn't skinny, but was just right. He could feel her in his arms when he held her, when he squeezed her and when his dick pounded in and out of her. He couldn't wait to hear her call his name. Kissing her breasts he said, "When you cum I want you to sing my name from the pit of your stomach; scream it in such a melody that the fuckin' windows feel to crack." Placing his hands around her waist he sat her on top of the piano. As her heels hit the keys a lingering chime traveled throughout the room. "Lay down," he whispered.

Yuri lay on the piano and felt Britt's hands gliding up and

down her middle, causing her clit to throb and her mind to wish he would just fuck it or suck it. But he needed to do something before the thought of it all caused her to cum. "Look up," he said, pushing two of his fingers inside her.

Yuri looked up and saw the large, lit mirror above the piano. This was the first time she'd seen her new body in full view, all the other times she felt too self-conscious to stare at herself. "You see yourself?" Britt asked, now slipping his fingers out and running them across Yuri's lips.

"Yes."

"That's who I want. Nobody else. Understand?"

"Why are we discussing that?"

"Because I see the fear on your face. And you get too emotional, too impulsive, and I want it to stop. My plans aren't to hurt you. I'm feeling you . . . to say the least . . . but you got a husband and I'm in between. We both have to remember to play our positions, but as long as you're honest with me, I'll never leave you alone. I don't give a damn about Jeff being at home."

"I just get confused. . . ." Yuri paused, she didn't want to say anything that would make Britt think twice about them being together one day.

Before Yuri could go on, Britt massaged her breast. "Shh . . . no more confessions."

"Britt—"

"Not now," he whispered. "Shhhh . . . sit up a little." Yuri did as she was told and her breasts were directly in Britt's face. "I want you to suck your nipple with me." Not sure exactly what to do, Yuri lifted her left D-cup breast and placed the nipple in her mouth.

"That's it, baby," Britt whispered. After watching for a few moments, Britt started to kiss Yuri's other neglected breast, teasing the nipple with his tongue. Shortly after tantalizing her right nipple on his own, he worked his way over, slipped his tongue in Yuri's mouth and after softly biting her tongue he worked his way around the hard and swollen nipple she sucked on, eventually stealing it away. Feeling Britt suck her breast was like a breath of fresh air; it was simple yet so serene, so natural yet so powerful.

Stroking his dreads she closed her eyes and began to imagine what they could one day be.

"Slide back," Britt said, slipping her nipple from his mouth and twirling it between his thumb and index finger.

Yuri kept her eyes closed and slid back.

"Now open your eyes," Britt continued, "and look at me."

Yuri opened her eyes and Britt was now lying over her, dipping his fingers into her pussy, pulling out her erotic candy. "Taste it." He stuck his fingers into her mouth.

"Uhmmm," she moaned.

"You like to taste that pussy? That's my pussy. My sweet, sweet pussy . . ." He took his fingers from her mouth and circled his fingertips across her clit. Placing his pussy-covered index finger back to her lips he demanded, "I want you to suck the candy off my dick."

"Whatever you want, baby." As Yuri turned him over and began to ride him, her pussy slapped generously across his thighs. The sound of her skin clapping against his drove Britt insane. As the nut began to rumble in his belly, he knew he couldn't let her think she was working this scene—after all, he'd told her to sing his name, and she hadn't called him once. So, he flipped her over, pulled her ass onto his shaft, and fucked her from the back wall of her pussy until he felt like the walls would collapse. "Don't nut without singing my name," he said, biting the back of her neck.

He felt her pelvis start to contract. "What the fuck I just say?"

"Britt," she panted.

"That didn't have a melody. I said sing the shit," he said, as his scrotum slapped against her ass. "Sing it!"

"Britt . . ." she sang in a baritone, yet fighting the urge to scream.

"No! Sing that shit higher."

"Britt . . ." she attempted in alto.

"Higher!"

"Britt . . ." Soprano.

"Higher . . . !"

"Britt . . . There's a quiet storm . . ."

"I said sing that, sing that shit!"

"Britt!" she spat out like Patti LaBelle hitting her highest note. "And it never felt like this before. . . ."

"That's it, baby," Britt moaned. "You there. Awwl shit."

As Yuri sang, she could feel Britt's nut dripping from her pussy and running down her thighs. "Turn over," she told him.

He complied and now she lay on top, continuing to sing and kissing him on the forehead.

"Why you making me love you . . . ?"

Yuri lifted the soft hairs on Britt's chest with wet kisses, leaving a damp trail down to his dick. Working his eroticness into her mouth she could taste her pussy-made candy. The taste was bitter and the texture was sticky, but she would eat it a million times if he asked her to. Being that she wasn't able to quite express how her heart felt, she traded off by providing him with the epitome of exotic pleasure. Pushing her thoughts of Jeff interfering and Troi stealing him out of her mind, Yuri licked and sucked with every blessing her mouth had to offer.

He did his best not to scream; massaging the back of her neck he sang, ". . . Every day is Christmas and every night is New Year's Eve . . ."

· · ·

"Yo," Britt yelled into the bathroom, as Yuri stepped out of the shower. "What's taking you so long?"

"What?" she yelled back, slipping on the pin-striped pajama button-up he gave her. She loved how his smell lingered in the collar. "Just so you know, my pussy is sore." She walked out of the bathroom, her thick thighs fully exposed and the bottom of her ass cheeks bouncing graciously, flashing her silk panties.

Britt slapped her on the ass as she walked past him. He flashed a huge smile, showing all his teeth. "Come here and let me kiss it for you."

Yuri walked over to him and expected him to laugh; in an effort to beat him to the punch she mushed him in his head. "You play too much."

Ignoring her, Britt bent down, moved the seat of her panties and kissed her pussy. Yuri bit the inside of her cheek and did all she could to stop her mouth from confessing every bit of her love for him. "You'll have a bitch kill you."

He gave a sly smile, he knew she was hung up on his charm. "I can't help it if I'm the shit."

"Oh, you real caught up on your own sack right now. Is that why all we do is fuck?" She sat on the bar stool across from the cooktop where he was standing.

"And that's an issue because . . . ?" Britt opened his cabinet and placed his pressure pot on the lit stove.

"Well . . ." she stalled.

"Exactly; leave the shit alone." He placed the goat meat he'd left marinating overnight in curry herbs and spices into the pot.

"Just one question."

"What, Yuri?"

"So what's different this go-round than the last time?"

"I appreciate you more."

"Really? Why?"

"Because you gotta big ass"—he laughed—"that's why. Now, what I tell you about confessing? Leave that shit alone. Please."

"Oh, I can't stand you." Yuri reached for the bottle of Rum Punch sitting on the counter in front of her and poured herself a glassful.

"Me?" Britt started to chop up fresh vegetables to make fried rice.

"Yes, you," she said, as she walked over, jumped on the counter and watched him cook. As Yuri went to take a sip of her drink, Britt motioned for her to place the rim of her champagne glass to his lips so he could take a sip. After swallowing he said, "I want you to stop being so emotional."

"Why do you keep saying that?"

"Because you're too jumpy. Just chill out and go with the flow: Let me be good to you and let you not expect anything to go wrong with it. Be a'ight with happiness."

"You're confusing me." She did her best to muster a laugh. "I thought you didn't want a commitment."

"I didn't say commitment. I said chill."

"Well, how do you explain you asking me 'why you making me love you'?"

"Look, don't push. We're good the way we are."

"Uhmm hmm."

"You know . . . you my man and shit, like my dude, we niggahs—"

"Okay—"

"Don't cut me off—"

"Sorry."

"Now, where was I?"

"You were just getting to 'we've been friends forever,' " she said sarcastically.

"Exactly. See, we here." He pointed to his chest and then to hers. "You know how we do—"

"Yeah, we chill."

"Yup." He took another sip of her drink. "We talk real shit. That's why I say you my man."

"Yeah, that's me, a fuckin' man."

"Like I said, we good. If we start confessing too much, about how we really feel, it's gon' lead us to doin' a buncha unnecessary shit."

"Unnecessary shit?" Yuri said, caught off guard. "Like what?"

"Like we'll start sweatin' each other. Gettin' mad and blowin' up each other's spots. And I'm not feeling that. So . . . we gon' stick"—he placed his lips against hers—"to our original plan. Best friends with hidden benefits. Nothing extra."

Instantly Yuri felt an iron fist begin to compete with the tears in her throat. Suddenly she was hustling like hell not to have her crushed feelings jump out and kick Britt's selfish ass for being so stupid and not understanding that she would give it all up for him. . . . All he had to do was ask. "Best friends don't ask me not to fuck my husband."

"Can't you do something else with this dude? Go to the movies. Read a book. Rent a Katt Williams tape and make him laugh. All I'm saying is don't fuck his ass."

"Anyway," Yuri said as she jumped off the counter and sat down at Britt's piano. "Enough of that." She started to play around with the keys.

"Yo," he said, happy she'd cut the conversation, "play something."

"A'ight, let me see. . . ." Quickly, Yuri thought of a tune and started to play.

"Oh, hell no," Britt said removing his rice from the stove. "What the hell you playing the theme song to *Good Times* for?"

"Ahh haa!" Yuri laughed so hard that drool fell out the side of her mouth. "Okay, okay, a couple more, a couple more. Name this one." She started to work her fingers across the keys.

"*The Jeffersons,* silly ass."

"Okay, I got you on this one."

"Girl, please. I live and breathe music, that's Biggie's 'One More Chance.' "

"Wait a minute, is yo' ass American on the low? What else you know? You know where bin Laden at?"

Britt laughed as he cut his food off and started fixing their plates. "Do you want a roti or just rice, crazy?"

"Both, but don't make up my roti; put the roti skin on the side. Oh and I want some Kuchilla too. Oh and a Shandy."

"You know you ain't West Indian, right?"

"Keep on talking, you know you gon' want some of this American pussy later. Anyway . . . name this tune." Yuri started to play the piano.

" 'The Sweetest Taboo'; that was ole-girl shit."

"Who?"

"Troi." As soon as he said it, he knew he'd hurt Yuri's feelings. "Yo, I'm sorry."

"Whatever Britt. Troi will never go away." Yuri rolled her eyes toward the ceiling, "Fuck it." She got up from the piano and started collecting her things, "Since that's ole girl's shit . . . since that's what you think, go get her ass and have her sing to you!"

"Yuri," he said sincerely, "I said my fault."

Doing her best not to cry, Yuri spat, "That was our shit! Our fuckin' song, not that bitch—me and you! That was the first song I ever sang to you! But you know what? Fuck you, fuck this and fuck that bitch! I'm leaving!"

"Where you going, Yuri?" He walked over to her and blocked her path.

"Move, you stopping me is not gon' work this time."

"Yuri, wait nuh," Britt said as his Trinidadian accent slipped in between his words. "Fuh real," he grabbed her hands and held them to his mouth. "I'm sorry, like for real I am. It's all about you. Fuck Troi. I shoulda never said that, my fault. I'll never forget the first time you sang for me. Never." He held her to his chest. "Don't leave, baby, I want you to stay."

Yuri inhaled Britt's scent and then she exhaled as if it

were her last breath. Thoughts of love and confusion tore through her mind. "All right," she mumbled, "I'll stay."

"You love me, girl?" He grabbed her around the waist, picked her up and carried her to the breakfast bar.

"No, I can't stand you." She suppressed a smile.

Britt kissed her on the side of her forehead. "Stop letting your imagination lead you a million places. Just ride with me for a little; worry about everything else later. All you need to know is that I got you. For real I do."

"You love me, don't you?" Yuri smiled, looking at Britt pinch a piece of his roti skin and pick up his meat.

"You a'ight, niggah." He waved his hand from side to side. "Now eat that food."

"Remember the first time you cooked for me I thought this was some animal called roti's skin?" She pointed to her plate. "Not until I tasted it did I know it was bread."

"You a ignorant motherfucker." Britt laughed. "I don't even know why I fuck with you."

For hours Yuri and Britt lay suspended in their own world. They ate from each other's plates, drank from the same glass, played hands of strip poker, where they each took pride in Yuri losing every time.

The only invader allowed in was the heavy rain that beat against the multitude of windowpanes and the low humming of CD 101.9's sultry jazz mix. Yuri tried desperately to think of a way she could confess to Britt about her wanting him for the rest of her life; and Britt tried his best to push how he really felt out of his mind.

"Yo." Britt looked at Yuri as she lay across his bed watching a DVD of his last performance. "Don't forget to give me a heads-up when you about to go home."

"Why you all over the stage like that?" Yuri asked, pointing at the high-definition TV, Britt's question not yet registering. "What you just say to me?" was her delayed response.

"I said give me a heads-up before you go home."

"Why, you gon' miss me?"

"Man, please." He did his best to dismiss her. "Now," he said with a frown, getting up from the recliner to sit on the bed between her legs, "I was doin' my thing. What's the problem?"

" 'Cause you doin' some Puffy and Yung Joc shit. Hunching your shoulders and carrying on. And what's with all the rubbin' on the dancer's ass?"

"You ain't complain when we performed and I was rubbin' all over yo' ass." He laughed.

"Yeah and you were planning on fuckin' me. Or is that what I see going on?"

"Here you go."

"Oh, you fuckin' bitches on the road?"

"You fuckin' niggahs at home?"

Knowing that she'd been appeasing Jeff with pussy, Yuri asked, "Why you stuck on me fucking Jeff?"

"I'm selfish." He turned over and lay on top of her. "You know you got to be bad to be stretched out in this motherfucker like this."

"Oh here you go with that dick swole."

"Dick swole." He turned her over and placed her directly on his hard dick. "Yo, you chillin' in my shirt,"—he started to unbutton it—"I'm cookin' for you." He kissed her on the lips and massaged her waist. Looking at her body he moaned, "You dangerous."

Yuri quickly peeped at the clock and saw that it was approaching eleven P.M.

Britt knew by the diversion of her eyes that she was count-ing the time, which was why he pulled his shirt off her and gave instructions, "I want you to ride my dick, let me nut in you real quick and then you can go home to your husband."

Jeff is gon' lose his damn mind, Yuri thought as she started to kiss Britt's chest, before sliding down on his dick.

"Stop thinking." Britt placed his hands around her waist and assisted her with gyrating.

After they'd pleased each other once more, Britt looked at the time. "Twelve A.M. You 'bout to roll?"

"In a minute." Yuri placed her head on Britt's chest, doing her best to keep her eyes open.

The Shark Bar closes at one A.M., she thought, settling on the lie she would tell Jeff. *So I have a little time to play with.* "Are you about to go to sleep?" She looked at Britt.

"Naw, I'm 'bout to light up this big head, check out these fake Puffy moves you were talking about."

"Okay, wake me up in a hour."

"Yuri, you sure you don't need to be getting home now?"

"Hold up . . ." She raised her head from his chest, and caught a slight attitude. "My space in line is up or some-thing?"

"What?"

"I mean, hell, let me know if Troi is coming over."

"Oh man, please." He sighed. "Here you go with that shit. I just want you to get home at a reasonable hour so this dude don't flip."

"Britt, please, Jeff ain't gon' do shit but get mad, play Al Green and go to sleep."

"No wonder you cheatin'." Britt laughed, as Yuri placed her head back on his chest and drifted off to sleep.

* * *

A few hours later, Yuri thought she was lost in a dream when she heard her cell phone ring. She opened her eyes and expected Jeff to catch an attitude because her phone was ringing so late at night. "Don't start, Jeff," she said before he could comment.

"Hello." She groggily answered the phone.

"Oh, wait a fuckin' minute." Jeff laughed in disbelief. "Yo' ass is sleep?"

Yuri sat up in bed and looked around the room: grand piano, keyboard, studio equipment. Britt. *Oh shit.* Realizing that Britt must've fallen asleep and forgotten to wake her, her heart started to race as she checked the time: three A.M. *Goddamn.* "Jeff . . . I got caught up."

"Caught up in what? That niggah breathing in your face or his dick ramming you in the ass?"

"Nae-Nae . . ." She paused thinking of what to say next. Before Jeff could go on, Yuri's other line beeped. "Hold on."

"Yur'ray." She knew it was Nae-Nae. "What the fuck? Britt's dick that big you gotta suck it all damn night? I told you a million times not to be selfish and share with me. And now look, Tina, you got Ike blowin' up my ma'fuckin' spot. Asking me have I seen you. I wanted so bad to say 'No, niggah. And apparently you either. All I see is this down-low dick I'm 'bout to tear into. Now stop hatin'.' "

"Tell me you didn't say that." She peeped over at Britt, and couldn't tell if he was still sleep or not, so she whispered, "What'd you tell him, Nae-Nae?"

"I told him we were at Fantasy Island, had too much to drink, so we came here and both fell asleep."

"A'ight, thanks. Bye." She clicked back over. "Jeff, look—"

"Look at what? What kinda lie you 'bout to tell now, Yuri?! The one Nae-Nae just fed you? Just tell ole boy to man-up, get on the fuckin' phone and let me ask him where he wants your shit dropped off."

"Damn, Jeff, what the hell did I just tell you!" she screamed. "Shit. I'm on my way." And she hung up.

"Check this." Britt turned over and faced Yuri, who was scrambling to get dressed. "I'ma kick some realness to you. First of all, calm down and take the I've-been-fuckin' look off your face." Yuri took a deep breath and Britt continued, "When you get home, don't say shit. Trust me. Let the nig-gah blow off some steam; and at most you say, 'My fault, I was wrong, I'm sorry, and it won't happen again.' "

"Britt, please." Now she was fully dressed. "That will never be enough for Jeff. He gon' badger the hell outta me until I tell him something that sounds close to what he wants to hear."

"What I just tell you, Yuri? This ain't no hard-dick advice, this some best friend shit. Walk in the door and shut the fuck up. Bottom line is, you're wrong, learn how to eat that shit sometimes. Now, don't underestimate his ass, jump bad and cuss him out. Let him do all the talking, get his shit off and when you go back to sleep, keep both eyes open."

"Ha-ha." Yuri said, kissing Britt on the forehead before she headed out the door. "I'll call you later."

At least a thousand wishes and whys floated through Yuri's mind as she raced from midtown into the never-sleeping streets of the Upper West Side.

Hating that her game was fucked up and her emotions didn't keep her pawns in check, she prayed that Jeff bought whatever Nae-Nae had to say. And then maybe she could muster enough wetness, close her eyes real tight, hit Jeff off with some guilt-ridden pussy and cap the night.

Doing her best not to jingle her keys in the lock, Yuri quietly opened the door. As soon as she entered she could see smoke rising from Jeff's Cuban cigar. Miles Davis's horn played quietly in the background as Jeff flipped the lights on.

"I'm sorry, Jeff, my fault, I overslept," Yuri spat out quickly, hoping to put an end to Jeff's premeditated argument. "Okay? So . . . I'ma head to bed."

"I don't advise you to catch no sleep around me." Jeff puffed on his cigar. " 'Cause right about now, I'm one crazy motherfucker. I have thought of so many ways to quietly knock yo' ass off it ain't funny. So don't sleep. . . . I'm beggin' you, please, don't sleep on me."

"Oh . . . kay . . ." Yuri said, thinking for a moment about what would come next. "Jeff. Relax, take it down a notch, please. I said 'my fault.' "

"When did it become your fault? When you overslept yo' fuckin' time in this niggah's bed. Huh?" Jeff mashed his cigar in the ashtray. "When did it become your fault? When you couldn't think quick enough about what lie to tell? What, you used to fuckin' this niggah when I'm at work, on a business trip? What, this yo' first time being bold about the shit? So tell me, Yuri, did you make a day of the dick? Did you enjoy it? 'Cause trust me: Whatever lie you 'bout to tell me better be so sweet that it'll make me think there could never be another motherfucker."

"I'm not going through this." Yuri attempted to walk away.

Jeff quickly rose from the couch and blocked Yuri's path. "How long you been ridin' this niggah's dick?"

"Get the fuck out my face, Jeff!" Yuri did her best to shake off the fear she felt creeping up. "I told you I was at Nae-Nae's when you called. We went to the Shark Bar, he had too much to drink and I didn't want him driving home alone. So I went back home with him and fell asleep."

"He said y'all went to Fantasy Island."

"We went there first."

"He said you had too much to drink."

"We both did."

"You fuckin' lyin'."

"Well, if I'm lyin' "—she pushed past him—"then stop asking me shit. So fuckin' sick of you harassing me! Now I can't go out and you not be in my goddamn neck?! You just make me fuckin' sick! Stupid ass!"

Before Yuri could storm toward their bedroom, Jeff grabbed her by her arm. "Get yo' ass back here; I ain't finished talking to you. You think you gon' walk in here at damn near four o'clock in the morning and hit me with some 'I'm sorry, my fault' shit? What kinda lame-ass game you playin'?"

"I said I was sorry; now get the fuck offa me." She snatched her arm away. "You have lost yo' paranoid-ass mind puttin' yo' hands on me!"

"Lost my fuckin' mind? I lost my fuckin' mind the day I looked at you and thought you were decent, but you ain't shit. You've lost a couple of pounds and think you gon' out slick me? If you was so slick, bitch, you wouldn't have fallen in love with some side niggah, trick! See, Yuri, you ain't cut out for cheatin'. You too goddamn insecure and confused. That niggah didn't even know yo' fat ass before, so let's see if it's still all good when you gain your weight back, whore."

"Fuck you!" she spat.

"Oh, now I got your attention. . . ." Jeff watched as her breath seemed to float away and her eyes started to water. "What, I know your fuckin' feelings ain't hurt? Or you scared? You've been married to me for damn near seven years and you scared of me? You ain't the one sitting here wondering where I'm at. You not sitting here trying to figure out what went wrong, where did I fuck up, was it the size of my dick or the fact that I'm sterile—"

"It's the fact you cheated on me with some nasty infected bitch and expect me to accept the shit because you have a son you wanna take care of. And now that I've decided that I want to move on with my life, you can't take it."

"What you want me to do, Yuri? My son has already been born."

"Whatever, Jeff." Yuri attempted to walk away again.

"I'm talking to you!" He grabbed her so tight that he practically pushed her into the wall. "You think this is a fuckin' game?"

Yuri was too scared to move, yet too scared to be still.

As if he'd been in a trance and was now having an out-of-body experience, Jeff saw himself standing over Yuri with intentions of smothering her. "I'm so sick of promising you that I will play God and kill you. I swear somebody got to pack their shit, and since I'm the one footin' the bills, you decide where you going."

"You know what? Not a problem, 'cause I'm not some lil' uneducated groupie bitch that has a need to sweat yo' ass. I got a job, motherfucker, so don't be too confused. Besides I been dreaming of the day I can leave you!" Yuri picked up the keys to her Touareg.

"Where the fuck you think you going with my keys?"

"Your keys?" Yuri asked, confused.

Before answering, Jeff sat back down on the couch and lit another cigar; no matter how broken his heart felt, his brain knew that financially he had the upper hand. "Yuri, don't play dumb. Basically, this conversation is over." He blew the smoke toward the ceiling. "Tell whoever dick you suckin' to go buy you another car, 'cause that truck outside is mine. As a matter of fact, all you own in this motherfucker is a pack of cigarettes and a pair of size-sixteen jeans."

Yuri stood in the middle of the floor, stunned. Where was the Al Green CD that she and Britt had laughed at earlier?

"And I'm not about to keep arguing with you," Jeff spat. "And I'm not gon' beg you to stay, if that's what you're thinking. The decision is up to you. You can either skip yo' ass up outta here or act like you got some fuckin' sense. Now"—he rose from the couch—"I'ma head to bed."

"Jeff—"

"Kiss my ass. . . ." Jeff said calmly as he walked away and waved his hand.

Yuri opened the frosted French-glass doors that led to the rooftop terrace and watched the glowing New York City skyline around her. She walked over to the terrace bar, poured herself a glass of Dom and lit a cigarette.

Doing her best to balance the pain of loving Britt against the desire to leave him alone, Yuri stared at the view, and wondered where she would go. Her mother's, perhaps? But her mother lived in Chicago and she wasn't ready to leave New York for Illinois. Besides, when she told her mother she was messing with Britt, her mother warned her not to mess up her marriage for a piece of dick, to take her nut and run, 'cause that's all Britt was cut out for.

But Yuri felt like nobody knew Britt the way she did. They'd never seen him cry. They'd never seen him be sweet and cook her food, rub her feet, or sing to her. All they saw was the newly famous reggae artist. But he was more than that. He was not only her lover, he was her best friend. And yeah, maybe she could let go of the dick, but how would she walk away from the friendship?

But then there was Jeff, who'd been there since she was eighteen, had an unwanted abortion and was broken-hearted. He didn't ask her who broke her heart, he just stepped in and filled the void. . . . Yet when he asked her to marry him, she was hesitant because she didn't want to marry a man who she'd settled for. She wanted to genuinely be in love with her husband. She wanted that love jones; cloud nine, Zora and Franklin, Vera and Taj fiction—erotic book shit. The kinda love that makes you eat, sleep and dream your man. The kind of love where even your man's funkiest smell is sweet cologne. The kind of love where the newness never leaves. . . . But her soul-mate resources were limited and, like she'd been taught, you gotta take what you can get, so she did. . . . And now she was paying for it.

Still, Britt's shiny armor was far from being neon or electric, and for the most part he was a selfish motherfucker; stuck on singing a song and banging out a nut. And it seemed that everything they did revolved around him: when they made love; when they saw each other; what type of relationship they had; if and when she could ever tell him she loved him and no longer wanted to be his "man," that she wanted to be his woman, his wife, who he looked forward to seeing, to being with. Not some chick he could freak on the piano and it was all good.

Yuri took a deep breath and picked up her cell phone. Continuing to watch the view, she dialed Britt's number.

"Yeah," Britt said, answering the phone. She could tell he was dead asleep.

"Britt."

"Yu." He sniffed. "What time is it? I'm sleep, man. Call me later."

"I can't, I need to talk to you now."

"What?"

"Me and Jeff really had it out. . . . and I can't keep going through this."

"Through what? If you didn't do what I told you to do, then you brought it on yourself."

"It's not about you," Yuri snapped. "It's about my marriage and me making up my mind what I need. Do I need to be Jeff's wife or do I need to be—"

"Be what?" Britt cut her off. "With me?"

"Well." She sighed. "Yeah."

"Oh, now that's a choice?"

"It's coming down to that."

"A'ight . . . and . . ."

"I was thinking that maybe—"

"Listen," Britt cut her off again. "I don't need speeches, ma'. Plus, this the second time you said the shit, so if you cool wit' it, then I'm cool wit' you being this niggah's wife full time. For real, it's cool. Like I always say: If you can't play your position, change your position. So trust me, I'm good. Plus"—he yawned—"I don't have time to teach you a game that you obviously can't play. It was good while it lasted, and that's about it. Now, I'm going back to sleep and you get to handling them marital duties and being faithful."

Yuri sat there speechless. She could barely breathe and the tears streaming from her eyes made it hard for her to see. "You know what?" Yuri's voice trembled as she pointed her index finger toward the air. "I don't know who the fuck you talking to. 'Cause truth be told you the fuck confused. Every day it's something different from you. One day you want me and the next day you don't. Who has time to deal with this bipolar bullshit? I got one crazy niggah. I don't need two."

"Cool, that's exactly what I'm saying. Finally, we understand each other."

"Fuck you, motherfucker. You just said earlier as long as I was real wit' you, you would never leave me alone. Now here you come with this bullshit."

"Listen, I'm not leaving you alone. You called me. See," he sighed, "you too fuckin' confused."

"I'm not confused. I want you."

"Yuri, what you really trying to do to me? You got love for me but guess which one of us belongs to somebody else? Do you even hear yourself? It's a catch-twenty-two and somebody gotta lose, so I'm good and I'm not a sore loser. Remember we're not seventeen and I ain't fuckin' you for the first time. For real for real ma', you don't even know me. And let's keep it that way."

"I don't know you?" Yuri said surprised. "You have really lost your fuckin' mind; its obvious that you couldn't think of shit else to say. I know you better than you know your damn self; as a matter of fact you're the confused one. You're the one that keep coming and going."

"And where we going, ma'?"

"Nowhere."

"Exactly."

Yuri could feel her eyes start to burn. "You been straight up fuckin' using me." She said more to herself than to him.

"Using you? Check this, Yuri, I'm single. I don't have no commitment other than my music. I could fuck a million chicks a day and nobody could ever pick up the phone and call me home. I'm grown, boo. My mother lives in Trinidad and I don't have a wife. So what I'ma use you for? Pussy? Please, it's sweet but it ain't like that."

"I don't believe this. You don't love me, you don't even care about me—"

"If you can say that, then that proves you don't know shit about me."

"Please, I know what I see and what I see is me lonely if I keep fuckin' with you."

"Beautiful," he said cutting her short, "it's been real. I'm glad you were woman enough to call; 'cause one way or the other it was gon' have to be done. So I'm up." And he clicked off the line.

* * *

Okay, Yuri, she said to herself, clutching the phone in her hand. *You gotta understand that he's a man and men say stupid shit. Maybe he was hurt. . . . Or maybe he just didn't give a fuck. . . . Goddamn, why am I fooling myself? I'm always making excuses for this sorry motherfucker, when I got a man crying and practically begging me to love him. What am I really doing? To hell with Britt. Let this teenage crush go! What am I looking for? Acceptance? Recognition? For somebody to scream* You're good enough? *Please. I'm killing myself. So . . . fuck him—fuck you, Britt!* She did her best not to scream, but couldn't help it. *You know what, Yuri? Keep on playing yourself for a dick-dumb fool and see don't you be alone. If you wanna do something, call Britt back and tell him to kiss your ass. Otherwise, be a woman about your shit and call it completely quits. Get your clit under control and show your heart who's boss. You got this, it don't have you.*

Yuri walked back to the living room and lay on the couch. Before she could talk herself out of crying, she began to wail with such force that her stomach started to hurt. *You still the same stupid-ass little girl,* she cried. *So goddamn dumb!*

"What you doing out here?" Jeff asked, standing in the doorway, fully dressed for work. Yuri opened her eyes and, as if they'd been waiting to be freed, tears streaked her face. "What?" Jeff went on. "No white horses saving the day?"

"Jeff, can I speak to you for a minute?" She wiped her face.

"I'll do you a favor and give you two."

"Look." She faced him. "We've been together for too many years to end our marriage now."

"Our marriage ended a while ago."

"Jeff." Yuri remained calm. "All I know is that I'm here and I didn't leave, because I need you. I love you, you're my husband. I can't tell you anything else, because anything else would be a lie." Yuri paused for a moment, she'd never spat out so much bullshit in her life; she hoped that if the time ever came she would be able to remember it all. For a moment she wondered if Jeff had done as much or more lying, when he was fucking around with Kathy. "Baby," she continued, "I'm still Yuri. I'm still me, and let me tell you what I know." She stood up, walked over to him and grabbed his hand. "I know that you are my husband; and I know that sometimes I act crazy, but it's because I'm confused. I am. I wanna . . . be . . . with . . . you. But I need you to trust me." Yuri felt guilty saying this with a straight face, especially knowing that if she had somewhere else to go, she would leave this miserable motherfucker all to himself. "Last night, I was dead wrong, I shoulda called. Or how about I shouldn't have let the shit happen, and it won't . . . again. All I'm saying is that I really don't wanna give up now. I wanna try and make our marriage work."

"Yuri." Jeff caressed her face and wiped the tears falling from her eyes. "Let me ask you something, baby."

"Anything."

"Shootin' game is a motherfucker, ain't it?" He turned to go back into the other room. "I'ma give you another chance," he threw over his shoulder, "but know that, after this, there will be no more."

Drae

Drae lay in her California king-sized bed not quite asleep or awake. Her swollen cherry was throbbing and her pussy cried tears. She loved the turbulence of a building orgasm. The tossing, the turning and the flipping in her belly. She grabbed Hassan's hand, squeezed it and said a prayer hoping that his caressing her pussy and whispering in her ear was his way of bringing them back to where they once were.

"Damn, baby. . . ." She moaned, her sleepy eyes still closed. "I missed this soooo much." His touch was unbelievably soft. The way he circled his fingertips ever so lightly across her nipples, taking his tongue and licking each of them as if they were melting. His plush lips enveloped her nipples and he sucked them so intensely that she swore her titties had a clit.

"You like that baby?" Hassan whispered in her ear.

"Yes," Drae cried, tears now sliding from her eyes. "Don't stop."

"I'm not gon' stop." He wiped her tears as she felt three fingers traveling inside her; maneuvering their way through her hot flesh.

"I want it to just be me and you, baby," Drae said, as the sensual touch reminded her of Naz. She did her best to push Naz out of her mind. After all, no matter what, she wanted her marriage to work. And she needed some sort of normalcy in her reality; otherwise she stood to lose it all. She was tired of the porno auditions and the unconventional sex. Now she wanted simple shit, like missionary position, stretch marks, babies, Chinese food and slow jams.

"You gon' fuck me, baby? I mean, really fuck me?" She felt a wet stroke to her clit.

"Don't I always fuck you?"

"No, baby"—she squeezed her eyes tight—"you don't. You been holding back on the dick . . . and that's what I want."

"You don't want this . . . ?"

She felt a warm tongue pressed against her clit. "The right side," she instructed. "Lick the right side . . . it'll make me cum." Drae's legs began to shake involuntarily, something that always happened before she reached her peak. As she grabbed Hassan's head to push it in deeper, his hair felt like silk and the length of it went on forever. Instantly Drae's eyes popped open and she saw a redheaded white woman eating her pussy, while Hassan was playing with his dick and whispering in her ear, telling her how much he loved her. Drae's heart felt as if it had cracked and fallen into a puddle of piss on the floor.

She scooted backward on the bed until she bumped the back of her head on the headboard. The white woman's lips were glazed with Drae's pussy. The woman sat on her knees and looked at Hassan. "Is this supposed to happen?"

After a few moments of blinking her eyes and assuring herself that she wasn't dreaming, Drae raised up and slapped the woman so hard that she fell off the bed. Her neck jerked and her eyes popped out. "What the fuck you call yourself doing?! I'ma kick yo' fuckin' ass!" Drae went diving behind her, landing on top of her and whipping her ass like Laila Ali would do Britney Spears. Drae punched and kicked the woman as if she were fighting for her life. There was red hair swinging everywhere. And although some of it blinded Drae, she continued to drive the ass-kicking home as she swung her arms like runaway bats. After a few moments of being entertained, Hassan pulled the two women apart. "Chill, it's too early in the morning to be fighting." He laughed holding Drae back. "Besides, it's not that fuckin' serious."

"It ain't that fuckin' serious?!" Drae spat. She looked at Hassan and threw a punch at him, but he blocked it. "What the hell is wrong with you?! I was goddamn 'sleep and this is what you do? I'm thinking it's you, but got some bitch sucking my shit! Oh my God." She began to gasp. She leaned against the windowsill and did her best to catch her breath.

"Don't act like you never had a bitch sucking your clit before."

Drae knew that this was it: no more auditions, no more of this life. No more, period. She was beyond tired. How and why would her husband do this to her? Didn't he care about what she wanted? Or was all of this more important than she was?

"Why are you acting like this?" Hassan looked at Drae as the tears drenched her face.

"I'm your wife!" Drae screamed. "Not some jump-off! Some side bitch. And you're pimping me, you're really fucking pimping me." She said more to herself than to him, "What the fuck am I doing?!"

"You gon' tell me that Kimmie wasn't fulfilling your fantasy?"

"My fantasy?! Me? Mine? This has nothing to do with me, this is all about you. The directing the porno,"—she held her right hand out as if she were counting on her fingers—"the auditions, the men coming in and out of here, the nasty-ass carpet munchers that you insist on sucking my clit—all of this is yo' shit. The next thing I know, you gon' want me to watch you trading in the loaded dildo for a niggah dicking you in the ass—"

As if lightning struck, Hassan slapped Drae so hard that she stumbled. "Kimmie, wait outside!" Hassan yelled.

"You ain't got to wait, you can go the hell home!" Drae screamed as she jumped on Hassan. Hassan did all he could to hold her off him. After seeing that his attempts were failing, he swung Drae across the room. "Sit yo' ass down!" He looked at Kimmie. "I said leave!" She grabbed her things and scurried out of the room.

"I'm done. This is over," Drae said, pushing herself off the floor. She thought about reaching for the knife they kept under the bed and slicing his throat, but quickly changed her mind. "Either you stop doing this porno shit or I'm leaving you!"

"Oh, now you wanna leave?" Hassan raised his eyebrows. "And go where? To do what? To teach? That dumb-ass job ain't got you living like this—I don't know why you would wanna be a teacher anyway—"

"I'm not a teacher, I'm a guidance counselor!"

"And who the fuck is you guiding? A buncha young-ass tricks and hos? You just a fuckin' fake. You think you one thing when you really something else! Now you tryna front on me and my shit? You ain't complain when you was nuttin' all over the place. You know you liked them niggahs fucking you. You liked that freaky shit. Look me in the face and tell me Nasty Naz ain't fuck the shit outta you. Tell me that, swear on your mother that you ain't still thinking about that niggah."

Drae didn't respond fast enough, so Hassan continued, "That's what I thought. You ain't shit, Drae, but a ho'n-ass gold digger. Ya raggedy, bitch! Now, how's that for your sanity?!" He flicked his hand. "Step." He sat down on the edge of the bed and crossed his legs; the only thing missing was a cigarette.

Drae was shaking so bad she could feel hives taking over her body. Only God knew how bad she wanted to leave, but how would she do that when Hassan was her everything. Everything she ever dreamed was riding on his being her man. "Don't expect me to be a part of this shit no more. I'm done."

"Whatever," he said nonchalantly. "Whatever."

Drae went into the master bathroom and locked the door

behind her. She held the lump in her throat for as long as she could, but the weight of her fear exploded like an asthma attack. Her chest heaved up and down as she fell to the toilet and cried for what felt like forever. She held her head in her hands, her temples began to pound. For the moment, she felt as if she'd been robbed and she herself was the thief. She robbed herself of loving, of living and being free. Instead she chose to be locked up in a world of bullshit, and now she had nowhere to go. And since she was too weak to kill herself, she had no choice but to fight with life. But life was kicking her ass and here she sat on the face of the shit bowl, wondering how and when all of this happened. . . .

· · ·

"And who is this niggah, Drae?" Yuri had asked when they were seventeen, sitting on the edge of Drae's bed.

"You should see him. He is so fuckin' fine and his pockets, oh my God, 'laced' ain't the word."

"You don't even know this dude."

"I know enough to know he's the one."

"I hope so, Drae."

"I don't hope, bitch. I claim."

· · ·

"Drae, it's me," Hassan yelled through the crack of the bathroom door and interrupted Drae's thoughts. She took a deep breath. "Listen, honey," he went on, "you know I hate it when you cry; especially when you cry like this. I'm sorry. A'ight?" he twisted the knob, but the door was locked. "Drae," he called again, "let me in . . . you hear me? . . . Drae . . ."

Drae wiped under her eyes with the tips of her fingers.

The lump in her throat had left some residue, but she figured she would cry it out later.

"Drae!" he called again.

Silence.

"Drae, stop playing."

Drae continued to ignore him. She looked at the clock: seven thirty. She had just enough time to shower and dress before heading to work. She washed, rinsed and wrapped herself in a towel. As she opened the bathroom door to step out, Hassan was there blocking her path. "I know you heard me."

She looked at him and noticed white residue underneath his nostrils. *He's high,* she thought as she pushed him out of her way.

"Why you gotta put yo' hands on me?"

Drae didn't respond. She walked into her closet and picked out an outfit. As she grabbed her clothes off the rack, she turned around and Hassan was directly behind her, causing her to bump into him. "Would you get the fuck out my way?" she spat.

"Say 'scuse me," he said as she brushed past him. "You just rude, huh? Ms. Teacher, Ms. Counselor, Ms. School Nurse or whatever the fuck you is. That's what you teach yo' kids in school, how to be rude? Them dumb motherfuckers." He walked up to her and pushed her slightly, almost causing her to fall on the bed. Drae gave him a quick and uncompromising glance. She was sure that this time, if a fight broke out, she'd be late for work, because she would reach for the knife under their mattress, and stab every demon that lived in this asshole out of him.

Drae regained her balance and proceeded to put on a chocolate brown Yves Saint Laurent wide-leg pantsuit with a sleeveless mint-green turtleneck underneath. She walked over to her dresser and sifted through her things for her Chocolate Cherries lip gloss and liner.

"Oh, so . . . you ignoring me?" Hassan asked.

Drae pulled out her makeup bag, sat at her vanity and put on a full face of Chanel.

"Drae . . . Drae . . . Drae . . ." Hassan stood next to her and screamed into her face, "Drae'yaaaaaaaaaa!!!!!"

She looked at him with her nostrils flared and rolled her eyes.

"You ain't gon' accept my apology, Drae?"

Silence.

"Fuck it, then. Here I am making a living for us, trying to get us to live right. I even looked for a church for us. You know, a couple that prays together stays together, now you know we need to pray, Drae . . . Drae . . . Drae . . . Drae. So you just gon' ignore me, right?"

"Pretty much," Drae snapped as she got up from her vanity, put her Elsa Peretti jewelry on and slipped on her ostrich stilettos.

"Oh . . . you a funny motherfucker? A funny-lookin' motherfucker." He fell out laughing. "I'm just playing." He pushed her on the arm. "For real, though, you ain't gon' accept my apology, Drae?"

Silence.

"Okay, fuck it then, fuck it then, fuck . . . it . . . then. You know what I'm saying? You just gon' ignore me. What, this a holiday called Ignoring Hassan Day?" Seeing that Drae continued not to respond, Hassan mushed her in the head. "Well, fuck you then, cracked-up bitch! That's why your mother's in hell sucking the devil's dick!"

Drae stopped dead in her tracks and immediately the residue of the previous lump in her throat filled her mouth. This time she wasn't ignoring him, she was speechless.

"I was just playing." He chuckled. "I guess you really mad now? So how much this attitude gon' cost me? What, I need to buy you a new Benz, some shoes?"

Drae took a deep breath, every part of her wanted to kick Hassan's ass, but instead of fighting a losing battle she took the blow he just dealt her in stride. Her mother was her world and he knew that, still, he took every opportunity he could to curse her.

Drae took one last look at herself in the mirror, slid on her mink, grabbed her purse and her totebag, and left the room.

"Drae!" he called behind her.

"Fuck you!" she screamed as she slammed the front door.

Yuri

Yuri took a strong pull off her cigarette, tilted her head toward the ceiling and blew smoke into the air. She and Jeff were celebrating their seventh wedding anniversary on the *Spirit of New York*'s evening cruise, which sailed for three hours around the island of Manhattan.

The deep waters splashed against the sides of the ship as it made its way past the multitude of red and yellow city lights that lit up the early evening sky.

Will Downing's "Moods" set the tone for the ship's spinning lounge that sat on the top deck and twirled around to show off spectacular views of the New York City skyline.

Celebrating their anniversary was Yuri's idea. After

all, lately Jeff had been treating her like a roommate with fuck benefits: saying very little to her, unless it was an insult; looking at her, rolling his eyes; and only touching her long enough to part her pussy lips and soothe his hard dick. And that had been only twice, both episodes on opposite ends of the same week. And at neither time was there a kiss, a fondle or a whisper. He treated it like a business transaction. He rolled over, advised her he wanted some pussy and she held her breath long enough to give him some. The last time, they simply looked at each other and, without saying a word, they both knew that fucking the other had become a done deal.

Nevertheless, Yuri was determined to make herself feel like she had a marriage, which was why she'd been ignoring Britt's efforts to reach her for the last month. She sent all of his calls to voice mail, ignored his text messages and dumped the weekly flowers he sent to her job in the trash. Besides, Britt needed to wallow in his own shit for a while.

She opened her purse, peeped at her cell phone and saw Britt had sent three new text messages: "Yo enough is enough. . . . Stop playing games and answer your fuckin' phone! . . . You begging me to come see about you. . . ."

Yuri read each message about three times before deciding to respond. "Kiss," she texted, "my ass."

Within seconds he texted her back, "I'm trying to."

"Then you'll have to work your way around my husband's dick." And she put her phone away.

"I doubt if there's a signal out here." Jeff sipped.

"What?"

"Weren't you looking at your cell phone? I doubt if there's a signal, he can't get through."

"Do . . . not . . . start," Yuri said sternly.

She mashed the last of her cigarette into the ashtray and stared at Jeff. She did what she could to find something intriguing about him. At least his Unforgivable cologne smelled delicious and he was easy on the eye. His tailored Gucci suit was impeccable and his loose silk tie gave him a certain sex appeal that, for a split second, reminded Yuri she was once attracted to him.

She picked up her Perfect ten and clinked Jeff's shot of Hennessy. "To our future."

"Yeah," Jeff said, "to the future."

Yuri ignored Jeff's spin on her toast. She sipped her drink and smiled at him. "So . . . Jeff," she figured she needed to say something, especially since for the last hour they'd been eating fried wontons, listening to Will and saying the bare minimum to each other. "Would you like to dance?"

"Naw . . ." He looked around the room. "I'll pass."

She did all she could not to roll her eyes; instead she turned around slightly and looked at the couples on the dance floor. She was happy that Jeff had said no, especially since the couples dancing actually seemed to be together. "Oh . . . kay," she said facing him again. "I was thinking . . . about kids."

"Really?" Jeff raised his eyebrows. "I have a kid."

"I mean *our own child*," she stressed.

"You mean one you can accept?"

"Exactly."

"He's an innocent little boy."

Yuri took a deep breath and assembled a smile. "Sweetie, where do you see us in five years?"

"Divorced," he said matter-of-factly, as he tapped on the table to get the waiter's attention.

When the waiter came to the table, Jeff took his index finger and moved Yuri's plate from in front of her. "You've eaten enough."

"What?"

"You heard me. When I got up last night I saw that you had eaten an entire bag of potato chips; and you're big enough, don't you think?"

"Miss," the waiter said, cutting through the obvious tension, "would you like to refresh your glass?"

"No, thank you." Yuri wanted badly to slap the hell out of Jeff, yet she didn't want to cause a scene; so she sat back in her chair and crossed her legs. Her black wrap dress revealed most of her thighs and her toned calves. Once the waiter walked away, Yuri clenched her lips and exhaled. "I'm tired of you always saying something about my weight, but when I start talking about your dick shooting water and that fuckin' Oreo cookie you got, you wanna argue."

"Nice, Yuri," he said sarcastically. "Now you're calling a five-year-old names. Real adult of you."

"You know what, Jeff? What . . . the fuck . . . are we sitting here for? As a matter of fact, what are we doing? I hate that I even suggested this shit; it's obvious you don't wanna be here and I'm not so sure . . . if I wanna be here either."

"No, what's obvious is that you're cheating, and the obviousness of it is what makes the shit so fucked up."

"Psycho's on the loose again." She popped her eyes wide open. "You're right, Jeff"—she smirked—"me cheating . . . is *sooooo* goddamn obvious. But, tell me, is it as obvious as the baby you had on me?"

He pushed his face close into hers. "Leave my son out of this."

"I just asked a simple question."

"Well, don't ask me any damn questions. Besides, it's your pussy, and if you handled your game correctly you would learn from my mistakes. Instead, yo' fat ass is so fuckin' silly that you doin' a buncha stupid shit. Insulting the hell outta my intelligence. And then you expect me to sit up here and play happily ever after? Celebrating what? A wrapped-up marriage? Mrs. McMillan, please."

"I swear, not even one night"—Yuri held up her index finger—"can we go without your brain running away and leaving you. Think . . . what you wanna think. Hell, maybe I should cheat so you can be right for once." She threw that one out there just to see what he would come back with.

Jeff fell out laughing, then reared back and pulled his loose tie even farther down his neck. "Sweetheart, you're killing me. You'd be better off convincing me that you wanna jump overboard." He slid his cigar out of his breast pocket and lit it.

"I'ma try my best not to even say anything, 'cause the next thing I say will come after I steal on yo' ass!"

And for the next hour and a half they both looked out the ship's windows.

As they left the pier and hopped in a cab, Yuri felt her cell phone vibrating. When she checked it, she saw she had ten missed calls—all from Britt. "Who was that?" Jeff asked, "ya niggah?"

"As a matter of fact, it was," Yuri snapped, slamming the taxi's door.

"Now, my wife, that's probably the one honest thing you've said tonight."

Before she could cuss him out and let him know she'd had enough, her phone rang again. This time she answered it. "Yes."

"You playing with me, right?" Britt spat.

"Hi," Yuri said in her best bill-collector's voice, "how are you?"

"You fuckin' that niggah?"

"Uhmm, last time I checked they were shootin' again."

"*Stop* fuckin' playing with me. Since when have we had an argument and you bounce?"

"You know," Yuri continued, "I believe that was my husband's idea. . . . He's a brilliant man."

"Hilarious. Now, where you at?"

"On my way home."

"Don't go home, come here. I wanna see you."

"Uhmmm . . . not."

"Not?" She could hear his disbelief.

"Not."

"Okay, go home. Please, go home. I gotta trick for yo' ass." And he hung up.

Yuri acted as if nothing happened and watched the dance of passing traffic. Manhattan was definitely the city that never slept. Even at eight o'clock in the evening there was a traffic jam, which was why Yuri and Jeff had elected to leave their cars at home. A decision Yuri was starting to regret; at least if she'd insisted they take her car, she could've pulled over and put Jeff the fuck out.

As the taxi pulled in front of their apartment building, Yuri started breathing heavy and immediately all the nerves in her body took cover and headed for her stomach. Britt was leaning against the front of the building, with his left leg propped up on the wall and both of his hands in his front pockets. He was wearing an army-green scully with his dreads resting on his shoulders, a white thermal, an army fatigue jacket, a pair of baggy jeans and Timbs.

There was a light coating of snow falling from the sky and some of the flakes landed and melted on his face.

Yuri started fanning herself.

"Why are you sweating?" Jeff asked as he handed the cab driver money for the ride and a tip. "It's the dead of winter."

Yuri couldn't speak, especially since she'd stepped out of the cab and her knees were incredibly weak. As she went to take a step, one of her legs gave way, twisting the heel of her Mary Jane stiletto.

"Dammit." She stumbled, trying her hardest not to look at Britt as he twirled the toothpick in his mouth, his tongue flicking back and forth. Just looking at him was making her feel faint, as she wondered what the hell he was doing here. Was he trying to swing his dick in her husband's face? Didn't he know better than to leave his post and show up at her front door? And he said *she* didn't know how to play this game; was *he* insane? It didn't matter that they were all from Brooklyn and went to high school together. What mattered was the here and now, what they were to one another today.

Okay, this is what she planned to do: see and not see him; in essence, wave her hand and keep it movin'. Hell, he was outside the building and she doubted it very seriously if he was bold enough to try and come in.

"Wassup, Jeff?" Britt said as he and Jeff gave each other a brotherly hug and handshake.

"Britt," Jeff said in an upbeat surprise, "it's been a long time. Congratulations on your CD."

"Thanks. And, yeah, it has been a long time. I've been try-ing to reach . . . your wife." He stared at Yuri. "I got a new CD dropping and you know this chick can sing her ass off, so I needed to talk to her about a remix."

"I stopped singing," Yuri snapped. "All I do is rhyme now." She fumbled for her keys to get into the building.

"Funny, I don't remember you having a sense of humor." Britt curled his lips.

"Oh, she a real Mo'Nique these days," Jeff said as he took Yuri's keys and opened the entrance door. "Britt, come on in."

"Thanks, Jeff, I sure will."

Yuri could've shitted on herself, suddenly she felt as if she had diarrhea. Britt walked in behind them and as Yuri walked past him he squeezed her ass.

"Would you like something to drink, Britt?" Jeff asked as he opened the apartment door and tossed Yuri's keys on the glass table. "Some wine, perhaps?"

"Yeah, that sounds good," Britt responded, while conve-niently standing in a position where he could unnoticeably stare at Yuri.

"Yuri, fix the man a glass and y'all talk about the remix or whatever. You'll have to excuse me." He looked at Britt. "I'ma need to grab a shower and change."

"No problem." Britt gave a sly smile. "I understand."

Yuri sauntered into the kitchen with Britt following be-hind her. She opened the wine cooler and did her best to play things off until she heard the bathroom door close. "What the fuck are you doing here?" she snarled.

"What's yo' problem, man? And don't shoot me no bull-shit."

"Right now, my problem is you trying to get me put out. And since my mother moved back to Chicago, my resources on where I'ma go . . . are limited."

"Well, I ain't fuckin' movin' until you talk to me like you got some damn sense." He slid into the breakfast nook. "And if need be, I will sleep here."

"Britt"—her hand began to shake as she opened the six-foot-tall wine cooler—"ou gotta leave."

"Really? I guess you didn't hear what I just said."

Yuri peeked at the doorway, she couldn't see too well through the frosted glass, but from what she could see she was able to make out the bathroom door still being closed. "Listen," she said through clenched teeth, "it's not about me loving you. Hell, I've loved you since the eighth grade, and no matter how hard I try, the shit won't go away. But I'm tired of being with you and not being with you at the same time. My marriage is about security and that's what I need . . . to be safe."

"And I guess calling you a buncha fat asses, jumping up in the middle of the night to see if you had something to eat and telling you he hates that you lost weight keeps you real safe. You damn sure," he said sarcastically, "will remain intact with that."

Yuri stood silent for a moment. She hated that Britt's words made sense. "Look, I can't take the chance you'll wanna be with me, when you won't even tell me you love me."

"So we're finished? You don't want me?" Britt slid out from the nook and walked up so close to Yuri that she backed into the glass door of the wine cooler. The melting ice smudged and soaked into the back of her dress, causing the material to lay against her skin like a fresh coating of paint. She hated that this turned her on. "Please move, go call Troi."

"I don't want Troi."

"You have to go home. Jeff could come out at any minute."

"Do I look like I give a fuck?" He pressed his lips against hers.

"What are you doing?"

"Tell me we're finished," he said while slipping his tongue in and out of her mouth. "Say it." He began to play with the sash on her wrap dress.

"Britt—please," she whined, snatching the sash from his hands and looking toward the door once more, her heart pounding so loud that she was sure Jeff heard it. "He gon' come out the bathroom and he gon' fuckin'—"

Britt cut her off by grabbing her face, cupping her chin and turning her around, "Fuck that niggah." He kissed her roughly on the lips.

"Oh, God." She broke the kiss and stomped her feet. "You gotta stop . . . for real. Please just leave."

"Is it me, or you don't get it? I ain't goin' no motherfuckin' where." He snatched her sash back, this time untying it, revealing her nude panty and bra set. He always loved the butterfly tattoo on her left breast, so he kissed it. Placing his hands around her waist he said, "Now, all you gotta do is tell me to my face." He ran his hands across her hard nipples. Biting them through her bra he said, "I'm listening."

Yuri's heart was beating so loud she felt it was only a matter of time before the thumping would burst her eardrums. She loved being pinned up by Britt in her husband's apartment, yet she was too scared to enjoy the risk of being caught. "I'm begging you, please."

"Don't beg, the shit doesn't work." He attempted to pull her panties down. "Step out of 'em," he said, as she snatched them back up.

"N-n-nooo, baby," she stuttered as her pussy dripped. "What are you doing?" she asked sternly. "You fuckin' crazy?"

"And you fuckin' tryin' me . . . now take 'em off, Yuri."

"No, Britt, stop playing." She gripped the strings of her bikini panties tightly.

"You not listening now?" He moved her hands. "You want me to rip 'em off?"

"Yes—no—baby, please."

"Then, take 'em off."

She did as she was told and he placed them in his left pants pocket. Playing with her pussy lips he said, "Tell me you love me and then swear that you won't do this shit again."

"I can't."

"You got a lotta ass-whippin's as a kid, didn't you, cause you hardheaded as hell." He unzipped his jeans and pulled his dick out through the slit. Rubbing the head of it against her soaked lips he said, "I swear to God I'll fuck the shit outta you right here." He picked her up. "Wrap your legs around my waist."

She nervously complied.

"Now tell me, or I swear I'll put my dick in."

"Don't do that," she moaned, desperately wanting to ride

his dick. She knew this wasn't right, but she couldn't help it. She not only missed fucking Britt, she missed his smell, his touch, the way he drooled in his sleep. She missed the hell out of him, and with him clutching her by the waist and threatening to fuck her, her mind was gone to a place beyond space.

"Stop being so fuckin' stubborn." He pushed his dick in and she screamed.

"Yuri!" Jeff yelled through the bathroom door. "You all right?"

"Yes." Her voice quivered.

"I dare you to tell him you love this dick," Britt whispered.

"No . . . yes . . . Jeff, I'm okay."

They heard the shower resume running. Britt stroked and said, "Hurry up and say it."

"I love you," she whimpered, "and this won't happen again."

"That's what I thought." He stroked her at least four more times before sucking his inner cheek and making himself stop. "Meet me in an hour so we can finish." He unwrapped her legs and placed her back on the floor.

Taking a deep breath and a sigh of relief that they didn't get caught, Yuri retied her sash as she looked down and spotted Britt's dick. It was the prettiest dick she'd ever seen, hard and long and thick like a fudge log, it looked so sweet she knew she could eat it. The more she stared the more her mouth watered.

"You wanna suck it, don't you?" he said more as a statement than as a question.

"Yes . . ." She bit the corner of her lip. "It's sooooo biggggggg . . . and it's sooooo thick . . . and if we get caught . . . I'm moving in with you."

Britt caressed her face as she squatted and rested on her knees. "Don't worry ma', I got you." She grabbed his dick and slowly worked it into her mouth; stroking each inch with her tongue and playing with his oozing precum.

"I knew you missed it." Britt rubbed the back of her neck and looked toward the bathroom door, the door was still closed and they could still hear the shower running. "Touch your pussy."

She did as she was told. She slid two of her fingers between her aching lips and twirled them inside. Simultaneously sucking his dick and smearing her juices all over her clit, she began to moan until she felt like she was going to cry.

"That fat pussy nice and wet?"

"Yes."

"Remember when I sucked it . . . it was like candy . . . wet, sticky and sweet. I started off by biting it and kissing it. Then I stuck my tongue into it and you came on my tongue. You gon' do that again, baby? You gon' fill my mouth with cum?"

"Yes."

"Damn, baby." Britt felt his nut creeping up and he knew Jeff's shower had to be ending at any minute. "Hurry . . . make us cum and he better not come before we do."

Flicking her clit and sucking his dick as fast she could, Yuri tried with all her might to have them climax together. As they heard the shower shut off, the nut rushed from the top of their heads and exploded. Britt's nut slid down Yuri's throat while her own made liquid between her thighs.

Quickly Britt slid his dick back in his pants and zipped them up. As he heard Jeff's footsteps nearing, he reached down to help Yuri off the floor.

"How'd you get on the floor?" Jeff asked as he walked in the kitchen and looked at Yuri, who was still on her knees and clutching Britt's hand.

"My foot." Yuri got up and limped over to the counter, she knew she looked disheveled but she tried her best to play it off. "I think I twisted it." She sat down and unbuckled her shoe. Feeling uneasy about Jeff staring at her, she asked Britt, "What about that chick you were seeing? How is she?"

"She got remarried on me." He smirked. "Listen, I'ma get ready to roll."

"Why you leaving so soon?" Jeff asked Britt, yet looking at Yuri. "Did she tell you what you needed to hear?"

"More than enough," Britt said, shaking Jeff's hand and turning to leave. "I can show myself out. Take care."

Yuri stood by the counter as Jeff watched her and she watched Britt. Once Britt closed the front door, Jeff said, "You still got a thing for him?"

Seeing an opportunity, Yuri exploded, "What?! I . . . have had . . . enough of you and your mountain of accusations. Now you wanna accuse me of Britt? Who's next, the doorman? Tell me something, Jeff, if you thought I was in love with Britt, then why did you let him in your house? Don't even answer that, because it doesn't even matter!" She slipped her shoe back on, grabbed her black clutch purse, and tucked it under her arm. "I need . . . to get away from you." She picked up her keys. "And, by the way, happy motherfuckin' anniversary." Forgetting that she just pretended to have a limp, she stormed out and slammed the door behind her.

As she headed to the elevator she spotted Britt. "Wait," she said to him.

Although his mouth didn't say a word, his look said a million. They each stepped on the elevator and faced the door as it closed.

Drae

"What I don't understand is why pussies is always hatin' on Nae-Nae!" Nae-Nae screamed as if he was making a public-service announcement.

It was Friday night and Drae, Nae-Nae and Yuri were hanging out at an uptown hole-in-the-wall called Queen of Sheba, a place where time stood still. Muddy Waters, Koko Taylor and Bobby "Blue" Bland were staples on the jukebox; naked black bulbs hung over the tables; there were no menus, but everyone knew what they served; and a good game of C-Lo was always going on.

"You feel me, Old Head?" Nae-Nae flung his wrist in the air and winked his eye at the owner's brother Randy, who everyone knew was a sixty-seven-year-old latent faggot.

"I'm sho' feelin' you, Nathan." He smiled at Nae-Nae, as he set three plates of fried chicken and waffles on the table. "And just so you know," he whispered, "Nathan, I love that you call me 'Old Head.'"

"Why?" Nae-Nae whispered back.

"'Cause Johnson finally gotta nickname." He blushed. "Let me know when you 'bout to leave, Nathan." And he turned to walk away.

"That's exactly why Raphael bust all the windows outta your car," Drae stated. "'Cause you a cheatin' motherfucker." She poured syrup on her waffle.

"Yuck," Yuri said in disgust, while stuffing chicken in her mouth.

"It must be in a pussy's nature to hate. And, for your information, Raphael was in the emergency room when my windows were bust out."

"How's Raphael doing?" Drae asked.

"He's doing a little better. Our sex life is on hold for a little while because his knees are still sore right now."

"Did I need to know that?" Yuri asked, putting her chicken down. "Now I can't eat."

"How did his knees get messed up?" Drae asked.

"He doesn't know." Nae-Nae rolled his eyes at Yuri. "He said whoever jumped him was so damn little he never saw 'im coming. Whoever it was had been there and gone before Raphael realized he'd had his ass kicked."

"Why is shit always happening to y'all?" Yuri frowned.

"Y'all just some drama kings." Drae sipped her drink.

"Speaking of drama, here come ya gurl." Nae-Nae arched his eyebrows as they spotted Troi. "I can't stand this bougie bitch . . . B.B.!" Nae-Nae screamed as she came to the table. "What in the world are you doing here?"

"Where else could I get chicken and waffles this time of night? Hello, everyone." She waved at Yuri and Drae before taking a seat.

"Oh, Yuri, look at you." She smiled.

"Hi, Troi, how are you?"

"I'm well, thank you. And Drae, Nae-Nae."

"Girl." Drae smiled. "You look good." Yuri kicked her under the table.

"Thank you." Troi favored the actress Meagan Good. She leaned on one foot and smiled extra hard at Yuri. "I'm claiming all the things I left behind. Yuri, how's Jeff?"

"About as well as your ex-husband." Yuri ate a piece of waffle.

"Ahh haa!" Nae-Nae laughed. "That's my bitch." He gave Yuri a high five.

"Troi." Drae gave Nae-Nae the evil eye. "Are you still practicing law?"

"Yes, actually I'm with Sony Music. Britt and I have been working closely together."

"Whew, Yuri." Nae-Nae wiped his brow. "Ring the alarm somebody!"

"So are you and Britt an item?" Yuri faked a smile. "Wouldn't that be interesting?"

"I'm not sensing that you feel some kinda way, am I, Yuri?" Troi asked. "Because I know how you felt about him in high school, but obviously you married the best man for you. So, you don't have an issue with me and Britt getting back together, do you?"

"Why would I have an issue?"

"I'm just asking. I mean, I thank you for being there for him, but I believe I got it from here."

Troi's order number was called as Randy motioned for her to come to the bar and collect her food. "Take care, everyone, our food is ready."

Troi's words stung Yuri like citrus piss invading a cracked lip. No, scratch that, it felt worse than that; Troi may as well have pulled out a blade from the side of her mouth and carved all of Yuri's arteries out, at least Yuri would have a reason for not breathing.

Feeling she needed to come up for air, Yuri headed to the jukebox; the hem of her denim gauchos swayed in the swiftness of her walk, while her stiletto knee boots clapped against the tile floor like drums.

After debating if she should call Britt and cuss him out, she decided, at least for now, she would drop a quarter in the jukebox and have Elmore James sing to her about muddy shoes.

She sat down on the stool next to the jukebox and watched the makeshift dance floor fill with people.

On the other side of the room Drae carried on. "That's what her ass fuckin' get. See, I knew he was gon' play her again."

"And what the fuck is Hassan doing to you, Drae?" Nae-Nae asked. "Don't forget who you talking to."

Drae slid her chair back. "Before I have to check yo' fuckin' chin, I'ma go play me a game of C-Lo!" The wedge heels of her Coach boots stomped against the floor and her toned thighs made a statement as her black miniskirt clung to her ass.

. . .

"I came to collect yo' money." Drae parted the huddle of squatted knees, curled backs and thick chestnut-, caramel-, onyx-, and mocha-colored necks. "Move aside." She bumped one of the men who'd just finished slamming his dice against the wall. She bent over slowly and dropped a hundred-dollar bill on top of the growing money pile. She knew all eyes were on her ass so she squatted for a few minutes longer and said, "I'm next."

As she stood up she looked dead in Naz's face. She couldn't believe it. And just when she'd decided she was chasing a dream and that all dreams did were end . . . there he was . . . again . . . and, of course, he was beyond beautiful: skin the color of a flawless chocolate diamond, mustache with sides that melted into a goatee.

He had the sexiness of Tyson, but the looks of the R&B singer Tank. If she had to give his beauty a name, she would affectionately call him a "pretty black niggah," a "don," or if all else failed, "one fine motherfucker" would have to do. He was the epitome of dapper: slightly baggy black cargo pants, black cashmere sweater with the hem of the white tee that he wore underneath peeking out nicely, and on his feet were all-black throwback Pumas.

Naz knew he was staring a few minutes too long to play it off, but he couldn't help it; either this chick was stalking him or there was something he was supposed to do with her. He just didn't know. If only she wasn't so fine or naturally gorgeous; or maybe a little more stand-up—a square—perhaps a librarian, a teacher or an usher for the church—or something—something that would convince him he wanted her for some other reason than a bomb-ass pussy. He hated that he remembered her real name, which was part of the reason that every time she ran across his mind he referred to her as Sunshine. It kept everything in perspective—but seeing her standing here now completely fucked him up.

Parallel to them, breaking their stare, the jukebox belted Koko Taylor as she sang, "I got what it takes to make a man forget his name and a bulldog break his chain . . ." Most of the time when Drae heard this blues classic, she grabbed something and sang, it didn't matter that she couldn't hold much of a melody . . . at least it didn't . . . up until this point. So instead of singing, she prayed that her nerves bore with her. She cleared her throat and watched Naz lick his seductive lips.

"You can't speak?" Drae suppressed her smile. "Cat got your tongue?"

"You tell me." He juggled the dice in one hand. "Does the cat still have my tongue?"

Drae knew it was only a moment before her pussy began to speak the language of wetness. "And before you flatter yourself, I'm not stalking you," she said sarcastically, feeling as if she needed to volunteer that information.

"Really?" He raised one of his thick eyebrows. "And I was just wondering that."

"Whatever." She flicked her hand. "You shootin', or what?"

"Stop asking me loaded questions." Never once taking his eyes off Drae, he sent the dice spinning through the air and hitting against the cement wall like cracking ice cubes. "Maybe, after tonight, you'll stop running."

"Running? From who?"

"Me." He quickly counted the dots on the three red dice.

"I wasn't running from you."

"Stop lying." He grabbed the dice. "Blow on these."

Drae gave a deep swallow and tucked in her shiny bottom lip as she tried to shake loose her nerves. "How you want me to blow on 'em?" she said low enough so that Naz was the only one who could hear. "You want me to deep throat it, or you just need a little tease?" She gave a seductive smile and winked, all while doing her best to stop her knees from shaking. The best thing about standing in Naz's face, especially since she never expected to see him here, was that she knew she was fly: black miniskirt, deep V-cut lavender sweater, abundance of cleavage, black Vickie Secrets fishnets and wedged-heel boots.

He held the dice to Drae's lips. "Surprise me. . . ." Drae gave her best I'm-the-shit performance, dredged up all the air in her body and blew it out as if she'd taken a smooth pull off a cigarette and was releasing the smoke.

"Oh goddamn," one of the onlookers said, and everyone in the crowd burst into laughter. "This niggah already won."

Naz shot the dice and came up short. "Looks to be your world, Sunshine." Naz handed them to her.

"I'ma spank dat ass." Drae smiled.

"Nah, I'ma spank *dat* ass." He gave her a sly smile.

As Drae prepared to shoot, the crowd of mostly old men seemed to come alive, now more than before. There were a million whistles, a couple of must-be-jam-cause-jelly-don't-shake-like-thats—and a few singing the chorus to the Commodores' "Brick House."

Naz stood behind Drae and his dick, along with a few others, was rock solid. But no one knew like Naz what a fine ass Drae really had to offer.

She squatted to the floor as if she were getting her eagle on in slow motion. The entire back of her body slid down the front of Naz's as if he was a stripper's pole. Once she reached his dick, she rubbed her ass in a circular motion. "Keep it up," he said as he squatted behind her. As she crouched a few inches from the floor she could feel Naz slip his hand up her miniskirt, pop one of the fishnets shielding her pussy, and slide two of his fingers in.

"Ooooh . . ." Drae was surprised as she unexpectedly tipped to one knee, almost hitting the floor. Naz grabbed her by the waist and pulled her back. "That's what you get for not having no panties on."

All Drae could do was close her eyes as the juice from her ill nana soaked his fingers and ran between her thighs. "Lil' mama, you gon' roll?" one of the men asked.

Drae tried to get her focus back on the game. She prayed that no one could see what Naz was doing, otherwise she would be embarrassed as shit.

"What happened to your panties?" Naz sucked lightly on her ear.

"I knew you were gon' be here," she lied. Although they were in a crowd, Drae wished that Naz would take his hand and palm her pussy instead of teasing her with his wet fingertip.

Drae held the dice in her hand and then placed them over her shoulder. "Hit it right in the center, baby."

"Unless you wanna be fucked," he said with a laugh, "you better quit playing with me." He gave the dice a smooth blow.

She shook the dice in a closed fist. "Am I the one playing," she asked, looking over her shoulder at his face, "or is it you?" She did her best to keep her balance.

"A'ight now," he sighed. "You gon' mess around"—Drae could tell his dick was hard by the sound of his voice—"and I'ma fuck the shit outta you."

"Well . . ." she said, basking in the motion of his movement, "how you wanna fuck me, daddy, like this?" She rolled her hips to the right. "Or like this?" She rolled to the left. "Or is this it?" She bounced slightly up and down, not too high for everyone to notice, but high enough for him to get the point. Her wetness flowed like rain and made his dick feel like it was going to explode.

"Cut that shit and roll them fuckin' dice." He pumped his fingers faster, sliding them in and out. Drae knew at any minute she was about to cum. Doing her best not to scream, she shot the dice against the wall. "Five! Motherfuckin' five!" she screamed, panting at the fact that she'd just cum and simultaneously won the dice game. Her inner thighs felt sticky and she could only imagine what Naz's hands looked like. "I told you I was gon' spank dat ass!" She jumped up.

He simply smiled, knowing that it was truly the other way around.

"Spank me!" someone in the crowd yelled. "And whip it real good!"

Everyone burst out laughing.

Drae caressed Naz's face. "I sure hope you know now to take your beating like a man." She licked the juice off the fingers he had had in her pussy. "Now give me my money, please."

Naz bent down, stacked the bills one on top of another and stuffed them into her bra. "You got that."

She threw her ass into extra motion as she turned to walk away. Drae took a series of deep, nervous breaths. If only she could get the butterflies in her stomach to stop moving around.

Instead of heading to the pool table where she spotted Nae-Nae and Yuri, she stood still for a moment and wondered where she could go and scream in peace. Naz had started her pussy juices to flowing and since she was too shy, outside of a porno audition, to tell him what else she needed him to do, she decided to take matters into her own hands. After standing for a few seconds too long, she walked swiftly through the swinging doors that led to the single-stall women's restroom.

After closing the door, she grabbed a hand full of paper towels and wet them with warm water. She dabbed a little soap on it, pulled her stockings down, and washed between her legs. The warm water on her clit made her remember Naz's fingertip.

Drae checked in the mirror to be sure her hair was still tight and her clothes were still fly. She figured she'd been in the bathroom long enough and just knew there was probably a line of annoyed women waiting to fix their wigs, play with their weaves or get a good piss on. As she opened the door and stepped out she bumped into Naz's chest. Instantly his Eternity for Men cologne filled her nose.

"You know we not finished." He pushed her back into the bathroom and locked the door behind him.

Drae tried to speak but there were no words to say; she lifted his shirt above his head and snatched it off. "You don't understand what you do—"

"Shut up. Now ain't the time to talk—my dick is hard and I warned you I was gon' fuck the shit outta you."

He kissed her before spinning her around to face the mirror-covered wall and placing her hands on the glass. He placed his hands on top of hers and started biting her up and down her neck, over and over again, almost as if he was obsessed with tasting her skin and having her scent buried in his nose. "Sick of you always fuckin' teasing me and shit."

Drae started breathing heavily—his raspy voice drove her insane. The pain of his bites made her forget her name, and the tingling in her pussy souped her up for what was to come. Her pussy cried like never before. She felt like a druggie, a fiend, a bitch snortin' a line called whipped-by-a-dick.

"I'm tired of thinking about this fat pussy." Naz lifted the back of her sweater and bit a trail that galloped over her ass and in between her ass cheeks. His tongue splashed back and forth over her behind, causing her to scream. He jacked up her skirt and ripped her fishnets so he would have full access to her pussy.

She screamed again. He placed his hand over her mouth, as she called his name. "You may as well stop screaming, 'cause you been begging for this dick."

All Drae could do was lick in between his fingers.

"You fuckin' teasin' me and shit." He pushed his hard dick into dripping wetness. For a moment he closed his eyes and did his best not to cum on the spot. Drae's pussy was undeniable, the warmth of it, the soft flesh, the expanding wall that clapped around his dick . . . and what seemed to make her pussy so fuckin' good was that she knew how to pop her inner muscle so it grabbed the head of his dick and teased it with the possibility of going farther . . . and farther . . . so far up into her pussy that he knew he could one day send his nut soaring out her mouth.

"I'm tired"—he forced himself to open his eyes and slap the sides of her ass—"of us running into each other . . . knowing we wanna fuck."

"Naz—"

"Shut up, you talk too much." As the sound of his dick slapping against her ass triumphed like a band, there was a knock at the door.

"Drae?" Yuri said. "Are you okay?"

"Yes . . ." Drae struggled to say. "I'm cumming!" she screamed.

"All right, we'll wait," Yuri said.

"Did I tell you to cum?" Naz pumped her harder than before. "Did . . . I . . . tell . . . you . . . to . . . cum? Stop . . . being so fuckin' grown."

"Okay, daddy" was all Drae could say. "But yo' dick is so big . . ."

"What you say, Drae?" Nae-Nae asked. "Did you say something about a dick?"

Drae didn't answer, instead she thrust her ass onto Naz's shaft and they began fucking like a boot-camp drill team: relentlessly, and both of them breathing as if they'd run out of air.

After Drae came again she could feel Naz's pace quicken. As she felt his dick begin to take up residence in her stomach forcing all the cream in her coochie to slide out, he grabbed her by the hair and splashed off on her ass.

He kissed her on the back and her hands held on to the edge of the pedestal sink. They were silent for a few moments, staring at each other's reflection in the mirror.

"Damn, Sunshine. I swear on everything I love you a bad motherfucker." He kissed the back of her neck, then grabbed the roll of paper towels.

Before moving, Drae looked once again in the mirror and stared at his face. She was tempted to thank him, but instead she tore a sheet of paper towel and cleaned herself with it.

They were quiet as they fixed their clothes and made sure they were composed again.

"I guess you need to throw those away." Naz laughed, pointing at the fishnets in her hand.

"Seems so." She smiled.

"We have to stop meeting like this." He kissed her on the lips. "Give me your number, since you too scared to call me." He slipped his cell phone from his pocket and Drae entered it. He opened the bathroom door and Nae-Nae, Yuri and a whole line of women were standing there with surprised and pissed looks on their faces. However, they all had one thing in common, their eyes were glued to Naz's body.

"Be easy, Sunshine." Naz tipped his head at the women. "Excuse me."

"Oh my God!" Nae-Nae screamed recognizing him from the strip club, "Nasty Naz, is that you?" He looked at Drae's face for confirmation. "I knew it! You two"—he pointed at Yuri—"is some bold-ass cheatin' bitches and I'm tired of y'all stealing my men. Hold my place in line, Yuri." He ran behind Naz. "Hold up, I got some singles!"

Yuri

Three A.M. and Yuri's head pounded like thunder as she beat against Britt's apartment door. Images of him fucking Troi and telling her how much he loved her ran through Yuri's mind; and the more time went on, the more obvious it became the visions weren't going anywhere.

Her feet were killing her and her stomach roared. She knew at any minute she would throw up, something she'd been doing all week. At first she thought it was nerves and her body getting sick of being next to Jeff, but now she knew it was a premonition of being in a fucked-up position: her loving Britt and his loving Troi.

"Britt!!" She pounded over and over again, the sides of her fist swollen and her eyes flooded with tears. This was the exact opposite of what she swore to herself she would do. Her plans were to keep it all together, be a bad bitch with confidence and control. She was supposed to light a cigarette, utilize the doorbell, and when he opened the door, haul off and smack the shit out of him. But somewhere amid the visions of him licking the pinkness of Troi's pussy, pulling her hair back and telling her he loved her, all of Yuri's calm and collected plans went out the window and now her adrenaline was pumping from sheer emotion.

"Dammit! Open this door!" Yuri rapped repeatedly.

"What the hell . . . is yo' problem?" Britt opened the door. He could tell she'd been crying, as she brushed past him and into his apartment. He locked the door behind her and she turned to face him. The entranceway was dark and the only light came from the neighboring high-rises and the view of the Brooklyn Bridge. Britt stood with his white, plush terry-cloth robe hanging open and his hard dick sticking out from beneath. "What's wrong? Somethin' happened?"

Yuri stood silent for a moment. She hated that even in the midst of tears and darkness she appreciated his beauty. She loved to stare at his hard dick and imagine all the things she could do with it, but now instead of her seeing herself sucking it, she imagined Troi caressing it into her mouth. "You still in love with Troi? You been lying to me all this time?!"

"What?!" Britt stood still and stared at Yuri.

She knew he was pissed, but compared to how she felt she didn't give a damn how pissed off he was. Hell, he was the one in love with someone else. Not her. "What you gettin' pissed off for—it must be true! No matter what, you will always love her ass!"

Britt glanced at the digital clock on the wall behind Yuri's head. "You for real? You ain't wake me up for a quick fuck, you woke me up to ask me some stupid shit? You know how long ago it's been since I've even thought about that broad? Man, please." He walked past his piano and over to his bed.

"Don't fuckin' 'man, please' me!" she yelled, walking behind him and pushing him in the back. "I'm talking to you."

"A'ight now," he warned as he took off his robe and crawled into bed.

"Answer me, dammit!" she screamed pushing him on the shoulder. "Do you still love her?!"

"I'm going to sleep, Yuri. Now, if you want some dick, come lay yo' retarded ass down. If you wanna argue over the most ridiculous fuckin' shit I've heard this year, then lock the door behind you."

She flicked the lights on. "You must be fucking her! What, are y'all laughin' at me? You talkin' about me? Is that why she said y'all were getting back together tonight?!"

"What? Ain't nobody said no shit like that."

"You fucking her?"

He simply turned over in bed.

"You know how many years I've been in love with you, and this is what you do? How could I let you do this to me again?! You could've left me at home with my damn husband! At least I was used to his bullshit!"

Britt sat up and pressed his back against the headboard. The flat green sheet was draped across his lap and his arms were locked behind his neck. Truth be told, at that moment he wanted to snatch Yuri by her fuckin' throat and ask her if she was listening to herself, but instead he stared at her and sized her up with his eyes. "What you scared of?"

"I just don't want my heart broken!" Tears drenched her face; she hated that her collected cover was blown.

"Then, what are you here for? If I'ma break your heart, why we keep doing this? We go through this same shit over and over again."

"So you still love her, is that what you're saying?"

"Would you stop asking me that dumb shit! It should be obvious that everything between me and Troi is dead. I can't believe," he said, exasperated, "that I'm fuckin' you, and you worried about another woman. What kinda game is that, Yuri?"

"This ain't a game to me, this is my life!"

"And you lettin' another chick play with it?"

"She threw it in my face that you two were getting back together."

"And you believed her. You ain't think to ask me?"

"Remember, you were the one who wanted to marry her!"

"So? We were kids—"

"Well, tell her that, 'cause she damn near said you were an item!"

"Shut up, I'm talkin', don't be interrupting me. You shoulda interrupted Troi and told her to kiss yo' ass! Instead of coming over here to me, going off and causing problems between us. Troi is not the one I'm in love with, and I don't appreciate having to explain that shit! Now, what you really wanna do? Huh? You wanna be with me?"

"Yes."

"You love me?"

"Yes."

"Then, leave that motherfucker."

"What?!" She knew he was furious, but when did leaving Jeff become part of this equation?

"Don't fuckin' 'what' me! I'm sick of this shit. Leave that motherfucker, right now! Call 'im and tell 'im you leaving!" He reached for the cordless phone on the nightstand. "Call 'im right now and tell 'im you coming to get yo' shit because you leavin' to be wit' me."

Yuri's heart started racing. She knew Britt was serious and, yeah, she wanted to leave Jeff, but right now at this minute? And it had nothing to do with money in the bank, assets, shared bills, or the apartment they lived in. . . . it was about what she was used to, what she'd come to accept and expect. There were no expectations with Jeff because there was nothing there. No love lost, no loved gained, nothing, just some furniture they bought together and a few groceries from the bodega. Shit, didn't Britt understand that she couldn't give up everything she had when he wouldn't even hold a straight conversation about whether he loved her or not, when all they did was fuck, and when after all of these years they'd never even been on a real date? And suppose Drae was right, then what? What would happen next if she left Jeff and was made to look like a big-ass fool?

Britt dialed a series of numbers and pointed to the phone. "Here, tell him!"

Yuri stood silent. She could hear the phone ringing.

"Take this fuckin' phone!"

She backed away.

"Tell this motherfucker"—his eyes widened—"you leaving, tell 'im that you love me!"

Britt walked over to Yuri and shoved the phone in her face, "What de muthascunt I say?! Tell him!"

"Britt, please," she begged softly while holding her hands together in a prayer position.

"What the fuck? You begging me?" He laughed emphatically. "You snortin' bullshit, you know that? You got game out the ass, yo' shit is just convenient."

"Britt, please," she pleaded quietly again.

"My man, tell me, what you whispering for?" He stepped back. "This the same game you shoulda had when Troi was playing wit' yo' head. What I told her ass is that I shoulda been with you when I had a chance. And that was after she volunteered to make me forget all the pain she caused me. Did she tell you that I told her to step? To leave and that we were strictly business? Did she tell you that? Naw, she fucked with your head and made you play yourself by coming over here."

"Britt, hang up the phone."

"Oh, hang up the phone?" He mushed her in her left temple. "Think you slick, talking soft so this niggah can't hear you? I thought you was bad, though, barging over here at three o'clock in the morning, ordering me around about a buncha nonsense, claiming you love me so much but you won't even leave this niggah." He clicked the phone off. "I hadn't even called yo' damn house. I would never give that motherfucker the satisfaction of you playing me. But let me tell your selfish ass somethin': Don't you ever in your fuckin' life"—he pressed his forehead against hers—"come over here rearing up at me about some bullshit, until you ready to leave that sterile-ass niggah. Until then, you get what the fuck yo' greasy-ass hand call for!"

"I will leave him."

"Bullshit. Now you can stop acting like the sick-and-in-love victim. Yo' ass is grown and you know what's going on. Now, if you gon' swing with me, then stop making demands that you yourself can't keep. And next time tell Troi to stay in her fuckin' lane, 'fore I catch her ass." Britt walked over to his bed and propped the pillow behind his head.

Yuri bit her bottom lip and wiped tears from her eyes. She tucked her purse securely under her arm and headed toward the door.

"Where you going?"

"I just—I figured I would . . . I would leave . . ."

"My man"—he sighed—"cut the light off and come here."

"No . . . I'ma just go. . . ."

"Damn, man, quit with the dramatic bullshit. We ain't on TV, just get in the fuckin' bed!"

Yuri cut the light off and placed her purse on the nightstand. She stood on the side of the bed where Britt lay.

He grabbed her around the waist and pulled her on top of him. "Just lay here." He put her head to his chest.

"Britt—" She felt him running his fingers through her hair. "You think this could last forever?"

"Shhh." He closed his eyes. "This is forever."

Drae

It was a record-breaking eighty degrees at four o'clock on a Thursday afternoon. Until now March had been in a deep freeze; it'd snowed twice, rained almost every other day, and the days in between the spring breezes felt like arctic air.

Drae had just gotten off work and stepped into her candy-apple convertible Roadster when her cell phone rang. She hoped like hell it was Hassan. She'd been waiting all day to light his ass up; especially since he'd been lying all week, had been home only twice since Sunday, yet called every day around the same time for her to fry him chicken, which he never managed to eat.

She looked at the cell phone and noticed it was a private number. A menacing smile ran across her face.

"Let me explain this to you," she answered, "when I catch you, I'ma . . . fuck . . . yo' ass up!"

"Dayummm, Sunshine. It's like that? To hell with 'Hey, how you doin',' huh?"

Instantly her heart skipped four beats at the sound of Naz's voice. She swore she could smell his cologne through the phone. "I thought you were—never mind—sorry about that—and yes, how are you?" For the life of her she couldn't figure out why she felt so nervous. She hadn't felt this giddy over a man since she had her first orgasm.

"It's been a minute." As he spoke Drae could hear him smiling. "Wassup?"

"You, that's wassup."

"True."

She laughed at his arrogance. "There's really no need for you to suck ya own dick."

"Funny." He chuckled. "Listen, me and my boys are down here at the court on Prospect. Why don't you come through and be my cheerleader?"

"So, what, you tryna get a date?" She was doing her best not to spit out "yes" too fast.

"It's your world ma', I'm just a squirrel tryna get a nut."

"I bet you are."

"What, you ain't know."

"Bye, Nasir . . ."

"Be good, love."

• • •

After Drae parked, she quickly took off the blouse she wore underneath her red Donna Karan seersucker pantsuit. She buttoned the two buttons going down the middle of her suit jacket; this way the contoured look would accent her waistline and compliment her abundance of cleavage.

When she walked onto the playground, Naz was dribbling the ball on the court and his friends were talking shit to him and laughing.

"I hope you don't fuck that fast," one of Naz's friends joked.

"Don't talk about your daddy like that," Naz retorted.

Drae took a series of deep breaths before she settled on what she would say when she walked up to him. Yet the closer she got, the more nervous she became. Just being in his presence mesmerized her.

Staring at him, she realized being dapper must've been a part of his style, because every time she saw him he worked it out: slightly baggy basketball shorts, a wife-beater and crisp white Uptowns on his feet.

Instead of sneaking up on him like she'd planned, she sat down on the cement park bench across from the court and cleared her throat. Naz, who'd just passed the ball, turned around and smiled. "Give me a minute," he said to his friends.

One of his friends looked at Drae and said, "And then give me one."

Naz sat next to her. "Sunshine . . . what's good, love?"

"You."

"All day."

"Okay." She blushed. "I take it you came riding in on your own dick today?"

"Nah, I was waiting for you." He kissed her on the forehead, and looked her up and down. "Only you would come to the playground in a red seersucker pantsuit. You too fly for words, ma'."

"Oh, daddy, you mean that?" She pouted her smooth and shiny lips.

"Daddy, yeah a'ight." He laughed. "This probably ya first time on the playground, huh? You ain't never play outside as a kid, did you?"

"Excuse you, my friends and I were always outside."

"Doing what? Playing dress up?"

"Hopscotch, thank you."

"You can't hop."

"I can so hop." Drae laughed as she mushed him on the shoulder. "Me and my crew owned hopscotch."

"You and who? The chick who looked at me like I stank when we got caught coming out the bathroom? And the punk who was chasing me in Queen of Sheba with dollar bills? What a whack-ass crew."

"Whoool." She playfully drew back her fist. "Don't get bodied, niggah."

"You think you tough?" He wrapped one of his arms around the back of her neck and placed her in a pretend choke hold. "Do somethin'."

She rummaged through her bag. "Let me see if I got a knife."

"A'ight, a'ight"—he let go—"I ain't fuckin' wit' you, but yo, ya man, lil' dude, what's his name?"

"Nae-Nae."

"Nae-Nae . . . what the fuck? I shoulda known." He shook his head. "Anyway, yo, my boys was lookin' at me like 'You know this kid?' I had to be like 'Yo, son, I promise you I will rock yo' ass to sleep if you don't step da fuck away from me.' "

"I should kick yo' ass saying that to Nae-Nae."

"Ya boy's retarded, I hope the shit ain't contagious." He paused, tilted his head down and looked Drae in the face.

"I'ma hurt you." She laughed. "Now, what he say?"

"That niggah was like 'Oh, you a killah? I like killahs.' Man, I just left him standing there."

Drae fell out laughing. "Let me just warn you now, Nae-Nae is relentless."

"Why you warning me? That's your friend. Why would I see him again? Is that a slick way of saying I'ma see you again?"

"Do you want to see me again?"

Naz looked up at the court, where his friends were still playing. "You know I'm going back on my word, right? I swore after my daughter's mother I would never mess with another married woman."

"You have a daughter?" Drae was surprised.

"Yes."

"How old?"

"Five."

"And her mother was married? Why was she cheating?"

"What, you got some morals?" He shot her a sly look.

"You being funny? You must wanna be cut."

"You my niggah, you know that?" He smiled. "But she cheated for the same reasons most chicks cheat: he treated her like garbage, cheated on her, beat on her. Ridiculous shit."

Drae arched her eyebrows, especially since the story was beyond familiar. "How'd you meet her?" Drae scooted closer to him; he placed his left hand in her lap and she started playing with his long fingers.

"I'd just started dancing at this lil' club in Jersey called

Cheetah's," he said, enjoying her touch. "She was in the audience and snuck backstage. . . . Sound familiar?"

"Ha-ha-ha."

"Anyway, I kicked it to her and we went from there. I got to know her, fell in love with her, and since she was the married one I played the game by her rules. When she got pregnant she was scared as hell and told me leaving that niggah wasn't an option. So, she lied and told him the baby was his. After that, we left each other alone."

"Were you hurt?"

"Hell yeah, I even stopped dancing and got a nine-to-five."

"Where?"

"Verizon."

"Doing what?"

"Telephone repair."

"All that body climbing a pole, I woulda lost control." Drae laughed.

"Your freaky ass probably would've too. Anyway, nine months later, she called me crying, said she couldn't do it anymore. That he knew the baby wasn't his and I needed to come get her, or else she was putting her up for adoption."

"What?" Drae said in disbelief.

"Yeah, I was living in a studio and shit. Verizon wasn't paying me nothing, not compared to what I made when I was dancing. I mean a nine-to-five worked for me by myself, but now I had a kid and I wasn't about to see her go through no bullshit. So I got back on my grind and revamped my hustle, which was exotic dancing."

"And pornos—was a hustle?"

"Yeah." He chuckled. "A short-lived one. Hassan—that niggah too wild for me. Some of the shit he was doing, I wasn't about to touch. Needless to say, I'm back where I started."

"So dancin' . . . that was your hustle. You act like you were on the block, paleeze."

"Let me tell you somethin', every thug ain't got to sell drugs."

"Don't knock it till you try it," she teased.

"What the fuck, you holdin'? Let a niggah know so I can bounce."

"Yeah right."

"Plus"—he laughed—"I'ma tell you a secret, and I better not ever hear this shit again."

"Who I'ma tell?"

"Punk-ass Nae-Nae."

"Pussies is always hatin' on Nae-Nae."

"Pussies—what? You callin' me a pussy?"

"No, baby." She did her best not to laugh. "That's Nae-Nae's shit."

"Nae-Nae's hatin' on pussies? Know what?" he quickly said, answering his own question. "I don't even wanna know. Now, you wanna hear my story, or what?"

"Cock Diesel, would you go on?!"

"Cock Diesel? Don't be so formal, 'daddy' is good enough." He shot her a sly smile and Drae's eyes widened in a pleasant surprise.

"You really giving yourself a head job today," she said. "Now would you please come on with the big secret?"

"Anyway, when I was younger . . . I tried selling drugs."

"You did not get me amped just to hear that shit. . . ." She mushed him on the side of his head. "This better be a good-ass story. So what happened when you tried to lock a block?"

"I kept getting arrested."

"Arrested?"

"Every goddamn day," he said, exasperated.

"Shut up." She burst out in laughter. "You lyin'?"

"I'm dead-up serious. It was like when I stepped on the block with dirty pockets, Five-O was right there runnin' 'em. After a while my brother was like 'You may as well in-vest in a pair of handcuffs.' Even the cops was like 'Man, please give this shit up, ain't nobody gettin' arrested but you. And you a lil' niggah, we don't want you.' "

Drae laughed so hard she cried. "I'm sorry for laughing, I am . . ." she stuttered. "I am."

"It's cool, the shit is funny. Face it, every niggah on the block can't trap that motherfucker, 'cause my black ass stayed on the come-up; even my mother was like 'Nasir, this is ridiculous.' "

"Is that why you started dancing?"

"Believe it or not one of my boys' moms got me into dancing."

"Ya boy's moms?"

"Hell, yeah. This chick was on me. I swear, I would come to see my boy and his moms would stroll through the house naked."

"And where was he at?"

"Who knows? But some kinda way, he was never there. And his moms was bad, she was forty-something years old and I was nineteen, but she was tight. And I had never really had no pussy before. I mean, I fucked a couple o' chicks in the hallway, snuck a couple of afternoons in my bed, but that was it."

"So you fucked her?"

"I fucked the shit outta her. And she kept my black ass too. I was the freshest lil' niggah on the block. I had more gear than her damn kids. Anything I wanted, she got it. She used to manage this lil' club, I forget the name, and she told me I should try dancing, the women would love me. I did and everything fell into place from there."

"Damn."

"Now, back to you, since you all in my business. What's up with your husband? 'Cause I'm not tryna see both of y'all."

"You won't have to."

"Really? And how is that?"

"Why, are you worried about him? Look, I'm sitting here with you and we kickin' it. Take that shit for what it is. Right now it's about me and you, and if you feelin' me and I'm feelin' you, then what he got to do with us? Just flow wit' it."

Naz looked at Drae long and hard before he fell out into complete laughter; his legs were gapped open and his defined arms fell in between. "You gamin' me? Please tell me you did not just try and run no shit off on me."

"You gotta admit that was good, though, right? Give it to me," she said, holding her fist out for a pound. "I had my shit together."

He gave her a pound. "Now," he said in a serious tone, "what's the story with you and this niggah?"

"Look." She crossed her legs and sat back. Naz spread his arms across the park bench, with his left arm hanging over Drae's shoulder. "Hassan and I have been together since I graduated high school, and when I first met him, he felt different to me. Everything about him felt perfect. He was better than I ever dreamed any man in my life could be. He was a fantastic lover, a wonderful friend, he listened, shit, he did more for me than my own daddy, who raised me. He paid for me to go to college and everything."

"So, if he was this great dude, then where do the pornos come in at?"

"That shit snuck up on me. He always told me he did movies, but I didn't know it was pornos . . . at first. I guess I didn't really ask either. I was so caught up in everything he was doing for me; and it wasn't the money, the clothes, the jewelry or the house, at least not at that time, it was how he made me feel. He made me feel like ain't shit else matter but me. And not since my mother died had I felt that way. So one night he asked me to do an audition and I did."

"Real talk?"

"Real talk."

"I can't believe you did that."

"Where was I gon' go? He was all I had. And, yeah, I had a degree, but my degree didn't make me. I thought Hassan did. So I had to balance the risk of me leaving him against losing my life. So I did what I had to do."

"So you punked out?"

"No, I was seeing things for the way they were."

"What? A buncha lies?"

"I didn't see it that way. I saw it as survival."

"Survival or caught up?"

"Both."

"What about now?"

"Honestly, life is kicking my ass, but I'm in my own zone right now, trying to get it together."

"So, if Hassan was so perfect, when did he change?"

"I don't know. I wasn't paying attention, I wanted to avoid the shit. I was too busy covering up for this niggah being fucked up, you think I took time to pinpoint exactly when he changed? Hell, one night I went to sleep with Prince Charming and the next morning I woke up with Flavor Flav."

"Delicious, Flav gon' kick yo' ass."

"Anyway," she said, playfully rolling her eyes, "here I am with a husband I can't stand. We fight, he talks to me any kind of way—"

"Fight? He puts his hands on you?"

"Well . . . yeah, he has . . ."

"Why would you allow him to put his hands on you? You could stop that. You should stop that."

"Woulda, coulda, and shoulda are all friends and they have left the building. The only one still standin' is me."

"Look, ma', I'm feelin' you, I am. But this is too much drama."

Immediately Drae's heart sank, she started to think maybe she'd told him too much. "Besides," he continued, "I promised myself I wasn't going back down the married-chick road—"

"Cool, then don't." Rejection was always easier if she could cut the shit short. "Let's enjoy the afternoon, you buy me some ice cream"—she pointed to the Mister Softee truck—"and we part, no love lost."

"Why did you cut me off?"

"I didn't cut you off." She stood up.

"You did, but it's cool."

"Okay, Nasir, what?" She sat back down. "What were you going to say?"

"Nothing. You 'bout to bounce?"

"You puttin' me out the playground?" Drae asked, surprised.

"I told you this was your world."

"Well, I want some ice cream."

He pulled out a twenty-dollar bill. "Here, go get it." He pointed to the truck. "And then go home."

"Now you being rude?" She did all she could to fight off her smile. After having her heart broken momentarily, she realized she had him in the palm of her hand.

"You know what, you're right," Naz assured her. "Have a seat, I'll get it."

"You should know by now that I like chocolate." She licked her bottom lip.

Instantly Naz's dick was hard, but he tried to play it off. He walked toward the truck and grabbed one cup and one cone of ice cream.

"This isn't chocolate," she said, as he handed her the cone.

"I figured you needed to get used to vanilla."

"No problem, vanilla tastes good slidin' down my throat."

Naz shot her a "Stop fucking with me" look and Drae smiled. She leaned back on the bench, crossed her legs and started licking her ice cream, purposely letting the melting sides slide between her full cleavage.

"Oh damn." She sucked her teeth. She arched her back and held her titties in his face as if she were Betty Boop. "Can you get this for me?"

He twisted his lips at her. "Drae"—Naz couldn't help but smile—"why you fuckin' wit' me?"

"You have all the napkins."

Naz took a napkin in his hand and wiped the melting cream from her cleavage.

"Oh, goodness," she said. "It's soooo sticky. Do you have anything wet you can squirt down there?"

Naz didn't respond. He simply looked at her and continued eating his ice cream.

"You wouldn't happen to have an attitude, would you?"

"Nah." He licked his ice cream off the spoon. "I'm cool."

"I thought so . . . wait— Baby," Drae said sounding as if she was in a panic, "you have something right there."

"Where?"

"Right here . . ." Drae moved in close to his face, took her tongue and slowly licked off the ice cream that had melted down his chin, leaving a trail of kisses down his neck and stopping at his chest hairs, which peeped up from the top of his wife-beater.

"What are you doing?"

"I was helping you get the ice cream off." She took her thumb and ran it across his lips.

"I wish I could fuckin' resist you. I'd leave you sittin' here."

"You can't resist me?"

"Nah, and that's a dangerous spot to be in with yo' ass, 'cause you don't give up."

"Would you want me to?"

"I don't do drama."

"You don't have to do drama, just do me."

Naz couldn't help but smile. "There you go." He took a deep breath. "We got one time for me catch fever and this is a wrap."

"I thought you didn't do married chicks?"

"You're married?" he asked sarcastically.

"Maybe not forever."

"Look, I'm feelin' you, I am. But I got a daughter and I'm not trying to get into no crazy shit, a'ight?"

"So what are you saying?"

"I'm saying that if we gon' do this, it's gon' be by my rules this time."

"And what are those?"

"We have to take it slow—"

"Okay. All I ask is that you be honest. Believe me, I've been lied to enough."

"I will always be honest with you." He pressed his chest against hers. "Now that we've established that, can we arrange for me to get some pussy tonight?"

She pressed her lips against his. "I was just thinking that."

Yuri

Every time Yuri looked at Jeff she hated that she wasn't ready to leave him. She couldn't stand to lie next to him, couldn't stand the smell of him, the look of him or the thought of him. And she hated that corny-ass Caesar he rocked, that Mr. Clean fuckin' earring he had and those hot-ass suits he wore . . . day in . . . and day out, and those ridiculous-ass Italian ties with the dice, the stripes and the eagles flying.

Not to mention he snored too hard, coughed too loud, sneezed too much, wasn't freaky enough and the sound of his Prada penny loafers (with actual pennies in them) clacking against the hardwood floor more than pissed her off.

Jeff leaned against the bathroom door and stared at

Yuri. Earth, Wind & Fire preached in the background as the lingering smoke from his dead cigar snuck in from the hallway.

"I can't take that smell," Yuri said, almost in a whisper, as she sat on the edge of the tub, holding the sides of an old mop bucket, where she'd been vomiting and having hot sweats for the last hour. She was too weak to stand, which was why she threw up in a bucket as opposed to the toilet. Unfortunately, vomiting and waking up next to Jeff had become a morning ritual she couldn't seem to get rid of. When she first started getting sick, she thought she had the flu, but after a week straight of Theraflu and no change she diagnosed herself with a stomach virus, which by now should've run its course.

"What's the problem, Jeff?" Yuri asked as she looked toward the door. "I'm holding you up from going to work or something?"

"Give the attitude a day off, Yuri, it's obvious you're really sick, and I decided to stay home and check on you. I scheduled a doctor's appointment for tomorrow."

"You . . ." she said in disbelief, "scheduled . . . a doctor's appointment for me?"

"Yes, I'll drop you off on my way to work."

"Why, Jeff? You want some pussy or something—" before Yuri could continue, she was throwing up again.

"Yuri, drop it." After she finished vomiting he touched her forehead. "You feel like you have a slight fever. What do you think is wrong?"

"I don't know." She wiped the sides of her mouth. "I'm just sick. Ever since I ate Chinese food a week or so ago at work, I've been sick as a dog." For the first time it ran across her mind that maybe she had food poisoning.

"You need to get in bed," he insisted.

"Why are you being so nice?"

"I'm not. I just don't want you dying on my watch."

"Hilarious, Jeff."

"Yuri, just come get in the bed. This is ridiculous; we don't hate each other, do we?"

She stared at him. "I don't think so."

He helped her up, she rinsed out the bucket and they walked to their bedroom, where she could tell he'd been strolling down memory lane with the multitude of records he had sprawled on the floor. She hoped he didn't pull out his beat machine or, even worse, take out his Kangol hat and microphone.

Yuri crawled into bed. "What are you listening to?" She pointed to the records on the floor and the record player he'd hooked up.

"Five Star, 'All Fall Down,' " he said, pulling the covers up to her chest and tucking in the sides.

She fell out laughing.

"What are you laughing for?" He couldn't help but admire her smile, framed by two deep dimples. "This used to be my jam and you used to sing it to me; that's how you hooked me. Don't try and forget."

"Oh please, I hooked you because you wanted some of this young inexperienced pussy," she laughed. "Remember when you rapped and I was your backup singer?"

"I sure do, you were the Mistress of the Mic."

"And you were MC Ice Right. Whatever happened to our group?" she snickered.

"Life. Life fucked us up, caused us to get married and mess up a good thing."

"Jeff," she said, taking a deep breath, the smile she wore immediately leaving her face, "why do you always have to bring up shit like that? How come you never go with the flow?"

"I don't know what the flow is anymore." They each stared at the other in silence. "I'ma run to Duane Reade," Jeff said, breaking the troubling monotony, "and get you some medicine. You want some soup?"

"I don't have an appetite."

"That's a new one. . . ."

"See why we don't get along? Damn, Jeff," she said, exasperated. "It doesn't stop."

"You're right. My apologies, that wasn't called for."

"Apology accepted," she said halfheartedly.

"Well, you *have* to eat something."

"Jeff, I'm *not* hungry."

"I'm getting you some soup and that's the end of it."

"If you insist." Yuri lay in bed and watched Jeff leave the room. When she heard the front door close, she turned over and called Drae.

"Hello?" Drae picked up on the first ring.

"What the hell is all that noise in the background?"

"I'm in the playground."

"Why?"

"Remember that guy from the club?"

"The one-night stand you were fucking in the bathroom?"

"He wasn't a one-night stand. Anyway, I'm on a mini-date with him."

"Are you cheating on your husband? Oh, we have to talk."

"Yes we do."

"Look, I called because Jeff is being a little too nice. So if you don't hear from me by eight o'clock tonight, bring your ass over here and make sure I'm not bodied and bagged."

"Well, I hope I'm your beneficiary," she chuckled. "And if you are bodied and bagged, how am I supposed to get in the house?"

"The Venus statue by the door—look behind it, there's a spare key. Now, good-bye." And she hung up.

• • •

"Yuri," Jeff said in a whisper, "wake up." He sat on the edge of the bed, handing her a tray with Tylenol Cold & Flu, chicken noodle soup, saltine crackers and a single red rose on it.

"This is sooooo sweet," she said, smiling. She couldn't bear to tell him that she couldn't take the smell of the rose, so she bore with it. "Thank you. Make sure you keep on being sweet," she teased.

"How I'ma keep being sweet when you know as soon as you get well, you won't be home?"

Yuri looked at Jeff as if she could strangle him. "Is it even safe for me to eat this?"

"I'm not gon' hurt you, Yuri, I'm simply making a statement." He sat down on the floor and she noticed he had a bacon, egg and cheese McGriddle sandwich and an orange juice.

The smell was making her sick all over again. "Jeff," she said while praying she didn't vomit, "what you wanna ask me?"

"Ask you?" He sipped his juice.

"Yeah, what is it?" She placed the soup tray on the

nightstand. "You got something that's been on your mind and I'm giving you the opportunity to just ask me."

"Yeah, right."

"I'm serious as hell, Jeff. I'm not gon' snap."

"I'm not trying," he said as he took a bite, "to argue with you, Yuri."

"What did I just say? I promise I won't snap, I won't go off, none of that. I'd rather you just ask me than say a buncha slick shit."

"All right . . ." It was obvious he was stalling. "Do you . . . still love me the same way you did . . . when we first . . . got together?"

"Do you still treat me the same way?"

He paused. "Maybe not."

"Then, maybe I don't feel the same way."

"So what, you're not in love with me anymore?"

Yuri stared at Jeff and she knew by the look on his face, the one underneath the smug smirk that attempted to say he didn't give a fuck, that his heart sat bleeding on his sleeve and his mind pleaded for her to say something he desperately wanted to hear. "I still love you, Jeff." She barely got out "But I'm not sure . . ."

"Sure of what?" he said anxiously.

"How long I can keep loving like this."

"Like what?"

"Like we mad-ass roommates. I wanna be desperately in love. I wanna look at my man and see my whole world."

"So that changed? You don't look at me and see that?"

"Oh my God, have you been fucking yourself or what? Do you see how you treat me? You don't treat me like you still want me. I'm with you but I'm dying for attention. You depend too much on me just waking up every morning being in love, as if the air holds some type of keep-me-sprung magic."

"Excuse me, what about you? Since we being honest how about you owning up to the part you contributed to us being in this situation."

Yuri sat quietly for a moment. She'd never really thought about taking any responsibility for their marriage falling apart: after all, he was the one with the bastard child. But then again, she was fucking Britt and perhaps her part in that didn't make her and Jeff much different. "Yes, Jeff, I know that I haven't made it easy to try and rebuild our marriage, but what you did really hurts. And every time Kathy calls here or your son comes over, it just takes me back to that day when I found those child support papers. I mean how would you feel? You're in the hospital, I'm looking for insurance papers and guess what I find? A child support order. What the fuck do you think happened to me that day? Do you know how much I cried, how loud I cried, how quiet I cried, how plain and simply fucked up I was?!"

"Yuri, you never wanted any kids."

She sat up in bed. The space between her throat and her esophagus ached, "And what . . . the fuck . . . does that have to do with you fucking that bitch and getting her pregnant? Nobody told you to go strolling through the trailer park picking up trash!"

"She's not trailer park trash, Yuri."

"You defending this bitch?!"

"No," he said defensively, "I'm just saying you're being a little harsh. Whether we like it or not she's Jr.'s mother."

"Do I look like I give a fuck?! Her being Jr.'s mother was your choice; I didn't get not one nut outta that. Shit, for all

intents and purposes I'm Jr.'s fuckin' mother, half our in-
come is taking care of his ass. What the fuck does Kathy do?
That bitch doesn't even work. You provide health insurance,
she lives with her parents so she doesn't pay rent, and not
only do you pay child support, you pay Jr.'s tuition, pay for
all his birthday parties, Christmas, Easter, everything you
pay for. And you know what's funny?" Yuri couldn't believe
it, but she felt as if she was about to cry, "I was here first,"
she pointed to her chest. "We were a family, and then you let
this bitch and this little boy come and take over your life and
now I'm on the outside. It's like I'm the mistress and shit."

"So what you saying? You wanted to be Jr.'s mother?"

"Jeff please, I don't even want a dog named Jr."

Jeff blinked his eyes and cleared his throat. "Damn" was
all he could say. After a few troubling minutes of silence, Jeff
said, "You hate my son just that much?"

"No, I hate what you did."

"So the problems come back to being Jeff's fault again? I
fucked up. I'm taking care of responsibilities with my child,
Yuri—"

"Yes, Jeff, you are, but somebody, somewhere has to tell
me how the hell to be happy about that."

"I don't know what to tell you, Yuri."

"And I don't know what I wanna hear either."

They sat silent for a moment.

"A'ight," Jeff said, "I can accept that, but let me ask you
something, though, Yuri. Were you ever in love with me? I
mean truly, truly in love with me?" Although he tried to look
cool, she knew he wasn't ready for the truth.

"What did I just tell you, Jeff?" She couldn't bear to tell
him again she loved him. "Nothing will stop me from caring

about you, but you're so wrapped up in me being in the streets, that you're pushing me out there. You accuse me almost every day of cheating, so that I feel like either you're doing it . . . again . . . or I may as well do it—"

"I'm not cheating on you, Yuri. I learned my lesson the last time."

"When? When my GYN told me I had STDs that you and your eighteen-year-old mistress gave to me? Or when I found out you had a son?"

Jeff leaned back against the bed as if he'd fallen against a wall. "We'll never get through this."

"Maybe not."

"So we're done talking?"

"No, Jeff," she said exasperated, going against her better judgment, "we're not. I said we weren't going to argue and that you could ask me anything. So go ahead." She held her hands out in an "after you" fashion. "Continue."

"So it's cool?" He arched his eyebrows.

"It's cool."

"All right." He sat on the edge of the bed and scooted up next to her. "You haven't cheated on me?"

"Question or accusation?"

"Question."

"What, you want me to say yes?"

"I'm open to anything, Yuri, including the truth."

"Please."

"Look, all I'm saying is just be honest. I know there are times when I can be an asshole—"

"You know this?"

"Yes, and instead of talking, I accuse you. And just like when I cheated, I know there are times you need someone to talk to. Someone to be there for you and take care of you when you're stressed out."

"Have you lost your fuckin' mind?! She was eighteen, what the fuck were you talking about? How to be a child predator? The real deal is you wanted some young-ass white-girl pussy. Period. And you thought you had my ass in the bag because I was fat and confused."

"I'm not going through that again, Yuri. All I want to know is if you cheated, so we can deal with this. We're married, Yuri, and I'm in it for the long haul."

"And how long did you prepare that speech? Before or after you said you see us divorced in five years?"

"Why are you looking for an argument?"

"Jeff, listen." Yuri knew she needed to end this conversation, especially since Jeff was spewing a buncha bullshit. "All you need to worry about is that I'm with you. All that other shit is taking up too much mental space. Drop it. Please."

"I'ma always fight for you, Yuri." He brushed her hair out of her face.

"You keep on fightin', Ali," Yuri said sarcastically, as she closed her eyes and turned over. "Can we finish talking about this later?"

He turned the TV on and lay his head on her thigh. "Being pussy-whipped is a motherfucker." Jeff laughed.

"Shut up, Jeff," Yuri started to drift to sleep. "Just be quiet, please."

• • •

Jeff and Yuri had both fallen asleep when he was awakened by her moaning. At first he thought she was having a bad dream, but when she gripped the edge of the fitted sheet, and sweat dripped from both sides of her temples he knew something was wrong. He massaged her leg to gently wake her up, but she didn't budge. He thought for a moment she might have been having a seizure.

"Yuri," Jeff whispered; he didn't want to scare her awake. "You're having a bad dream?" She didn't wake, but she continued to moan. He felt wetness in the bed and for a moment he thought she'd peed on herself, until he held his hand up and saw it was blood.

Immediately he jumped up and looked at Yuri. There was no blood coming from her mouth, her hands or anyplace he could see. Maybe it was him, maybe he was bleeding. He hadn't seen this type of blood since his brother was shot. Jeff yanked the covers back and Yuri lay in a pool of red. "Yuri!" Jeff screamed. "You're bleeding!"

Yuri's heart raced as she jumped out of her sleep. She sat straight up and pressed her hands into the sheet. When she looked up at Jeff, the entire front part of him was covered in blood. As if someone were playing her life in fast forward, she looked down at the sheet and saw the bed was covered in red and the palms of her hands dripped as if she'd been playing in paint.

Neither one of them knew what was going on, but they knew they had to get her to the hospital. "Jeff—" Yuri panicked. "What happened? Oh God!" She thought she was dying. She could feel an excruciating pain in her lower back and abdomen.

"We have to go the hospital." Jeff did his best to hide his anxiety.

"Jeff!" Yuri started to scream. "What is happening to me?!"

"Calm down," he said sternly. "You think I'ma let something happen to you? I promised you I would always take care of you. Now," he consoled as he wrapped his coat around her, "let's go."

. . .

Jeff hated the emergency-room waiting area. He hated the sterile smell, the nurses, doctors, interns and orderlies all buzzing back and forth, as if they were happy to live in a world of others' misfortunes. He hated those hard-ass orange plastic chairs that suctioned his ass when he sat down and made a popping sound when he got up. He hated the flashing exit signs, the ambulance entrance and the signs that read: PEOPLE WILL BE SEEN IN THE ORDER OF THEIR EMERGENCIES.

Besides, every time he'd been in an emergency room he always felt doomed: his brother was shot, his father had died, and he had his skiing accident.

For hours Jeff paced the waiting area. He called Yuri's mother in Chicago to let her know what happened and she asked him to please call her back as soon as he found out anything. He called his own mother, who said a prayer over the phone with him. Then he called Nae-Nae and Drae to tell them Yuri was in the hospital. He replayed their wedding day in his mind, laughed at their first corny joke, remembered the first time she gave him some pussy and reconsidered the thought that their marriage was due to end.

"Mr. McMillan?" A doctor in a white overcoat with a tag that read DR. JOHNSON, walked over to Jeff and extended his hand.

"Yes." Jeff stood still, never noticing the doctor's extended hand; Jeff cupped his chin and waited for the doctor to begin speaking.

"Listen"—the doctor led Jeff to a more secluded waiting area—"the good news is your wife's fine."

Jeff took a deep breath and wiped the sweat from his brow.

"She's resting," the doctor continued, "and within the hour you two can go home. The unfortunate news . . . is she miscarried the baby."

"Come again?" Jeff could've sworn this was beyond hearing wrong. For a moment he wondered if he had just been spat on. "Yo," he said, momentarily releasing the ghetto in him, "what you say, son?"

The doctor stepped back. "I'm sorry to be the one to tell you, but your wife lost the baby."

"What . . ." Jeff fumbled over his words, trying to make out if his throat had been sliced and was making him speechless.

Misunderstanding Jeff's confusion, the doctor explained, "Mr. McMillan, your wife was expecting."

Jeff plopped down in one of the orange chairs he hated. Every time he went to speak, his tongue burned as if he had piss in his mouth. Truth be told, Jeff felt like slapping the doctor for GP sake; after all, he could've sworn this niggah said Yuri lost a baby. Whose baby? Yuri? Yuri lost a baby? Somebody somewhere had to be playing, because they had Jefferson McMillan fucked up. Just because he went from the projects to the Ivy League didn't mean he was a punk. He could push a motherfucker to sleep if need be, and perhaps this was one of those times. After all, who didn't know he was sterile? Who didn't know he spent a weekend with his mistress, had a skiing accident and split his nuts open? Yuri never let that shit die, so how could the doctor not know? "How . . ." He cleared his throat and stood back up. "How far along was she?"

"Six weeks."

It's not mine, it's not mine, it's not mine . . . it's not mine . . . it's not mine . . . He massaged the sides of his forehead; suddenly he had a migraine. The reality he swore he wanted to face had suddenly showed up and kicked his ass. Now either he had to deal with it or be done with it. "She was what? Are you sure?"

"She was six weeks pregnant. I apologize, Mr. McMillan. I'm really sorry to be the one to tell you . . . but your wife was so upset that I didn't think she would be up to explaining it to you."

"She knows already?"

"Yes."

"Did she tell you to tell me?"

"We never discussed it. I just assumed since you were her husband . . ."

Hell, Jeff being her husband didn't mean shit, the baby wasn't his. "Thank you, Doctor." Jeff nodded his head in dismissal. "Can I see her now?"

"Right this way."

Jeff walked into Yuri's room feeling numb. Looking at her he imagined some niggah, any niggah, the mailman, the cable man, a lil' young niggah flippin' burgers or an old niggah flippin' real estate, barge up in her raw dawg, as if she'd told them all about his dick not being able to shoot shit. He imagined them laughing at him and purposely planning to have this baby. A baby that everyone would consider the ultimate get-back-at-him-for-fucking-a-white-bitch scheme.

Now he knew for sure that she had to have known she was pregnant. That's why she'd been so sick, that's why she'd been gaining weight, sleeping, cussing him out, couldn't stand to smell anything. That's why she'd been treating him like there was nothing he could do for her other than get the fuck out of her face . . . all because she'd served his ass up some serious fuckin' payback.

"You gave me quite a scare, girl." He leaned against the side of the bed she lay in.

"You? I scared the hell outta myself. But the doctor said I'll be okay, that I can go home now."

"I was hoping to find the doctor so he could explain to us what was wrong." Jeff searched her eyes for any sign of fear, but what he spotted wasn't enough. "I wanted to be there when he told you. In case there were any special instructions. Matter fact, let me go and find him, so I can be sure of what you need to do." He started walking toward the door.

"Jeff!" she called.

He could hear her trying to get off the bed. He turned around. "Where you going? Take it easy."

"Why are you looking for the doctor?" she said anxiously. "I'll get the discharge instructions. It was just fibroids anyway. Something very common in black women."

"Why are you so anxious?"

"I'm sorry." She took a deep breath. "I'm still in shock, I guess."

"I understand." He handed her her clothes. He could tell she didn't want to keep talking. "Are you in a lot of pain?"

"No, not anymore." She slipped her clothes back on. "I've had two Motrin."

"The bleeding?"

"Still bleeding heavy, but nothing like before."

"So what did the doctor tell you?" Jeff asked.

"Fibroids," she spat out a little too quickly. "He said I have fibroids. It's common . . . African American women."

"You said that already."

"Well, I mean African American and Native American women."

"Yeah," he said distantly. "African American and Native American, huh? Interesting combination."

The room was silent as they both stared at each other just long enough to know the other knew the truth. Jeff thought about telling Yuri he knew about her get-back scheme, but he couldn't bear to spit out the words "pregnant" and "Yuri" in the same sentence. After all, she was his wife and how would he say—let alone accept—she was carrying another man's seed. That would mean she opened her legs, showed the face of her pussy and had another man's dick kiss it, while he nutted inside of her as if she were his own. As if she didn't have a husband, at least one they regarded as being worth anything.

On the drive home Yuri wondered how she could've been pregnant and not have known. Suppose she didn't have a miscarriage, then what? She'd be stuck nursing Britt's baby and convincing Jeff his sterilized dick had actually done something.

Once they arrived at the apartment building, they were both quiet until they got inside.

"Yuri," Jeff called from behind her, as she headed toward their bedroom. "Where are you going?"

"To bed."

"It's early. Come talk to me. I'll put some tea on for you."

Being that the guilt from her miscarriage was eating her up, she didn't put up too much of a fuss. Instead she sat down on the couch.

"Sugar?" Jeff yelled from the kitchen.

"What?"

"Do you want sugar in your tea?"

"Yes, sugar and lemon."

Jeff returned from the kitchen and handed her a cup of tea. The cup shook on the saucer, causing some of the hot tea to splash on the sides.

Jeff did what he could not to black out and whip her ass off the couch. Initially, he thought he could attempt to be diplomatic and handle this like an adult, but this shit here had put his manhood to the test. All the times she floated her fat ass in here, two, three, and four o'clock in the morning. All the times he asked, begged and pleaded with her to please tell him the truth, who was the niggah. He thought about how she answered her cell phone sleepy, when she was supposed to have been at the club. Was she in bed with the niggah then? Had his dick just literally come out of her mouth? And what about the time she said Nae-Nae and Raphael had a fight and her clothes were different when she came back home? What was she doing that night? Had she had a bath in the niggah's sperm? Hell, Jeff wondered, where was he when all of this baby makin' was going on? At home watchin' *American Idol* or jerking his dick to sleep?

After Jeff served her the tea, he pulled up one of their black leather Pier One dining-room chairs and sat directly in front of her. He sat so close that his breath made her eyes blink. "I love you, you know that, right?"

Suddenly Yuri didn't feel like drinking the tea. "And I love you too," she said with as much sincerity as she could muster. "And I really have to thank you for being there for me today. Not every man would take—"

Before she could continue, Jeff reared his hand back, squinted his eyes and hauled off and knocked the shit out of her. He smacked her so hard that her head moved back and forth like a Bobble Head doll that'd lost control. The hot tea splashed everywhere, specks of it hitting her eyes, burning her thighs and running down her legs. Immediately she jumped up to defend herself. He pushed her back down. "I wanna fuckin' talk," he spat, yoking her neck with one hand. "Can we do that?"

Yuri couldn't believe what had just happened. It took her a few seconds before she could open her mouth enough to scream.

WHAPP!!!! He smacked her again. "I'll kick yo' fuckin' ass you scream in here again. Now, whose fuckin' baby was that?!"

Silence. Instead of answering she sat there wondering how she could either kill him or get away; it was obvious that it had to be one extreme or the other.

"You want me to slap the shit outta you again?" He raised his hand. "Now, whose goddamn, rotten-ass dead baby was that?!"

"What are you talking about?!" she managed to scream. "Don't fuckin' hit me no more!"

"You still lying?!" He grabbed her by the neck and lifted her up off the couch. "I will kill you," he said through gritted teeth. "You still wanna lie, Yuri? You still lying?"

"No!" she screamed. "Let me go!"

"Bitch, please. Lettin' you go is the least of your fuckin' worries! Now I'ma ask you this one . . . last . . . time. . . . Whose . . . fuckin' . . . baby . . . was that?"

"Jeff—"

"That wasn't my baby, so what the fuck you calling my name for?! Are you trying to get yo' ass killed?! I swear to God that the next word better be this niggah's name"—he turned toward their picture window—"or I will toss you through that motherfuckin' glass!"

Yuri tried desperately to speak, but she was shaking so badly no words would come out.

"Let me help you out." He began walking her around the living room. Although she was fighting and screaming, he overpowered her, and when she managed to squirm to the floor, he slapped her again, wrapped her hair around his hand and began dragging her around the living room. "You fuckin' wit' Blake?"

Instead of answering she tried to dig her nails into his hand. Once she drew blood, he reached over with his free hand and smacked her so hard she could've sworn he broke her face. "You'se a hardheaded motherfucker. Now . . . we gon' try this again. You fuckin' Blake?"

"Who is Blake?" Tears and snot poured down her face and all she could see were the helicopter lights from the neighboring high-rise. "Jeff, please . . ."

Ignoring her plea he went on, "Bitch, is it Blake's?"

"Who is Blake?" She shook.

"The fuckin' mailman, bitch." He started dragging her around the living room again. "Raheem," he said more to himself than to her. "It's Raheem's?"

"Raheem?"

"Oh, you know Raheem, bitch."

"Jeff, please stop!" If she could get on her knees and beg him she would.

"You fuckin' Raheem?" He started dragging her again.

"Who is he?!"

"Radio Raheem, bitch. Who the fuck you think it is?! You know that niggah is the cable man, he's in here all the god-damn time!"

Yuri couldn't believe this was happening. Everything seemed to be spinning. As Jeff went to lift her off the floor by her neck, he heard her cell phone ringing. Robin Thicke was singing "Lost Without U," causing Jeff to stop dead in his tracks. He held Yuri by her neck and for a moment that felt like it went on into infinity, they were both silent. Both of them knowing that the shit had finally clicked. "That's that niggah. There he go right there." He let her go and went for her cell phone, which rested on the coffee table. "Britt . . ." Jeff read the caller ID. "Britt?" He chuckled in disbelief as he answered the phone. "So tell me dawg, you fuckin' Yuri?"

"What?" Britt was obviously caught off guard.

"Man-up, niggah."

"Jeff . . ." Yuri said in the background. "Give me the phone."

"You crazy, Yuri? Give you the phone? Bitch, do you get it? I'm two seconds from killing you."

"Bitch?" Britt said calmly, yet in disbelief. "You called her a bitch?"

"What the fuck you gon' do about it, niggah? You weren't here when that fuckin' dead-ass baby died in my bed! Did I call her a bitch? Who the fuck you think you talking to?"

"Jeff, please give me the phone," Yuri begged.

"Bitch, what I tell you?"

"I'ma ask you nicely," Britt said, doing his best to remain calm, yet letting Jeff know he wasn't playing. "Don't call her a bitch no more. Now put Yuri on the phone."

"Put her on the phone? You think this is a game? I'ma kill this bitch!"

"You know what? You done went too motherfuckin' far!" And he hung up.

"I'm sick of being treated like a fuckin' joke!" Jeff threw the phone across the room, shattering it into pieces. "I done went too motherfuckin' far, but he fuckin' my wife? I'ma kill 'im!" Jeff started pacing back and forth across the room, snapping his neck from one side to the next. "Motherfuckers laughing at me," he repeated. "Y'all think Jefferson McMillan is a joke, but y'all niggahs the joke. A baby? A baby, Yuri? You . . . got . . . to be fuckin' kidding me. How was you gon' come up in this motherfucker with a baby, Yuri?"

"The same way you came up in here with one!" Now that Jeff had started pacing the floor, Yuri had a moment to collect herself. She wondered if she had enough time to race in the kitchen, get a knife and stab this motherfucker for putting his hands on her.

"You talking, Yuri? You want me to beat the shit outta you again?!"

"I wish you fuckin' would, and one of us will die up in here today!"

As Jeff raced toward Yuri, Drae flew through the door,

practically twisting her ankle as she fell in. "Yuri!" she said as if she had run up all twenty-five flights of their stairs. "I heard you screaming!"

"You fat-ass filthy fuckin' bitch!" Jeff rushed Yuri, knocking her to the floor.

Drae did what she could to break them up; and when she saw Jeff had taken a step back and seemed to be making his way so he could stomp Yuri, Drae pulled her out of the way, and jumped on top of her.

"Both y'all bitches is trash, so what the fuck I care about tossing you out with this bitch! This no-good tramp, who nobody liked except me is fuckin' Britt behind all our backs. This bitch is fuckin' Britt!" he said in a rage of disbelief. By the look on Drae's face, Jeff could tell she already knew. He couldn't believe everyone knew but him. It was official: They were all laughing at him. "You fuckin' bitches! I should fuckin' piss in both y'all's faces! Y'all cunts think I'm some type of joke?! Get the fuck out, before I throw y'all out that window!" Jeff picked up the coffee table and threw it across the room. "Get the fuck out!" Feeling they weren't moving fast enough, he grabbed Yuri by her waist and Drae grabbed on to her feet. She thought for sure he would be throwing her out the window.

Somehow Jeff had Yuri and Drae both lifted off the floor. And as if he were the bionic man playing football, he took them and threw them out the front door, their bodies making a thud as they hit the wall.

Jeff came out into the hallway, where building security, who'd received a complaint about someone fighting, blocked his path as he prepared to tackle the women.

Yuri had never seen Jeff like this; he had gone completely crazy.

Just as security thought they'd stopped Jeff dead in his tracks, he started coming in their direction again. Out of fear, Yuri and Drae took cover and the police who were coming out of the elevator now pulled out their guns. The security guards moved Drae and Yuri out of the way, causing them to fall to the floor, while the police were able to catch and handcuff Jeff before he attacked them again.

"Yo, my man" floated over Yuri's shoulder. Britt walked over to her. "Can you stand up?"

"Yes." She nodded her head as Britt lifted her from the floor. Looking at the bruises on her face, he stroked her cheek. "I can't believe this motherfucker put his hands on you."

"I swear to God I'ma see you, Britt!" Jeff screamed.

"You see me now, motherfucker," he said, pushing Yuri to the side. "Now what you wanna do?!"

"Okay, time to break this up," the police officer spat. One of the officers turned to Yuri. "Miss, I think you need to get some things and leave for a while."

"I don't want anything," Yuri nervously responded as she grabbed Britt by the hand. "I just wanna go."

"Yeah, we gon' go after you get yo' shit," Britt said, never taking his eyes off Jeff. "You ain't got to be afraid of no-fuckin'-body."

Security escorted Yuri and Drae into the apartment. Yuri pulled out her Marc Cross luggage and took all the clothing, shoes, jewelry and purses she could; and what she left, she would have to do without. She picked up the keys to her Touareg and walked back out the apartment door.

Yuri watched the police read Jeff his Miranda rights as they arrested him. She had never seen so much hurt in Jeff's face. She could tell he wanted to cry and scream at her: Why? Why all of this? Was what he did with the white bitch this bad? Did she hate his son this much? And, yeah, he'd beat her ass, but look at what she did. Before this he never put his hands on her, all of his punches flew out his mouth.

She never wanted to see Jeff in this predicament. She simply wanted to one day get the courage to walk out. No hard feelings. No unsettling good-bye, just some yesterdays lost behind them. But this? This had gone too far. He didn't deserve to be going to jail, he didn't deserve those handcuffs squeezing his wrist, he didn't deserve any of this. Nevertheless, here she stood with Britt making the shit worse.

"You have to come to the precinct by the morning," one of the officers said, "and officially press charges."

Yuri stared at the officer, already knowing that he wouldn't be seeing her again. She just wanted this day to end. It was apparent that the fairy-tale ending of her marriage wasn't going to happen, so she needed to simply say good-bye by turning her back and walking away.

Drae looked at Yuri and shook her head. She had fresh bruises on the side of her face from being slammed into the wall. Yuri knew that Drae wanted to spit out "I told you so," but for whatever reason she didn't.

Yuri looked at Britt and then she looked at Jeff, who had tears pouring down his face.

"Look," Britt said, "you know I'm not one for speeches. So if you got some kinda special way you wanna say good-bye to this motherfucker, hurry up and do it, so I can get the fuck outta here."

"I don't have nothing I wanna say." Yuri swallowed. "I'm good." She turned to Drae. "I'm sorry you had to go through this, but thank you for being there for me."

"Yuri," Drae spat, "save it. 'Cause I don't even wanna hear it."

Drae

Drae couldn't believe what she was seeing. She had to be dreaming. Hassan sat on the edge of the bed with a glass dick stuck between his lips and a butane lighter burning underneath it. He opened his mouth and clouds of smoke floated out.

"Have you . . . lost every bit of your fuckin' mind?" Drae snapped as she stood at the door, ready for work. She was dressed in a red-and-white mud-cloth wrap skirt, a sleeveless white tee, a denim midriff jacket, and canvas Coach espadrilles. This was the last week of school and she was helping some of the students get their working papers for summer jobs. "You strung the fuck out?!"

"Strung out, strung the fuck out on what, Drae?"

"On the glass dick in your mouth!" she snapped.

"I'm not strung out, maybe I just like dicks in my mouth."

"I'm not even gon' fuckin' address that."

Hassan took one last pull from his pipe and then looked at the black burn mark underneath. "Where the fuck you been, Drae?" Hassan spoke in a raspy voice, his eyes half closed. "You know how much money I done missed messing with yo' ass?"

He stood up, placed the pipe and lighter in a black velvet bag and tucked it in his dresser drawer. "I have had auditions lined up all week, and I know you been getting my fuckin' messages. But word is, you done filled my position and now you playin' Captain Save a Ho. Gettin' stand-up niggahs locked up and shit. Is that what you do in yo' spare time, Drae? Play GI Jane, bust up in niggahs' houses and shit, playing Batman and fuckin' Robin? I wish y'all two bitches would try that shit up in here, and I would take and whale on yo' asses!"

"I didn't know fiends had that much energy! I can't believe that you a fuckin' fiend." She shook her head in disgust. "Where the fuck do I get off at? When does this shit end?" Drae looked at him as if he had the answers. "You just a twisted-ass niggah! I have got to get away from you."

"And how long you think you gon' live, when you leave? You think I'ma let you go, fuck another niggah and fuck my money. Then maybe I need to ask you what the fuck you smokin'? If you want some extra dick, then tell Naz he welcome over here. Let me see him fuck you again. Otherwise, if I see you with that niggah again, I'ma kill you."

"Naz? What are you talking about, who is that?"

"Girl, I will bust you in yo' fuckin' mouth if you try to tell an unnecessary lie—just know I've seen the shit. A'ight? Anyway," he snorted, while scratching the side of his neck, "it's some niggahs downstairs with hard dicks you need to see."

"What?"

He could tell she was caught off guard. "What the fuck you surprised for? You got work to make up."

"What?"

"Audition: Take Two, bitch."

"What?"

"Say 'what' again and I swear I'll bust you in yo' fuckin' lips. Now say I won't. Say it. . . ." When she didn't respond he said, "I didn't think so."

"Whatever, Hassan." She grabbed her purse and oversized bag for work. "I told you this ho's retired; find another bitch to pimp."

"I married the bitch I was gon' pimp. As I was saying, before you so rudely interrupted me, I lined up a threesome audition. You need to drink a lotta water, 'cause I want you to pee on one them niggahs. Now, Captain Save a Ho, get out there and handle your business."

"Aye, aye! Captain Save a Ho will be right there!" She saluted him as she walked out her bedroom door. "You keep right on waiting."

He ran up behind her and hooked her neck in the crook of his arm. "What the fuck did I say you was gon' do bitch?!"

"Get . . . offa . . . me!" she gagged.

"Not until you suck them dicks and get fucked in the ass! You not gon' fuck up my money. You wanna spend the shit, but you don't wanna get down for it? Oh, you gon' do what the hell I say."

"Hassan!" a high-pitched feminine voice yelled. They could hear her feet pounding up the stairs. "What is taking so long?" She stood at the door and her eyes locked with Drae's. It was the same woman from Fantasy Island.

"Is this a dream?" Drae asked as Hassan let her go. "You brought this bitch to my house? Are you serious?"

"Did I give you permission to come up these stairs?" Hassan barked at the girl. "What the fuck is on your mind? Didn't I tell you I had some business to take care of?"

"You that goddamn disrespectful"—Drae was in absolute disbelief—"you bringing bitches home? You really strung the fuck out!"

"You can slow up with the bitches, homegirl." The girl looked at Drae as if to say "now what." "My name is Crystal and I work for him, and I damn sure wasn't here for you. Matter fact, I didn't even know you were here, you ain't been here."

"You been in my house before? On an ordinary day I would've kicked yo' fuckin' ass," Drae snorted at the girl. "But since today is a certified nightmare I'ma let you live and suck the Satan's dick." She pushed Hassan away. " 'Cause I'm done with this bullshit. It's over, Hassan. I swear to God I'm done." And she walked out the door. When she got down the stairs and into the living room, she saw the two men Hassan had waiting for her staring at each other and playing with their dicks.

* * *

A half hour later Drae was at work. She signed in and walked into her office. Doing her best to push her morning out of her mind, she closed her office door, opened her file cabinet drawer and popped four Motrin in her mouth. She had a migraine that felt like a hammer and chisel had invaded her skull. She was determined not to go back to Hassan, that today was it for their marriage. She would go home, get her belongings and leave.

She sat down at her desk and cut her computer on.

"Mrs. Shaw," the secretary called as she knocked on the door.

"Come in, Dotty."

"Mr. Shaw is here." Dotty had an extra-wide grin on her face.

Hassan stepped through the door with a long white box with a red bow around it. "Happy anniversary," he said grandly.

Dotty blushed and closed the door behind her.

Hassan turned the lock on the knob and then turned back to Drae. "Getcha shit!" He opened the box, which was filled with two garbage bags. "This is it for this motherfuckin' job! I'm sick of this! You staying home from now on! You got other shit to do!" With one sweep he took everything off her desk and knocked it into a garbage bag, her pictures frames and ceramic flowerpots breaking as they hit the bottom of the bag against the tile floor.

"What are you doing?!" She grabbed his forearm. She tried to control herself—after all, she was at work and didn't want to lose her job—but she was two seconds from smacking the shit out of him.

"Get the fuck offa me." He snatched his arm away. "And get some fire under ya ass! I said let's go." He walked around her office, taking the artwork off the walls and shoving it into the bag. The sound of the glass breaking hurt her ears.

"Hassan, please stop," she begged softly. "You're embarrassing the shit outta me."

"You gon' be even more embarrassed when I drag yo' ass outta here!"

When she saw him headed for the file cabinet that contained the students' records she ran in front of him, stretched her arms out and blocked his path. "What the fuck is in here, Drae, that you don't want me to see?!"

"It's not mine," she cried. "It's the students'. Their school records."

"You're lying, Drae!" He pushed her out of the way and started tossing the records all over the room.

There was a knock on the door. "Mrs. Shaw, are you okay?" The principal twisted the locked knob. "Mrs. Shaw, open this door, please."

"Principal Cox, it's okay. I knocked some things down by accident."

"Principal Cox?" Hassan frowned. "Nastiness just follows you everywhere you go, don't it? Why don't you tell Principal Dicks the truth."

"Are you sure you're okay?" the principal asked.

"Yes, ma'am." Drae mustered a laugh. "I'm fine. Hassan," she said diplomatically, sounding as calm as possible, "please, don't do this here . . . please."

"Sounding like a white girl ain't gon' cut it, Drae. You fuckin' with my money and you think I'm gon' let you stay here? I said get yo' shit, bitch! And let's go!"

Drae didn't move.

"Oh, a'ight." Hassan grabbed Drae by her arm and opened her office door. "I said you leaving!"

"Hassan, please," she begged as he yanked her backward

out of the room. There was a group of students passing by her as she was coming out of the office.

As one of the male students stopped to talk to her, Hassan loosened his grip. "You a'ight, Mrs. Shaw?"

"Yes, Derrick." Drae's heart was pounding as she looked toward the back door. "I'm fine!" She snatched away from Hassan and took off running. Immediately, Hassan fled behind her and some of the students in the group tackled him from the back, while others ran to the office, watched Drae run or screamed.

"Hurry, Mrs. Shaw, leave!" some of the kids yelled.

As Drae ran toward the back door she was halted by security. "What's wrong?"

Drae wanted nothing more than to disappear. She heard the crowd growing behind her. She turned around and the entire first floor of the school was in an uproar. Security was everywhere, the children involved in the fight were bloody and their clothes were tattered from tackling Hassan. Within seconds Drae heard police sirens blaring. For a moment she thought she was dreaming, so she pinched herself and begged God to wake her up.

"Mrs. Shaw"—the principal rushed toward her—"what has happened here?!"

"I'm so sorry," she cried as the principal looked at her, filled with disgust.

"This is completely unacceptable! You have placed our children in danger, and just how do you think we will be able to explain to their parents that they were injured because they were protecting you?!"

The police were standing at the other end of the hall, talking to Hassan. "Officer," he spoke calmly, "I was surprising my wife for our anniversary and it scared her, that's all. I was simply defending myself when the children attacked me; I think this is just one big misunderstanding. I didn't mean for anyone to get hurt."

"You still have to come with us," one of the officers said. "The school may want to press charges."

"I'll go, Officer, let's just not make this any more of a scene than it has to be."

Drae couldn't believe it. Was this the same man who was freebasin' this morning, trying to make her fuck strangers again and then practically dragging her out of her office making her leave with him, now acting diplomatic, like he had sense, when he was really crazy as shit? All she could do was cry as she looked at Hassan, wondering why. Why would he do this? Why couldn't he just leave her alone?

"Mrs. Shaw," the principal said, "I need to see you in my office."

As she walked past Hassan she wanted to slap the smug look off his face. He'd gotten exactly what he wanted, now she had no choice but to leave.

"You don't have to fire me," she said, when she stepped into the principal's office. "I'll resign."

"We weren't going to fire you . . . yet," the principal stressed. "You'll be suspended with pay until we have an administrative hearing to determine your career's future."

"I understand," Drae conceded. She stood up to leave.

"And let me give you some advice," she said as Drae approached the door. "I know a battered sister when I see one, 'cause I was one myself. Get out while you can."

Drae walked out of the building feeling like a zombie. She hated the day she met Hassan, hated all the time she got on her knees at night and prayed to God to let him be the one. Hated that she set her sights on his being her husband before knowing what it would take to be his wife. She hated always looking for security in no-good men. She hated this shit, all of it, and if she wasn't so weak and could stand the pain of dying she would slit her wrists, step to death and dare the niggah to show up.

Not knowing where else to go, Drae parked in front of Britt's loft building to see Yuri.

"Wassup, Britt?" she said as she stood at Britt's loft door. "Is Yuri here?"

"She stepped out for a minute, but she'll be right back."

"You mind if I wait?"

"Naw," he hesitated, "not at all."

Drae came in and looked around; she started to sit on the sofa, but changed her mind. Instead she stood by one of the large windows and looked onto the street.

"Yo," Britt said, "I'm getting ready to go, but let me say something to you real quick."

"I'm listening."

"Understand this: You may not like me, but stay out my business."

"What are you talking about?"

"You know what I'm talking about. You running back and telling Yuri shit about me and Troi, filling her head with a buncha shit that I don't appreciate. I don't know what Troi been telling you, but ain't nothing going on. Period. So stay in your fuckin' lane."

Drae stood there amazed, she hadn't thought about Troi since they last saw her at Queen of Sheba. She made a mental note to cuss Yuri out for involving her in some pillow-talk lies she was obviously telling. "After the fucking morning I've had, you just the excuse I need to go off! Me and you both know we been here before, Britt. Yuri may not know, but I know that you left her the last time to get back with Troi. So I know you ain't shit! You didn't impress me by showing up and saving her from Jeff like you Zorro and shit. Yuri is my blood, my cousin, and I'll be damned if I'ma let you or anybody else fuck her over. Now, if you are fuckin' the two of them, then I advise you to leave Yuri the fuck alone and let her get on with her life. Otherwise man-up, niggah, and handle your fuckin' business 'cause the next time she gets pregnant there may not be a miscarriage. And if I ever hear that you not owning up to your responsibility, then I'ma kick yo' fuckin' ass my goddamn self. Now get the fuck out my face!"

"What the hell is going on here?!" Yuri was in complete shock when she walked in the door. She was carrying two bags of groceries from the local bodega. Britt took them out of her hands and kissed her on the forehead. "It's nothing, baby, your cousin just being her wonderful self. Look, I'ma head to the studio. I need to meet with my manager, the record company wants to talk about giving me my own label imprint." He took the groceries, set them on the kitchen island and left.

"What the hell was that about?" Yuri asked Drae as she started putting the groceries away.

"Nothing. And why the fuck you lying on me? If you tryna catch that sorry motherfucker in something, leave my name out of it!"

"What are you talking about?"

Drae started hollering and screaming, "You know what I'm talking about!"

Yuri could hear the tears in Drae's voice. "What's wrong with you?"

Drae held her head down and began to sob uncontrollably.

"Oh my God, Drae, sweetie, what? What's wrong?" She ran around the counter to Drae. Yuri's heart was racing. "I'm sorry I lied. I just wanted to see if he would admit that it was Troi who keeps calling here and hanging up. Please tell me what's wrong." Drae shook her head no.

"Please tell me. Is it me?"

Drae continued to sob and shake her head no.

"Sweetie, please tell me."

Drae held her head up and wiped her eyes. "You know how, when we were younger, you always said you felt like you settled for men because you felt like no one would ever really like you . . . the way you were?"

"Yeah."

"Well, I always felt that I needed to find a man to save me. Like I needed to be rescued from this life."

"What life? Rescued from what?"

"I don't know . . . something . . . It's just that ever since my mother died, I've been looking for security, for someone to take me to happily-ever-after land. And when I found Hassan I thought he came to take me."

"And?"

"He led me to hell."

"Oh . . . kay. I mean you said he was rich and this big-time director. What is it, *National Geographic*? Isn't he what you always dreamed of? Does this have to do with you not being satisfied with where you are in life?"

"You don't fuckin' get it Yuri!" she screamed. "He's a

porn director. He does pornos, and he used me to do the auditions."

Seeing the look of shock on Yuri's face, Drae continued.

"Yes, I've been living a lie. There's no fuckin' *National Geographic* shit! He makes pornos. People fuckin' all over my house."

"And what do you mean you've been doing the auditions?"

"I was fucking the people auditioning! Dammit!"

Yuri sat on the bar stool next to Drae in complete and utter shock. "What?"

"He was my husband."

"You did what?"

"I loved him."

"What did you just say?"

"I thought I was ridin' for him."

"Ridin' where?"

"I don't know what to do, Yuri," she began to sob uncontrollably again. "My job was the only sane thing I had going on in my life and he took that from me. Now I have nothing, I think I'ma go crazy."

"Your job? Did you really have a job or was that a lie?"

"Yes, I had a job, but Hassan came to my job and made a scene. I've been suspended, but I know they're going to fire me."

"Oh my God," Yuri began to cry while hugging her. "My God."

They sat at the kitchen island holding each other. Yuri couldn't believe that Drae had been in so much pain and never said anything. "You have to know that you are not alone. I know we don't have a big family, but we have each other. You understand me? I'm here for you and I don't give a damn if we have to sleep in my car together; don't ever feel like you have no place to go. You understand me?"

"Yes . . . I do."

"I love you, girl."

"I love you too, Yuri."

They kissed each other on the cheeks. Yuri cooked Drae something to eat and after a few hours passed, Drae sat at the kitchen island looking out the window. Everything in Manhattan moved so fast, she wondered if she needed to go to a town where everything was slower; slow enough where she could process all her thoughts of how and why she stayed so long, why she did what she did. And how she'd fooled herself into thinking that Hassan was it.

Maybe she would be daring and go to Phoenix, but then again the heat might be too much. Maybe she could go to Atlanta, but she never liked the South. Maybe L.A. or San Fran, maybe St. Louis or Dallas or Murfreesboro, North Carolina. Just someplace, anyplace where nobody knew her and she could crawl under a rock in peace. For a moment Drae wondered: If she seduced death, would he promise to be sweet?

"Listen, girl, let me get going. I didn't mean to stress you out."

"You sure you're all right?" Yuri asked, surprised Drae wanted to go. "You don't have to go."

"No, I'm fine. I just have a friend I need to see."

. . .

Drae knew she was taking a helluva chance showing up at Naz's house without calling. But at this moment she needed to see his face, to find comfort in his arms. And she knew she was bouncing from one man's arms to the next, but she wasn't so sure she could face herself yet. After all, what explanation would she have for being in such a fucked-up situation?

Drae stood on Naz's row-house porch and rang the bell. She could hear music playing and she could smell burning charcoal and barbeque. When she peeked over the side of the railing, she saw Naz's daughter doing a dance and singing Bow Wow's "Shortie Like Mine," "Addicted to how we kick it . . ."

"A'ight, Sydney, calm it down."

"I'm being a good girl, Daddy?"

"Yes, you just a lil' excited right now."

"That's a good thing, Daddy?"

"Yes, Sydney."

"Hey, lady." She waved.

Naz peeped to see who Sydney was talking to. He was dressed in a pair of baggy jeans and a wife-beater. He held a spatula in his hand. "Somebody told me," Drae said as she leaned over the rail, "that this fine man lived here with his beautiful daughter. And I was so hoping that I would get to see them and show 'em that I have some barbeque skills myself."

"Is that so?" Naz smiled.

"Yeah." Drae hunched her shoulders. "That pretty much sums it up."

"Well"—his entire face lit up—"why don't you come show me whatcha got? The front door is open."

Drae couldn't help but admire his place as she walked through. There was nothing spectacular going on: no recessed lights, vaulted ceilings or heated floors. It was simply a home with a small entranceway, stairs leading to the second floor, a blue micro-suede living-room set, a small dining room, an L-shaped kitchen and a door leading to the back-yard. But it truly felt like a home.

Drae stepped into the backyard and Naz smiled at her. "What's good, ma'?" He kissed her on the cheek.

"Nothing."

"This is my daughter, Sydney. Sydney, this is Ms. Drae." They smiled and said hello to each other.

"So what brings you this way?"

"Nothing, just wanted to see you, that's all."

"I'm glad you did. Now, don't think you sittin' down. You said you got some barbeque skills and I wanna see." He tossed Drae an apron. "You got to show me how you get down."

"We do have a child here."

He gave her a sinister smile. "Handle your business."

"All right." She laughed. "Where's your sauce?"

"Right here." He held up a Kraft bottle.

"Oh Lord, I'ma have to school you. My daddy always said if you don't make it from scratch, then use Jack Daniel's. Anyway, give it here and let me hook it up."

"What you need? 'Cause I got it."

"Honestly," she sighed. "I just need a friend right now."

Not expecting that response, Naz said with a serious face, "You got that."

She slipped her shoes and midriff jacket off. "Now, I also need you to get me some honey, vinegar, sugar and a little milk."

"Milk?"

"I'm not eating that," Sydney said. "I'll just have me some chicken nuggets."

"Nah, Sydney," Naz laughed. "Let's watch Ms. Drae do her thing."

Drae took the barbeque sauce and doctored it up. Afterward she poured it on the ribs, steaks, and burgers that he had on the grill. When they were done, she served them.

"A'ight," Naz said, "I gotta admit this was da bomb."

"Yeah, Ms. Drae, this was good."

"Thank you." She flicked Sydney on the nose. "I saw you dancing when I came up. You like to dance?"

"Yeah, I take ballet and tap classes. Did you know my daddy can dance?"

"Really?" Drae laughed. "He must be pretty good."

"Yeah, he tap dances. He's going to be in a Broadway show one day, right, Daddy?"

"No."

"Daddy," she whined.

"You tap?" Drae asked.

"A lil' sumthin' sumthin'," Naz replied.

"So is that Naz's secret? He wants to tap dance on Broadway?"

"You wanna know my secret?" he asked.

"Yes," Drae responded.

"You sure you're ready for it?"

"Would you just tell me!"

"A'ight. I wanna be a regular niggah. Just regular. Go to work, come home, kiss my wife, play with my kids—"

"Kids?"

"Yeah, I would like another kid. I like being called Daddy. And I wanna wife, one day. To cook for me, take her shoes off and get pregnant." He laughed.

"Excuse me," Drae snickered. "Mr. Daddy of a Daughter. I would think you'd want your wife doing more than that."

"I'm just kidding. All she gotta do is be down for me."

"Can you handle it if she is?"

"I welcome the challenge."

"Ms. Drae," Sydney interrupted, "can you dance?"

"I can do a lil' sumthin' sumthin'." She winked at Naz.

"Like what?" Naz laughed.

"Can you Wu-Tang?" Sydney asked. "Or do the Old Man, or Chicken Noodle Soup?"

"She can't handle those, Sydney. Let's pick another one for her."

"Excuse you," Drae laughed. "Everybody can't compete with you and your little hip-hop group here."

They laughed. "Okay, Ms. Drae," Sydney said. "You wanna do the electric slide?"

"What about the cha-cha, Sydney?" Naz added.

"Yeah, that's it, Daddy, let's show Ms. Drae the cha-cha."

Sydney put on a cha-cha slide CD and turned it up. The three of them got up and stood in the middle of the backyard. "Follow us," Naz smiled. "The song tells you what to do." They started dancing and it wasn't long before Drae picked up on the dance and started doing it without any assistance.

"Now Charlie Brown!" the song sang. "Criss cross, everybody clap your hands . . ." And on it went until the sun started to go down.

"If nothing else," Drae said as they started to clean up, "I'm glad I came here today." She nodded her head toward Sydney, who'd sat in the patio chair and fallen asleep.

"Let me take her inside." Naz carried Sydney to her bed and he came back out with a bottle of wine in his hand. "You need this?"

"Yes." Drae grinned. "Oh yes."

They sat down at his patio set and Naz poured them two glasses of wine. "You ready to talk?"

"No. I just need you to be here for me, please. Just be here."

"I care about you. . . ." He pressed his forehead against hers. "I really do."

"Thank you." Tears slipped from Drae's eyes. "Thank you."

"Can you stay for a minute?" He kissed her on the lips.

"I can stay for a couple of minutes." She responded to his kisses.

Yuri

Today was the first day that Yuri didn't wake up and feel the emotional sting of losing her baby. It was also the first time since she'd left Jeff that she appreciated his not being anywhere around. There was no tension, no grunting, no wishing, no waiting or wanting to disappear. There was nothing to fuck up the atmosphere. She didn't look around and see Jeff's shoes all lined up perfectly, separated by color and style, and there were no Italian suits hanging meticulously in the closet separate from his jeans. For once she lived in a place where she was comfortable enough to be herself. There were no demands, no expectations, no comments about her weight; and this go-round, when she was told she had a fat ass, it was a compliment.

She looked over at Britt and silently thanked him for being everything she'd ever dreamed. She knew sex wasn't supposed to occur for six weeks after the miscarriage, but it'd already been four and there was no way she could continue to resist. Britt lay next to her with the flat white sheet draped across his hard dick. His bare chest was like a work of art, an undiscovered masterpiece that only she'd seen and could appreciate. And his thighs looked to be drizzled in the best chocolate the world had to offer. . . .

"I just want some," she said to herself while sucking on the tip of her index finger. She slid the sheet back and kissed his beautiful dick. It was the best kiss she'd ever given. Slowly Britt's eyes peeled open as he ran his hands through her hair. "Such a luscious dick, I couldn't resist."

He opened his eyes and gave a sly grin. "You like that dick?"

"I *love* that dick."

"You gon' get the pussy wet for him?"

"Uhmmm, is that what he wants?"

"Yes."

She lay on her back and looked into Britt's face. She took her wet index finger and circled it around her clit. Almost instantly her flesh came alive and began dripping with heat. She could feel shock waves float through her mind as she moved her fingers in a steady grind. Slowly she stroked her clit up and down, moving the tip of her finger like a tongue. Her clit started to swell.

"What does it feel like?"

"Hot . . . wet . . . and oh sooooo silky . . ." She quickened the pace of her fingers, dipping two into her pussy with one hand and playing with her clit with the other.

"You gon' nut on my dick?"

"All over it."

"You gon' put some on my tongue?"

"You want some?"

"Yes."

"Well, you gon' have to eat it for yourself."

"I want you to feed me."

Yuri took her creamy fingers and slid them into Britt's mouth. "What it taste like?"

"Candy, baby." He sucked her fingers. "It taste just like candy."

Sensing Yuri was due to cum any minute, Britt turned her around and placed her backward on his dick. He watched her ass roll back and forth, working it in and out—out and in—of her pussy. It was the prettiest thing he'd ever seen. This was a classic . . . watching her pussy leave more and more cream on his dick as it slid up and down. He took his hands, placed them on her ass and assisted her pussy with climbing up and down his long vanilla-covered pipe.

"Welcome home, baby." He closed his eyes and his nut exploded into her. "Welcome home."

Drae

This fantasy had been perfect and uninter-
rupted. Drae had stayed at Naz's, played mother to his
daughter every morning and made love to him every
night. She dressed in jeans, tees, Adidas sweat suits and
sneakers. She rocked her Louie bags while doing Sydney's soccer carpool, and she cooked: fried, baked, and
barbeque chicken, hamburgers, french fries and every
night a vegetable. She and Sydney baked cakes, cookies,
and surprised Naz, when he'd gotten sick one night,
with Get Well balloons the next morning. It was perfect
until this moment, when she sat on the edge of the bed,
watched the flowing traffic out the window and realized she'd abandoned her life.

It had been close to three weeks since Drae had seen

Yuri and Nae-Nae. She called them only once to let them know she was okay. She officially resigned from her job and did all that she could to erase Hassan from her thoughts.

Drae slid next to Naz on the bed and draped his arm around her shoulder. She didn't exactly tell Naz why she left Hassan; she just told him she wasn't going back and figured, for now, that should be enough.

Drae caressed the side of Naz's face and began kissing his neck. His scent was so seductive, yet she knew she had to leave. Otherwise, when she submerged into her life again, she wouldn't be the only one not knowing who she was.

She stroked his left ear and began sucking on his earlobe. "I need to leave," she whispered. Her warm breath tingling the side of his face.

Naz turned over to face her. "Where you going?"

"I'm not going back to Hassan." She looked into his eyes. "I don't want that life anymore."

"So then, what do you want?" He stroked her hair.

"I want simple shit." She smiled. "Like Chinese food, stretch marks and babies."

Naz threw his head back and laughed. "Sunshine wanna be called Mommy."

"Yes, I do. One day. And stop calling me Sunshine."

"I'm sorry." He kissed her.

"Why do you keep calling me that?"

"To remind myself that none of this is real." He caressed her breast and ran his index finger down the center of her body.

"I'm not real?"

"Uhmm, maybe you're real. At least, this is the realness you want, but you're not ready. You need some time to spend with yourself. Get to know what you want and like again. After that, anything is possible."

"So what does that mean?" She tried to sound playful and laughed. "You don't wanna marry me?"

He rolled on top of her. "It means that when you collect you and really get it together, where you've dealt with what's really wrong and what's going on, then you come back and kick it to me."

Now her laughter was genuine. "Kick it to you?"

"Yeah, I want you to be like 'Somebody told me that this fine niggah' "—he kissed her firm breast—" 'named Nasty Naz was here.' "

"And what you gon' say?" she asked as she felt him play with her clit.

She opened her legs and while he slid down her belly he said, "I'ma say"—he parted her pussy lips—" 'Sunshine, Nasty Naz has left the building. But Nasir is here.' "

She stroked the back of his head as he began licking her pussy like it was pudding. Chills ran up her back as she said, "And I'ma say, 'My name is Drae.' "

"What I'ma do without you?" He began to softly eat her pussy.

"I don't know," she said as her hips began to move with the motion of his face.

As Naz's mouth made love to Drae's soaked and wet middle, his hands felt like silk as he twirled her nipples between his fingers. Drae had melted over and over again as his tongue made her cum. She closed her eyes and imagined him being her man. She imagined this being real and not being a taboo moment. The last time she imagined this or even felt like this she was caught up in the newness of love. And love is not what this was. Drae was aware of that. This was a beautiful distraction from the real shit she didn't want to deal with and music she didn't want to dance to.

After tasting her pussy to both of their satisfaction Naz climbed on top of Drae and slid his dick in. For some reason, he didn't want to freak her or fuck her, he wanted to make love to her. And he knew better than to have thoughts like this. He knew better than to be holding her, pressing his forehead against hers and wondering if this was the moment when he was supposed to surprise her with the words, 'I love you.' He knew she needed to leave, and he needed her to leave, so that he could get back in check; his heart was slippin' and now wasn't the time to have love or any niggah that looked and felt like him, stepping up and rocking his world.

Slowly he stroked Drae, her soft and wet walls sending chills up his spine. His firm ass tightened with every stroke as he kissed her all over her face. "Don't let another niggah snag you. Gimme a chance first."

Drae opened her eyes and looked into his. "I'm not looking for nobody else. I'm just looking for me." She cupped his ass as he pounded his hard dick in and out of her.

"Don't forget me." He drove his dick in as deep as it would go.

She arched her back, "I won't ever forget you." She stopped talking long enough to moan, "But I'm not going away right now. I just know I can't keep staying in your house like this. I have some things I need to deal with."

"I'ma miss waking up next to you." His nut freed itself into her warm flesh.

"Me too," she panted as she came. "Oh God, me too."

Yuri

For most of the ride they were quiet. Yuri rolled down the window, leaned back and closed her eyes. The wind blew into her face and through her hair. She knew things had started to change since she first moved in. And maybe she noticed it when she cussed out the woman on the phone who turned out to be his business associate, or maybe it was when he asked if she had been going through his things and she lied and told him no. Or it could've been when she started thinking he was fucking all the girls in his videos. Or maybe he was simply tired of her and that's why he stopped coming home some nights. Hell, there had to be a reason, especially since, when she first moved in, it was all a dream come true. He was Cock Diesel and she was the new millennium version of June Cleaver. Although she worked, she always made sure the place was clean and there was food to eat. They talked until the wee hours of the morning, played Monopoly and Uno every other night, watched TV, sang, wrote songs together and made love everywhere . . . for however long they wanted, without worrying about the time or her needing to make up a lie because she'd stayed too long. It was exactly what she needed, and even when Jeff served her with legal-separation papers three weeks after she'd left, she didn't think twice about the choice she'd made. Her only regret was not leaving Jeff sooner.

"You got a problem with me going to the studio tonight?" Britt looked at her out the corner of his eye as he drove her to Nae-Nae's for his Vote for Sanjaya *American Idol* party.

"I got a problem with you going every night."

"I'm making a CD, Yuri."

"Cool. Hope you're making hits."

"You trying to be funny?"

"Do I look like I wanna laugh?" She faced him.

"You love me, don't you?"

"Not this time, Britt. I'm really not in the mood for that shit."

"A'ight, Yuri."

"Yeah, a'ight." Yuri was doing her all to keep her emotions in check, but she wanted to scream at him about why Troi was calling the loft, and why he was going in the other room every time his phone rang. And that she was tired of his being at the studio all night, coming home, gettin' some pussy and then falling asleep. No "Hey how are you," "I missed you," "How was your day," nothing. Just a nightly fuckin' nut that he acted like he'd been dying all day to lay.

As they pulled in front of Nae-Nae's, Yuri gave him a quick peck on the lips. "Pick me up by twelve o'clock."

"Yes, baby." He leaned over and opened her door.

She closed the door and watched him take off.

As Yuri crossed the street she noticed Drae's car was parked. Near Nae-Nae's stoop she saw a caramel-colored woman sporting larger-than-life white hoop earrings, who looked to be at least seven months pregnant, with a blond clip weave, belly shirt and a fitted denim skirt tucked underneath her stomach. Alongside her was a small boy, who looked no older than eleven. Yuri tried not to laugh, but for the life of her she couldn't understand why this kid was dressed like a Guardian Angel, with a red tam cocked to the side and a black karate suit on. Once she got a little closer she could swear that they looked familiar, yet she couldn't place them.

"Good evening," Yuri said as she stepped on the porch.

"I don't know who the fuck told you it was a good evening," the pregnant woman snapped. "Somebody better tell her."

"If she don't know," the kid said as he sucked his teeth and leaned to the side, "she better get the video."

"For real, though." The pregnant woman chuckled snidely as they exchanged high-fives. "She over here eye-fuckin' me and shit. Hmph niggahs is got Freeda Foreman fucked up."

"Straight hatin'," the kid added.

"What are you talking about, eye-fuckin' you?" Yuri said in disbelief. "I was just looking at how cute your kid was."

"Kid?" He turned around, and that's when Yuri realized exactly who it was. "I'm not no motherfuckin' kid, bitch. Oh, you got Squeak fucked all the way up."

Squeak and fuckin' Freeda from IHOP, Yuri thought. *What the hell are they doing here?!*

"Oh no she didn't, Squeak!" Freeda screamed.

"Yes she did."

"Oh hell no . . . she didn't. She ain't called you no kid, Squeak. Don't give it to her, Squeak. Don't even sweat that shit. She don't know 'bout you. Plus the twins is right here." She pointed to her belly.

"You right." His chest heaved up and down. "You right, and you know Squeak luv da kids."

"Excuse you?" Yuri said, finally coming out of the shock that they were actually here and talking about her. "Why are you even here? Didn't they lock the space monkeys up?"

"Space monkeys?"

"I ain't stutter," Yuri said, and turned to the side as if she were speaking to an invisible person. "Did I stutter? No, you ain't stutter. Didn't think so. Now if you got something you wanna say to me, then say the shit." She turned back to face them.

"Girl, please." Squeak looked Yuri up and down. "You don't want none of this."

"Whatever." Yuri pressed relentlessly on Nae-Nae's bell. "Nae-Nae better come on." Yuri said to herself, but loud enough for them to hear.

"Nae-Nae?" Freeda and Squeak said simultaneously.

Freeda turned to Yuri. "Nae-Nae fucking with you too, and here I thought you and that other girl was les'bens."

"Les'bens?"

"Now she don't know what a les'ben is, Squeak. It's a dyke!"

"Booyah!" Squeak jumped at Yuri.

"But I tell you what, Squeak, I know for sure I'ma floor his ass. That fairy niggah will never be the same. You know he playin' you, right?" She turned to Yuri.

"Playin' who?"

"Oh," Freeda laughed, "this ho must think she special. She really don't know do she, Squeak?"

"You smell that?" He sniffed.

"Smell what?"

"A dumb ho in the air."

"Okay, you know what, I'm not gon' stand here and y'all comin' at me crazy." Instead of pressing on Nae-Nae's bell, Yuri pounded on the door. "Where is this niggah at?! Been done fucked around and have me put you over my knee lil' man-child, and whip . . . yo' . . . motherfuckin' ass!"

"Man-child?"

"Hold your horses!" Nae-Nae screamed as he approached the door. "That is, unless you came ridin' in on one." Nae-Nae opened the door, wearing a pair of super-tight flame shorts and a Vote for Sanjaya tee shirt with the front twisted into a knot, showcasing the sunburst tattoo around his navel.

"Where the fuck have you been?!" Yuri screamed, barging past him. "I been banging on this motherfuckin' door out here with these two goddamn special-ed clowns and shit!"

"Yuri, calm down," Drae said as she and Raphael rose from the couch to see what was going on.

"I'ma see you, bitch." Squeak kicked his feet at Yuri and lost his balance, slipping onto his ass. "Special-ed my ass! We got feelings too!" he said as if he wanted to cry.

"Get up, Squeak." Freeda extended her hand. "You know you slue-footed."

"I swear to God!" Squeak went off. "I'ma see yo' gigantic

rotten ass again! You big bitch. I should get up from here and work yo' ass over!" He rose from the floor.

"Calm down, this ain't about you, Squeak. You can handle that tee-pee-lookin' bitch later. Lookin' like her name Eagle Ass! Now, Nae-Nae!" Freeda screamed. "Where you been, Nae-Nae?!"

"Why is yo' fishy ass worried about where Nae-Nae been?" Raphael, who was wearing tiger shorts, patent-leather combat boots, and the knot in his Vote for Sanjaya tee shirt twisted midway up his back, smacked his lips. "Where did she come from, Nae-Nae?"

"That's what the fuck I wanna know," Yuri snapped.

"What is going on here?" Drae asked. "What are they"—she waved her index finger—"doing outside of IHOP?"

"I'm his woman." Freeda pointed to Nae-Nae. "He came back and kicked it to me that day and we been on ever since. Tell 'em, Squeak."

"Not right now, Freeda," Squeak said. " 'Cause I really didn't appreciate that special-ed shit."

For a split second the entire room became silent and then everyone except Freeda and Squeak burst into laughter.

"His woman!" Drae laughed. "Birdman got a better chance of havin' a woman."

"Told you they were special ed. Dumb motherfuckers!" Yuri screamed. "I know this ho lyin' on Nae-Nae. You know damn well ain't no straight niggah rockin' all that patent leather."

"Tell them I'm your woman, Nae-Nae," Freeda said, sounding as if she wanted to cry.

"I ain't telling 'em shit. I'm Bishop Don Nae-Nae and these is my bitches!" He pointed to Yuri and Drae.

"I told you we was gon' have to kick his ass!" Squeak said to Freeda.

"I got this, Nae-Nae," Yuri spat. "I been wantin' to get at this sawed-off Chia Pet–lookin' motherfucker since I stepped in here."

"Chi-chi-chi-chia." Drae laughed.

"Both y'all stupid," Yuri carried on. "This niggah ain't never seen no goddamn pussy, let alone nut up in one. You lyin'-ass skeezin', Rainbow Shop–wearin' bitch!"

"Low IQ-havin' ho!" Drae added.

"Who you talkin' to?" Freeda turned on Drae. "Go suck a dick, you porn-star freak! What is yo' name, Moon . . . Star . . . Oh I forgot, it's Sunshine!"

"What—"

Before Drae could go on, Freeda snapped, "See, I shut yo' ass up! Now, who else want some?"

"Let me break it down for you, hood-ho. Don't you ever step up in this motherfucker"—Raphael threw his hips to one side—"thinkin' you 'bout to bring it, 'cause I will take off this motherfuckin' midriff and show all y'all niggahs the hair on my chest. Now, how you need to leave, on your own or my foot got to do it?!"

"You gon' let them talk to me like this, Nathan? You ain't talk to me like this when you was strokin' me and telling me I look like a queen."

"Now I know you lyin'," Raphael said, " 'cause this niggah don't stroke, he on the bottom, bitch."

"T.M.I. Raphael, please," Yuri said before she resumed cussin' Freeda and Squeak out. "You look like a queen, yeah, right," Yuri screamed. "What you look like is Shrek the drag queen. I don't know what's on your lil'-ass mind, but this niggah don't have no motherfuckin' money, so why would you be tryna put them kids on him?"

"These is Nae-Nae's kids!" Freeda screamed. "Tell 'em, Nae-Nae."

"I swear on the Rainbow God," Nae-Nae said. "Billie Jean is not my lover."

"Now look, Freeda," Squeak added, "he don't even know yo' name."

"But he the twins' daddy, Squeak!" Freeda screamed. "Nae-Nae know these kids is his!"

Everybody fell out laughing again. "If you don't get yo' Work-First ass outta here—" Yuri snapped.

"You telling her my business, Nae-Nae?! And I believed you when you said I looked like a queen."

"Freeda," Squeak called.

"A queen, Nae-Nae!"

"Freeda!"

"You know he said it, Squeak. You know he did."

"Come on, Freeda," Squeak said. "Get it together."

"But, Squeak."

"Don't cry, Freeda. You know I can't get high enough to wipe your tears. Told you we shoulda waited for *The Maury Povich Show*. I betchu he'll make this fairy-flamin'-pussy-actin'-small-dick-ass-freak tell the truth. He wanna act funny, walkin' around in flamin' drawls lookin' like a shitty-ass skid mark with a Vote for Sanjaya tee shirt on, and everybody know overgrown ass Jordin gon' win. Come on, Freeda, 'fore we have to slice these niggahs up."

"I'ma see you again, Nae-Nae," Freeda cried. "That's exactly why I bust out all yo' windows and sliced yo' tires."

"And that's why I had my crew jump yo' ass!" Squeak spat at Raphael.

"They had me jumped?!" Raphael screamed in disbelief.

"I promise, you will see me again." And she and Squeak walked backward out the door, Squeak hunching his shoulders at Yuri.

Once they crossed the threshold, Squeak pointed from his eyes to Yuri's, "I'm comin' for your throat, bitch."

"Call me when you jump that high." Yuri slammed the door in their faces.

"Oh Jesus." Raphael flopped down on the couch, as if he were due to faint. "Nae-Nae, where did them creatures come from? Who invented them?"

"I don't know."

"Nae-Nae," Yuri said, "if you went back in IHOP and got with that bitch, I'ma beat the gay off yo' ass!"

"Oh no," Raphael said as if he'd been defeated. "I don't even wanna imagine you with no fish. You promised you weren't gon' cheat no more, Nathan!"

"That heifer is crazy!" Nae-Nae tried to console Raphael.

"She better be," Drae said distantly.

"Look," Yuri said, as she sat down on the couch and kicked her shoes off, "the show is on and before you know, it's gon' be time to vote. We all know Nae-Nae don't even dream about pussy unless it's in a sex-change operation, so I'm convinced that bitch is crazy, especially since she and Tattoo attacked me and all I said was good evening."

"That's right," Nae-Nae said. "Let's watch some TV."

As everyone laughed and agreed with Simon's comments, Yuri called Britt several times on his cell phone, but he never answered. The last time she called him, she could tell he'd turned it off. And when she called the studio the phone just rang.

"All right now," Nae-Nae announced. "The phone lines are open and you know our standard: ten votes apiece."

"I'm gon' vote for LaKisha and Melinda too, Nae-Nae," Drae insisted.

"Real class, Drae. You gon' waste your vote on Big Country and a buck-toothed Bobble Head."

Drae ignored him and looked at Yuri. "You votin' already?"

"No."

"Well, who are you calling, then?" Drae asked.

"Nae-Nae got enough business for us to get into, I don't need you in mine."

"Shut up, Eagle Ass, before I get Squeak back in here." Drae laughed.

"Yeah a'ight, Sunshine."

"I wonder where they got that from?" Drae said, more to herself.

"They don't know what they're talking about!" Yuri closed her phone.

"I hope not, Yuri," Drae said, unsure.

A few hours passed and everyone voted, ate dinner, drank wine and recapped the evening. Before long it was going on two o'clock in the morning. "Oh damn." Drae looked at the clock. "I need to get going. I hope they haven't given my room away. Shit, I hope I didn't forget to reserve it all week."

"Where are you staying?" Raphael asked. "You know you don't have to stay in no hotel. You can stay with me and Nae-Nae. We just like to make love in the kitchen every once in a while."

"Here we go with the visuals," Yuri said. "If it's all that, Drae, you know you're welcome to stay with me and Britt. He wouldn't mind."

"Listen, thanks, but I'm okay. I'm on a personal vacation right now." She smiled. "And tomorrow I have a nice surprise planned for a very good friend of mine. So let me go." She grabbed her purse. "Don't you have to go to work, Yuri?"

"Yeah . . . I do . . . Will you give me a ride home?"

"I thought Britt was coming to get you."

"He got stuck at the studio," she lied. "But if you're not going that way, I could catch a cab."

"Girl, if you don't come on here."

Yuri and Drae grabbed their purses, kissed Nae-Nae and Raphael on their cheeks and left.

When they got in the car and started to drive, Drae asked Yuri, "You heard anything from Jeff?"

"I met him for lunch."

"Are you crazy?!" Drae turned and quickly looked at her. "Why would you do that?"

"Because we needed to talk. And we needed to talk with all the shit on the table, the truth and nothing but the truth. I don't know about you, but sometimes I need closure."

"Closure can be simply not looking back."

"Not for me," Yuri said. "Besides, we met at Darlene's, a lil' posh place in Manhattan."

"And?"

"And he told me he was sorry. Sorry about everything: how we didn't work out, about Jeff Jr. and Kathy, sorry for the way he treated me."

"And you?"

"I apologized for my part."

"And that's it, y'all are good friends now? What kinda ridiculous shit?"

"We didn't leave friends, Drae. We left satisfied that the shit is finally over. He said he may try with his son's mother again."

"And what did you say?"

"I said good luck."

"Do you have any regrets?"

"No," Yuri spewed too quickly for even her to believe it. "I just hope I'm not being a new fool for old love."

Drae pulled in front of the building. Yuri's eyes scanned the block for Britt's car, but there was no sign of it. "All right girl." Yuri leaned over and kissed Drae on the cheek. "I'll call you tomorrow."

* * *

The loft was pitch-black when she walked in. She didn't even bother to flick the lights on because she knew there was no surprise waiting, just the same ole shit.

As tears invaded her eyes, Yuri refused to cry. She went in the bathroom, showered, changed into one of Britt's oversized tees and went to sleep.

Hours later she felt Britt's warm breath on her ear. "I'm sorry, baby. I'm so, so sorry."

She awoke from sleep and looked into his face. There were streams of light coming in from the row of windows that lined the adjacent wall. His hands roamed all over her body as he continued to apologize. He squeezed her breast and began sucking her nipples through the tee shirt she wore.

"How could you forget me?"

"I'm sorry."

"I waited for you."

"I know, baby." He lifted her shirt and begin kissing down her belly to the heaven between her thighs. Licking her clit he said, "I got so caught up."

"Do you know how embarrassed I was?"

"I'm sorry." He licked her clit again.

"I think I'ma go, Britt, and get my own spot. Maybe us living together is too much. I really don't want you to break my heart."

"You wanna leave me?" He began to aggressively suck her pussy, opening it up and running his tongue up and down the sides of her vulva. "Huh? Tell me," he spoke in between pulling her clit through his teeth. "What I'm 'spose to do when you go?"

"But, baby . . ." she moaned. "I just . . . thought . . . maybe . . ."

"You don't want no babies with me?" He pressed his tongue against her clit as he spoke. "A little girl maybe . . . Bree . . . Sanaa . . . Lake . . . or a little boy? You gon' bounce even before we have a family . . . This ya home ma'. . . ." He took his tongue off her clit and stared at it. "Damn, I love this pussy." He stuck two fingers inside her, slid out her juice and sucked it off. "I would share, baby. But since you wanna leave me, I need to savor it." He stuck his fingers inside her again, pulled out more juice and sucked it off. "I'ma miss you . . . I don't know why you gotta go." He began kissing her clit and talking to it. "She wanna leave daddy. So daddy can't kiss you no more. You so nice and pretty and fat." He sucked it. "Don't leave daddy. Daddy's sorry."

Tears rolled down Yuri's cheeks as her legs began to shake. Britt always knew what to do to get her to cum. But the tears weren't about her cumming as much as they were about her not wanting to be thrown off-kilter. Already she was stepping outside of herself and accepting shit she would've cussed Jeff out for.

Feeling her cum working its way down her spine and through her belly, she ran her hands through Britt's dreads. "I love you so much. . . ." she said as he licked her dripping candy. "Please don't break my heart."

He rose from between her legs and lay on top of her, "I'm not gon' hurt you baby." He slid his dick in.

Yuri pushed back against Britt's stroke with her hips. If only she could feel like this wasn't bound to end. She hated the sinking feeling that always settled into her stomach during moments like this.

"Stop thinking." Britt looked into her eyes. "Too much thought is not good."

Yuri looked at him, her eyes still cloudy. She wondered where he'd been. Had he been with Troi and if so did he stroke her like this? Was he saying some of the same things to her or was he saying more?

"I don't want nobody but you," he whispered as if he were reading her mind. "I put that on my life, it ain't nobody for me but you."

Drae

The surround sound pumped the remix to Silk's "Freak Me" as Naz walked toward the door and the base vibrations welcomed him into the dimly lit presidential suite. He was at the Waldorf-Astoria to meet Drae.

The sensual darkness of the suite instantly made his dick hard. He didn't know where Drae was, all he knew was she was in here somewhere and he was to follow the long trail of white rose petals in between two rows of tea-light candles to find her. Once he reached the dining room he knew he'd reached his destination, as paradise came alive. White candles of different shapes and sizes flickered around the room, and there were white rose petals strewn about on the floor, the dining-room table and the fireplace mantel.

And then there was Drae, who topped it all off. She was standing on the open balcony, her back leaning against the black metal railing, as she sucked on a cherry-red Blow Pop, licking it seductively and staring Naz right in his eyes. The lights from the New York City skyline sparkled against her back and created yellow hues that glittered into the room.

She rocked a Yankees baseball cap with a white Purple Label button-up; the top three buttons were left open, giving subtle hints of her full cleavage. On the shirtsleeves were platinum cuff links, and around the collar was an extremely loose raw silk necktie, hanging slightly to the side.

Drae stood with one leg in front of the other. Her thick toned thighs glistened like honey and her three-inch metallic silver stilettos made her French-manicured feet look delicious.

The music continued to pump as Silk seemed to give Naz instructions when they sang, "Let me lick you up and down." He lifted his white tee over his head, revealing his beautiful chest, and started walking toward her.

Drae winked her eye as she sucked the lollipop and signaled for him to stop. She needed to digest how fine God had actually made him. "Go take your place at the head of the table, baby."

Naz smiled as he speechlessly complied. He stood at the table, the candles that outlined it burning before him. He folded his defined arms across his hard pecs, and admired Drae's beauty. . . . it was so fierce that it was almost ridiculous. He knew if he concentrated on her too long he would nut just by staring, so he pulled a blunt from his back pocket, lit it and watched her do her thang.

Silk's "Freak Me" blended into Jodeci's "Feenin' " as Drae began to dance. She started by tipping the cap off her head by the bill, shaking out her shoulder-length hair, walking over and placing the cap on his head. The bent bill fit like a half moon over his eyes.

As she moved her body like a snake dancing to an Indian flute, Naz pulled out a stack of bills, tossed some in the middle of the table and held the rest in the palm of his right hand, as the smoke rising from his blunt filled the air. "If you want it . . . come get it."

Drae stood at the foot of the table, slowly unbuttoning her shirt, revealing her beautiful breasts underneath, which sat upon her chest like full moons, complemented by hard chocolate nipples. She shifted the necktie, letting it hang around her neck, and laid it between her breasts.

Naz tossed more money, some of it floating in the air like mini parachutes.

By the time Drae had danced her way down to nothing, Naz had tossed well over two thousand dollars into the center of the table, and when his palm was empty Drae crawled across the table, onto the money, and made her way toward him. Once she was before Naz, she unzipped his pants and began rubbing his dick. She kissed him along his pubic bone, licking around his dick before easing it into her mouth. And just when she thought his dick couldn't get any bigger she felt it swelling in her mouth. Sucking his dick was better than she ever could've imagined. The sides rubbed against her cherry-flavored tongue and the tip hit against the back of her welcoming throat.

As she sucked his dick with the intensity of a perfectionist, all Naz could do was run his hands through the back of her hair, grip it at the root and nut down her throat.

Drae swallowed as Naz regained his composure. He mashed the remains of his blunt in the ashtray and turned Drae over, doggy style. As she rolled through the money some of it stuck to her back.

Naz bit her all over her ass, from one cheek to the next, tossing her salad in between. He ducked his head underneath her and sucked her pussy until she screamed. Afterward he took his fingers and played in her juice before sliding his dick in.

Almost immediately he felt his nut rush back to the tip. He hated it because he wanted desperately to savor the moment of bathing in her juices. "I want us to cum together." He bit her on the neck and then he started banging her ass with his dick as if he were trying to create new drumbeats. His scrotum slapped against her skin, as though it offered pleasurable punishment. Drae threw her ass onto his shaft like never before and Naz pumped his dick in and out, as if they were running a race and passing the torch back and forth to each other. The pounding of his dick in and out of her pussy lips had overtaken the surround sound and was better than music could ever be to his ears.

"I'm cummin'," Drae whined, her breathing extremely heavy.

"Damn, baby . . ." Naz continued to pump as Drae moaned. "This my pussy and don't ever forget that shit." He was spilling from his dick as he pulled it out and nutted all over her ass. Once he was finished he rubbed it into both of her cheeks, while taking his fingers and placing some inside her pussy.

He slapped her on the ass before literally picking her up

and carrying her to the bedroom. "Now, that's what the fuck I'm talking about."

. . .

"Nasir," Drae laughed, "just admit you pussy-whipped and I'll give you your money back."

"You fuckin' crazy. I don't know what you think this is, but I'll never be caught dead admitting no shit like that." He mushed her on the forehead. "Punk ass tryna play me." He lay to the side of her, as she placed her head on his chest. He reached for the blunt on the nightstand and lit it.

"You see yourself loving me, don't you?"

"You on your shit, or what?" Naz took a pull.

"Yeah." She took the blunt from between his fingers, took a toke and blew out the smoke. "I am kinda feeling myself."

"Well it's not like the world hasn't seen that before." He laughed.

"Yeah, a'ight." Drae handed Naz the blunt and began kissing down the center of his chest. "Pussies is always hatin'!"

Naz laughed. "Yo, that the same thing ole boy on the TV just said." As Drae slid down his body to suck his dick, Naz pointed to the TV. "That's one flamin'-ass niggah."

"Pussies is always hatin' on Nae-Nae" floated from the TV.

"Damn, you sound like Nae-Nae," she said, dipping her head beneath the covers and getting comfortable between Naz's legs.

"I ain't say that gay-ass shit." He paused. "Wait a minute, ain't that your boy?"

"Who?" Drae lifted the covers off her head and looked at the TV. Instantly her mouth flew open. "Nae-Nae?!"

As she rolled off Naz and reached for her cell phone, it

rang. It was Yuri. "This niggah." They started talking over each other, "Wait, wait," Drae said. "Are you watching *Maury*?"

"I'm . . ." Yuri spoke slowly, "going . . . to stab that gay-ass motherfucker! And his mother begged him to stop showing his ass and look at this shit."

The Maury Povich studio was rocking. Nae-Nae, Raphael and Freeda were onstage.

"Anybody," Freeda screamed, "can see that niggah ain't gay! He just doing this to make me jealous."

"Fishes is hatin', Maury!" Raphael screamed. "Fishes is straight hatin'!"

"He tryna say you stink, Freeda," Squeak yelled from the audience.

"Oh hell to nawl," Freeda stood up. "I gets my doosh on!"

"Sizzle, sizzle, niggah," Squeak yelled. "Guess she read yo' flamin' ass."

"Somebody step on him, please!" Raphael looked around. "Lookin' like a fake-ass action hero. Why don't you take that damn karate suit off and lose yo' lil' bitty self?"

"Lil' bitty." It was obvious that threw Squeak for a loop.

"Don't even worry 'bout that, Squeak, he don't know 'bout you. He . . . do not . . . know . . . 'bout you," Freeda consoled. " 'Cause we all know you will rock . . . this too-tall faggot . . . to sleep. 'Cause we all know that Nae-Nae ain't gay. Er'body can see he a thug!"

"He got on a patent-leather catsuit and some earrings," Raphael snapped. "This niggah is gayer than a fuckin' passion-fruit Pop Tart. He so damn gay that when he's dead, he gon' have to be buried ass up in order for anybody to know him."

"He just told you to kiss his ass, Freeda," Squeak yelled.

"That mofo just told you to kiss his big black sugar-fartin' ass! They playin' the hell outta you, Freeda."

"Do you have anything to say?" Maury asked Nae-Nae.

"My feelings are just so hurt," Nae-Nae's voice trembled. "I don't know what to say."

"These is yo' kids, Nae-Nae," Freeda insisted.

"I don't even know who you are," Nae-Nae responded. "It's obvious that a restraining order wasn't good enough."

"Restraining order? I don't give a damn about no restraining order!"

"Wait a minute," Maury intervened. "Are you saying that these are not your children?"

"Maury," Nae-Nae spoke somberly, "all I'm saying is that people are known for taking advantage of me."

Before Nae-Nae could answer, Freeda interrupted, "It's okay, Nae-Nae." She pointed to the newborn twins' picture up on the split screen. "I can do bad all by myself. I don't need you to help me take care of my babies. I make more than enough to see 'bout Petrone-Alizé-Malik-Kaareem-DiShawn Jenkins, the Second, that's my son. And you sho' ain't got to worry 'bout my daughter Caviar."

"Tell 'em, Freeda!" Squeak yelled from the audience. "Tell 'em!"

"Looka here, Funky White and the too-short dwarf, we 'bout to prove y'all wrong," Raphael insisted.

Maury held a manila envelope in his hand, with paternity test results inside. "So are you sticking by your man?" he asked Raphael.

"I sho' am."

Maury opened the envelope, "When it comes to Petrone-Alizé-Kaareem-DiShawn Jenkins . . ."

"The Second," Freeda added. "Don't forget 'the Second,' I added that 'cause it sound real fancy."

"Tell 'em, Freeda," Squeak yelled. "That shit there is distinguished."

"The Second," Maury continued. "And Caviar. Nae-Nae you are . . ." He stalled. "the father."

Immediately Raphael fell to the floor and passed out. Squeak started running around the studio, jumping up into the camera. "Told you! Told you!"

"All I want," Freeda cried, "is for him to take care of Petrone-Alizé-Malik-Kaareem-DiShawn Jenkins, the Second and Caviar."

"Awwwlllll!!!!!" Raphael screamed, now revived and lying on the floor, appearing to be having a series of convulsions. "Say it ain't so, Nae-Nae. Please say it ain't so."

"I swear on the Rainbow God, these pussies"—he pointed to Freeda and Squeak—"gang-raped me!"

"Told you he wasn't gay, Maury," Freeda spat. "Yup, told you!"

"I just had a weak moment," Nae-Nae pleaded.

"Where them Charlie Angel wannabe bitches at now?" Squeak screamed, jumping up on the stage and standing directly in front of the camera. "Attention Eagle Ass, Squeak is comin' for your throat, be'yatch."

"I can't believe this," Drae said, still holding her cell phone to her ear. "I am utterly embarrassed."

"Britt over here laughing," Yuri said, "but I see I'ma have to cut this lil' niggah up."

Yuri

"Why are you buggin'?" Britt asked Yuri as he slipped on black, tailored Gucci dress pants, a crisp white button-up, platinum cuff links and onyx square-toe crocs. His matching suit jacket lay on the bathroom vanity.

Sony Music, the company Britt was signed with, was having a CD-release party for one of their new artists and was also celebrating Britt's new reggae and soca imprint.

"Oh now I'm buggin'?" Yuri sucked her teeth. "I've seen the same number on the caller ID for the last week, seven days in a row, at some real funny fuckin' hours." She stood at the vanity, puckered her lips and applied

MAC lipstick and liner. "Don't start no shit, Britt." She stood up straight, dabbed Angel perfume in her cleavage, and ran her hands along the sides of her cream Versace tube-top dress, which clung to every one of her voluptuous curves like a magnet. "Understood?"

Instead of responding, Britt tapped her on the ass.

"I take it it's understood." Yuri slipped her yellow diamond studs in each ear, then sat down on the closed toilet lid, held her foot up and handed Britt the rhinestone Manolos he'd bought her. He placed her feet respectively on each pant leg, slipped her shoes on and buckled them around the ankles.

"Now," she said, "we're ready to go."

Britt checked his dreads, which were styled with a series of single cornrows in the front and hanging loose in the back. "What was up with those grandma drawls you had hanging up there yesterday?" He playfully mushed her on the side of her head. "I already told you we don't wear drawls around here."

"You so retarded," she laughed. "For your information, I was doing laundry. Didn't you notice your clothes had been washed . . . and the loft had been cleaned?"

"Yeah, I noticed you were performing your wifely duties."

"Yeah, niggah, I better be the wife and you better tell that ho who keeps calling your phone the same thing before I slide her ass."

"There you go tryna slide somebody. Don't be tryna take the conversation off them big-ass drawls. Who you sleeping next to in them?"

"Yo' ass. I wear them when I'm on my period and it's due to come any day—"

"It ain't come yet?" he cut her off. "According to my calculations it shoulda been here Tuesday . . . of last week."

"You keeping up with my cycle?"

"Hell, yeah. I'm not playing with you; as much as I be nuttin' up in yo' ass, I'm taking no chances."

"It's only a few days late."

"You better tell that niggah he got a curfew."

"Whatever." She picked up his socks and jeans from the bathroom floor. "Find a hamper for these, please."

"I wasn't finished with them."

"Stop lying." She laughed. "Yo' ass was gon' leave 'em right on the floor like you always do."

"You love me, don't you?" He grabbed her by the waist and turned her toward him.

"Yeah, too damn much."

"This all me, baby?" He ran his hands along the sides of her body.

"Yes, Britt, that's all you."

"That's what I thought, now give me a kiss." As they began to kiss passionately, flicking their tongues in and out of each other's mouth, Britt's cell phone went off. Ending their kiss, he looked at the number on the phone. Instead of answering he sent the call to voice mail.

"Now gimme some more." He pinned her against the wall, placed his hands under her dress and moved the seat of her panties over. As he slid two fingers into her silkiness his phone rang again. "Shit!"

"Don't answer it," she said, unbuttoning the shirt he'd just put on.

"No, I can't do that. All kind of people call on my phone; it could be my manager, anybody."

"You need to get you a business line."

"You right, baby," he said looking at the caller ID and sending the call to voice mail again. Before he could place the phone down, it rang once more.

"Okay," Yuri said, pissed, "who the fuck is that, Britt?"

"Nobody."

She took a step back. "You lying to me now? That's how we do? You want me to lie to you?"

"I wish you would fuckin' lie to me. . . ."

"A'ight then, who was that?"

"It was Troi."

She hoped he didn't see her heart skipping beats. "What?" she said as calmly as possible.

"Just listen. You know . . . when you were still with Jeff, me and Troi would kick it . . . from time to time, mostly about business, her marriage and that's it."

"Oh, now you admit you talked about more than business."

"If you gon' start accusing me, then I may as well let you tell me the story."

"Go ahead." She swallowed.

"Ever since you moved in, I deaded it."

"Before or after you fucked her?"

"She was getting divorced and having some problems."

"*Before* or *after* you fucked her?!"

"Yuri—"

Her heart stopped beating. "Just fuckin' tell me!"

"Goddamn." He attempted a smile. "You 'bout to slice me?"

"I am not . . . fuckin' playing with you."

"I didn't fuck her."

"How am I supposed to believe that?"

He was instantly aggravated. "Because that's what I just told you."

"And that's good enough?" She sucked her teeth.

"Hold it." He stopped dead in his tracks. "Let me check you for a minute. You were fuckin' married, Yuri. Matter fact, you still married and you was straight-up living with this niggah. When I asked you to leave the motherfucker, you played me the fuck crazy, went home and laid up in the niggah's face. So, quite frankly, it could be Kim goddamn Porter I fucked and you will never have a right to ask or accuse me of fuckin' anybody. As long as you was playin' wife to that motherfucker, knowing you was loving me, anything that went on over here was fair goddamn game. Now get that shit in order."

"Was all that called for? You acting like you had some pent-up resentment and shit. Or am I mistaken, and you just going hard for that bitch? Let me know, so I can step."

"Oh, here we go. That's why I didn't wanna tell you."

"Then, why you telling me now?!"

"I was being honest."

"Whatever." As she began checking her face in the mirror, she had a flash of him fucking Troi. "Did you fuck that bitch?" She turned to him.

"No," he said with conviction. "I said I deaded the situation. If I speak to her now, it's about business. She's an entertainment attorney for the record company, so occasionally I run into her. But it's nothing."

"Look," Yuri said as she popped her lips, "maybe I need to bounce while there are no hard feelings. I remember that

Troi shit and I'm not going back through it. Maybe Drae was right when she said if you leave who you love for who you screw, who you screw will leave you for the one they love."

"What the fuck is that?" He frowned. "Poetry? And I told you about telling me some ole ridiculous shit somebody said. I don't wanna hear it. 'Cause as soon as you turn your back that bitch'll be in my face."

"You sayin' Drae tryna get with you?"

"I'm sayin' Drae need to mind her fuckin' business and stay outta mine. And stop discussing us and what we do! 'Cause leaving me is nowhere in the game. So try something else. Now, if it'll make you feel better, when and if I run into Troi I'll ask her not to call me again. And to direct anything she needs from me to my manager." He kissed her on the forehead. "Straight?"

"Straight," she conceded.

"Now can I laugh?"

"At what?"

"At you, you had a look like you was 'bout to kick my goddamn ass." He fell out. "My baby straight gangsta wit' it."

"Whatever. Just know I haven't forgotten how much you used to love that bitch. 'Cause if my memory serves me correctly, had she not said no, you was 'bout to marry her fuckin' ass."

"My baby jealous?" He pulled her by the waist and buried his head in her breast. Kissing her cleavage, he said, "Don't sweat that shit. When I stop coming home, then you worry."

"The day you stop coming home is the day I'm leaving."

"That's the second time you said something about leaving. Let's just squash this Troi talk and this leaving bullshit, a'ight?" She could tell he'd caught a slight attitude because the vein in his neck started to stick out. "'Cause as soon as you try to get with another niggah I'ma fuck all y'all up."

"Awl, look at my daddy." Yuri kissed the thumping vein on his neck. "Mami sorry. What, daddy need to feel better?" She started sucking his bottom lip and feeling the imprint of his dick.

"I don't know." He pouted. "I ain't sure."

"Uhmmm, daddy dick hard." She stuck her hands in through the slit of his pants and played with it. "Daddy, it's soooo big. It's swelling, daddy. . . ."

"What you gon' do about it . . . to make the swelling go down?"

"I'ma ride it out."

"You gon' mess up your dress."

"Not if you take it offa me."

Britt glanced at the clock, hating to break up their act, then said, "I'ma be late, baby."

"Oh, you gon' be late?" She stepped out of her dress. "So you mean to tell me," she said as she lay down on the cool tile floor, the chill of it giving her back goose bumps, "you gon' leave all this pretty"—she opened her legs as wide as she could, moved the seat of her thong to the side, and with each word she spoke she dipped her fingers in her pussy and sucked it off—"you gon' leave this hot, pink, dripping wet pussy all by itself: no kisses, no dick, nothing. You just gon' drag it to a party?"

Britt unbuttoned his shirt and hung it over the bathroom door. "Mami know she wrong." He slipped his pants and boxers off. "She know that pussy is my weakness."

Britt lay between Yuri's legs and sucked her clit through the seat of her panties, causing her to cum so hard that the juice soaked through her thong and filled his mouth. After, he pulled her thong off, turned her over doggy style and slid his dick in. She cocked her neck to the side and watched him stake claim in her pussy. "Whose pussy is this?" He stroked.

"Uhmmm, I can't remember."

"Oh, you can't remember?"

"You gon' give it to me good, daddy. You gon' make me remember?"

"You know I'ma punish you."

With each hard and forceful stroke he slapped her on the ass. "You remember now, huh? You remember now?"

"Yes, I'm sorry."

He slapped her on the ass and pounded into her, "Say it again."

"I'm sorry." She could feel her nut stirring.

"You ain't sorry." He rammed his long pipe into her, causing her nut to run like a marathon over his dick. "And now you nuttin' on my dick."

"There I go again, daddy, being bad. I'm sorry."

"Prove it."

Yuri turned around and started licking the tip of Britt's dick. As soon as she got into a groove where she began swirling her tongue around it, he took it out of her mouth, and teased her across the lips with it, making her desire it more. As she inched up closer to suck it again, he let her tongue stroke it a few moments more before he slipped it back out of her mouth. "You not playing fair," she said as he ran it across her lips. "Let me suck it." He grabbed the back of her hair, guided her mouth to his dick and finally allowed her to deep throat it. "See, I'm not so bad, daddy."

He caressed the back of her neck as his nut shot out. "You ain't bad, baby, you just fuckin' right."

Two hours later, Britt's cell phone was ringing off the hook. "Shit, baby"—he looked at his caller ID as he helped her from the floor—"my manager done called me fifty fuckin' times. Come on, let's go. The limo should be downstairs!"

Yuri and Britt practically washed and dressed each other. He helped her slip on her dress and made sure her breasts were situated with pasties correctly, while she buttoned his shirt, zipped his pants, tightened his belt, made sure his jacket was laid just right and snapped his cuff links.

He gave her a peck on the lips. "You look good, baby."

"Thank you." She smudged the corners of his mouth with her thumb. "And you do too."

. . .

By the time they got to the party it was already jumping. There was music from the new reggae artist blasting. Dom and caviar were floating around the room on the shoulders of white-gloved butlers. The main course of steamed lobster tail was due to be served at any minute. Everyone who was anyone in the music business was in the place. From the likes of Jay-Z, Lauryn Hill, Stephen and Ziggy Marley, Mary J. Blige, Baby Cham and Sean Paul.

When the hostess made the announcement of Britt's imprint, he walked up to the podium and said a few words. Afterward, he returned to the table where Yuri waited for him.

"How'd I do?" he asked.

"You were cool." She took her napkin and wiped the sweat off his brow. "I'm the one nervous."

"Why?"

"I don't know. I just have this horrible feeling."

"You pregnant?"

"No, Britt." She gave him a quick peck. "No."

"Mr. Brittmond L'Overture Lake, the Third" poured from behind them as a soft caramel hand with French-manicured nails rested on Britt's shoulder.

"Troi." Yuri faked a smile. "Wow, look at you." Troi was standing there in three-inch pencil-heel stilettos and a hunter green Mychael Knight minidress, which crossed over her breasts, exposing her extremely flat stomach. "You see Troi, Britt?"

Britt shot Yuri a sly look to let her know he wasn't feeling her sarcasm. He nodded his head. "How are you, Troi?"

"No, the question is how are you two?" She smiled. "Am I seeing correctly? Is this a little couple situation going on?"

"It's cool," Britt responded. "This my man. We straight."

His motherfuckin' man? Yuri hoped Troi didn't hear her heart crack. *His fuckin' man? Is he serious?*

"Wow, look at you two!" Troi's smile was extremely wide. "Yuri, you look absolutely wonderful!"

"Thank you." Yuri wished she would hurry and leave.

Britt turned to Yuri. "Excuse me, baby. My manager is calling me." He turned to Troi. "Nice seeing you."

Troi sat next to Yuri and lit a cigarette. "Mind if I smoke?" She took a puff, not allowing Yuri enough time to answer, and went on, "What an affectionate term: his man. Must be nice for your position not to have changed much."

"Fuck you, bitch," Yuri said with conviction. "Everyone can't master going from hooker to housewife. Last I heard, you had that sewed up."

"How cute," Troi smiled at some people passing by. "But I always told you your feet were too wide to follow in my footsteps. Now tell me, how are Nae-Nae and Andrea?"

"Not as fine as you. . . ." Yuri joked, tilting her head toward Britt. "Now if you'll excuse, I believe, *my man* is calling me."

"But wait, Yuri. Before you step away I have to tell you: You look fantastic in that dress! I was going to buy me one, but the designer didn't make it in my size. I was so pissed— for a split second, I wished I could've gained fifty pounds so I could have it."

Did that bitch just call me fat? "I thought something was different about you. You lost weight? I didn't want to pry, but since the floodgate fell open, I have to ask, are you sick? If so, accept my condolences. I can tell you don't have much time to live—it looks as if your diagnosis ends with positive."

"It's been real, Yuri."

"Uhmm, it certainly has."

For the rest of the evening Yuri did her best to fake smiles as she and Britt took pictures, ate and drank. He could tell something was wrong with her, but he chalked it up to her being pissed about seeing Troi.

• • •

"Don't say shit to me" was the only thing Yuri said during the entire ride home.

"Yo, my man," Britt said as he and Yuri walked in the door of his loft. "What the fuck is yo' problem? Why you sweatin' that shit?!"

Silence. She began to undress.

"You hear me talking to you?" He placed his suit jacket on the piano and it fell to the floor.

"You allergic to a fuckin' hamper or somethin'?" She picked his jacket up. "What the fuck is your problem?! I just cleaned up in this motherfucker and I'm sick of picking up behind you. I ain't your damn mother and especially not your fuckin' wife. I'm just ya fuckin' *man,* remember? We cool." Yuri rolled her eyes so hard they looked as if they would pop out.

"Yo, ma'." He twisted his neck. "You can roll 'em, but you can't control him."

"Do I look like I'm fuckin' laughin'? This shit is not funny. Everything between me and you is a joke! This fuckin' relationship is a joke. But hold it, I just remembered we don't have a relationship—we motherfuckin' boys! But the strange thing is I don't remember your manz and dem sucking yo' dick. Next time, go tell Beanie Sigel to give you some head."

"But, mami," he said jokingly, "don't nobody suck my dick like you." Expecting a laugh, Britt was in shock when he saw tears come to Yuri's eyes. He stood still for a minute. "Yo' my man, baby. I'm sorry." He walked over and grabbed her, pulling her into his chest. "I shouldn't have said that. My fault."

Yuri pushed him off her. "Get off me!" She fought, pounding her fists into his chest to get away. Tears were streaming down her face.

In order to make her stop hitting him and have her stand still, he grabbed her tightly by the forearms and pulled her against his chest again. "Yo, I swear to God on everything I love, including you, that I was just playing. It's all about you. Troi don't mean shit. It's nothing, just business." He kissed her on the forehead and held her tight. "You know you my heart, and ain't nothing coming between us. You know it didn't mean anything when I called you my man."

"Exactly." She pushed away. "It didn't mean a fuckin' thing."

Drae

Leaving Naz alone wasn't the easiest thing to do. Drae thought staying in a hotel for a while would do the trick, but all it did was help her spend a small fortune of Hassan's money, which she started to stack a few years back.

Once Naz dropped Sydney off to school, Drae stopped by, and as soon as she stepped in they began making love on the floor.

"Ma', I don't even know what the fuck I'm doing with you," Naz said as if he were dreaming. He held Drae's breasts together and licked her deep chocolate nipples, as if they were melting. "Word is bond, you got me fuckin' going."

"I got you going, or this hot, pink pussy is sending you on a trip?"

"I'm not sure." Naz placed a trail of soft bites down the middle of Drae's body. "Get on top of me."

"Baby," she whined, "I wanted you to eat my pussy. My clit"—she started rubbing it—"is aching."

"I got you, ma'. Naz always do." He kissed her pussy lips. "Now," he said as he lay beside her, "come 'ere."

Drae kissed her way on top of Naz, running her hands all over his chiseled chest. Sucking his nipples and rubbing her clit against his hard dick, she said, "Now I want some of this."

"I want you to sit on my face first."

"Really." Drae smiled, more than happy to comply.

"Uhmm hmmm."

"That's where you want me to nut at, in your mouth?"

"Exactly."

Drae eased her way up to Naz's mouth and sat on his face. She worked her pussy over his lips as if she were riding his dick. Naz's tongue licked every inch of her pussy as if it were racing against itself. Her feeling heightened with each stroke of his tongue, all she could do was arch her back, place her hands behind her and on his knees. Tears ran down her face as her nut began to ease its way between his lips. She could feel him envelope her vulva. He held it so tight in his mouth that, when he released it, a popping sound came out.

"Now ride it." He smacked her ass.

"I'ma ride the hell out of it." Drae kissed her cum off his lips. She slipped her tongue into his mouth and kissed him as if she were fighting for dear life. He bit her top and bottom lips and then he sucked her chin.

"Ride this dick like you own it."

"I don't own it?" She stroked.

He cupped her ass. "Naw, I don't think so."

"You don't think so?"

"Naw, you ain't done shit to make me think you deserve it."

Drae began riding his dick and throwing her hips with every inch she had to offer. She could feel her clit slapping against the front of his dick, climbing up and down his rigid wall as her G-spot rained sticky pallid cum all over his rock-solid member. Instead of screaming his name, she said, "I see you still don't know whose dick this is."

He opened his eyes and gave her a half grin.

Drae eased off his dick, turned around, stood over his body, pressed on all fours and slowly eased back down on his dick, leaving her creamy cum mark all over it. It was feeling so good, all Naz could do was close his eyes. "Uh-uh, open your eyes and watch this pussy work this dick," Drae insisted.

Naz placed his hands around the base of his dick and every time Drae's pussy slid down on it, he slipped two fingers inside her. "Goddamn, this shit is bananas. Oh . . . my . . . God . . ." His toes began to curl.

"You better not nut up in this pussy until you tell me who it belong to."

He ran his hands all over her ass. "Sunshine . . ." he moaned. "Oh, goddamn, work it, baby." She popped her inner walls. "I see why you a star," he carried on.

"Whose dick is this?" She held her ass in the air.

"It's yours." She slid back down.

"Whose dick is this?" She held it the air again, teasing him.

"Oh my God, baby, it's yours!" he screamed. "Sunshine,

it's yours." His nut raced to the tip as she sat on his dick and took him on a trip he would never forget.

• • •

After Naz came, he fell out exhausted on the floor. Drae lay to the side of him, propped up on one arm and running her index finger up and down the center of his chest. "Naz?"

"What ma'?" He wiped the sweat off her nose.

"I have to ask you this."

"Anything."

"What did you mean when you said you see why I'ma star?"

" 'Cause, Sunshine, that's what you are." Naz looked at Drae, confused. "Right?"

"It depends on what kinda star you're talking about. And why do you and the rest of America," she said, agitated, "keep calling me Sunshine?"

Naz turned on his side, facing Drae. "Drae . . . for real, it's me. You don't have to front for me, it's cool. I know what you do for a living. That's how I met you."

"Know what I do for a living?" she questioned. "I'm a high-school guidance counselor. At least I was until recently."

Naz tried not to laugh in her face, but it started to ease out the side of his mouth. He began to laugh so hard that he fell onto his back and bellowed out.

Drae squinted her eyes at him and curled her upper lip. "What the fuck are you laughing at?" She sat up. "Did I just crack a fuckin' joke?"

"Naw," he said, laughter still seething through his teeth. "Fall back. It's good ma'. I'm saying though, if you wanna role play, just let me know. You can be teacher and I'll be the naughty student. Just don't spank me on my ass, 'cause I ain't beat for all that."

"You know what, niggah," she said, tempted to mush him in the head, "fuck you. Here I am, laying up with you, and you laughin' at me? Oh, you done pissed me off."

"Ma'," he said as he grabbed her forearm, "calm down. What's the attitude about? We both know you do movies."

"Movies? Pornos?"

"Yes."

"Are you serious? All I've ever done were the auditions, and I hate I did that shit."

Naz looked intently at Drae, as if trying to figure something out. "Drae, when we got down"—he pointed from his chest to hers and back again—"that wasn't no audition . . . that was a movie."

"What?" she said in complete disbelief. "Niggah, please. Now, if you wanna role play, that's all you gotta say."

"Are you serious?" His eyes revealed a deep level of confusion. "Did I miss something?"

"You missed a whole lotta shit if you think I been out here doing movies!" Drae wasn't sure why, but her heart started racing and she started to get a sinking feeling in her stomach. "You scaring the hell outta me, Nasir, and I don't think this shit is funny."

"Drae, baby." He held both her hands between his. "You been doing pornos."

"What . . . ?" Tears filled her eyes. "Stop saying that. It's not true."

"Baby." He wiped her tears with the back of his index finger. "I wish I was fuckin' lying, but you are a porn star."

"No, I don't believe this."

Naz rose from the floor, his tight ass swaying in the wind as he wrapped a towel around himself, then left the room and came back with a DVD. "Look at the jacket." He tossed it to her.

Drae looked down and began to read, "Ain't No Sunshine 'Til She Cums, from the chronicles of Hassan Shaw . . . from the chronicles of Hassan Shaw . . ." Drae flipped the DVD over and she saw a picture of Naz's dick entering the back door of her pussy. She tossed the DVD across the bed, as if someone had just handed her poison. "No, this is not so. This is not happening to me. There were no cameras in my house."

"Sweetie—" he wiped the stream of silent tears pouring from her eyes—"there are cameras all over your house."

"What?" She was still in disbelief.

"In the recessed lighting. All over your house are recessed lights and inside all of them are cameras."

"How do you know that?"

"Everyone in the industry knows that. Hassan has the fliest studio around."

"Studio?" she cried. "That's my house."

"No, baby, that's a stage."

Drae sat still for a moment that felt like forever. Suddenly every audition that she'd ever done ran through her mind. She thought about the times the actors seemed so scripted, almost remote controlled when they spoke, how she chalked it up to their being nervous and inexperienced. And then it was Lee-Lee Lickme, Naz and the white girl eating her pussy. She remembered Freeda, who'd called her Sunshine. Sunshine, a ho with da bomb pussy from *Harlem Nights*. Sunshine, a bitch selling pussy. "Nasir, who is Sunshine?"

"You. That's your porn name."

Drae's entire body ached. "I don't believe it! You're lying." She got up and started getting dressed. "You're fuckin' lying. Hassan is a lotta things, but he would never do this."

"Drae—"

"Fuck you!" She picked up her purse and headed toward the door.

Naz blocked her path. "You can't run from this." He grabbed Drae and pulled her close.

Her voice trembled as she tried to speak. "Get off me. This some bullshit and I'm not dealing with it! I'm done with you, do you understand? We're over!" She pushed him in the center of his chest. "Move, dammit!"

"This is not about me."

"So," she said, the snot running from her nose, and trying to state with confidence, "it was only one?"

"My baby." He ran his hands through her hair. "You need to come with me."

Naz threw on a pair of jeans, a white tee and a pair of Jordans. Drae was quiet as they drove down the West Side Highway. Once they were in the Village he was able to find a parking spot not too far from where the store was. Drae noticed that the store's windows were all painted black and the entrance was concealed by a steel door. When they walked in, the young woman behind the counter looked shocked. Her eyes were beaming as she stared at Naz and Drae.

"Why is she looking at me like that?" Drae whispered to Naz, her tears still stinging the edges of her eyes. For the first time since she did the initial audition, she felt dirty. She felt as if she were in a brothel selling a fine piece of ass. "I think I'm ready to go."

"No, I need you to see this." He led her to a back wall where there was a collection of Hassan's movies, from his early works to all of the movies he'd ever done with Drae. There were DVDs of her taking a shower, playing with herself, fucking him with a loaded dildo and shooting off on his ass, Lee-Lee Lickme sucking her pussy, and one marked bestseller—the one she did with Naz.

As Drae felt herself about to faint, she heard someone yelling. "Sunshine! Sunshine! Oh my God!" a young woman with a sleeve of tattoos panted. "I can't believe this. I'm like your biggest fan. You're the reason I tried other chicks. The way Lee-Lee licked your pussy, I couldn't resist. You don't," the girl said with a blush, "do private parties, do you?"

"What?"

"I mean, I noticed you never give, you only receive; and it's cool, I love the taste of pussy."

As Drae thought this was the part where she needed to smack the girl, someone else approached her. "I heard that you lived in New York. Someone said you did something at a school. But I didn't believe it!" the young man screamed. "I swear to you, the way you fucked him with a loaded dildo made me wish I could turn my chick out like that. Damn, if I get a tattoo needle, will you tattoo my dick? All I want is *Sunshine* on it."

Drae knew it was time to leave, she'd gotten the point and needed to go home so she could break down in peace. But before she could walk away a small crowd surrounded her. "I am such a big fan!" Someone shouted.

"You got the prettiest titties I've ever seen!"

"Can I kiss your pussy?!"

"You still fuck him with a dildo?"

"I promise, you won't have to eat me back, I just wanna taste your cum!"

"How come you never show at the award shows?"

"Let me call my cousin and tell him you're down here. He always jerks off to you."

And on it went.

Drae felt like her head was spinning and her body was giving way. Something was wrong, something had to be wrong. All she could see were lines waving in front of her eyes, and she could no longer breathe. She needed to leave, she just didn't know where she would go, but she had to get outta here. Drae took a deep breath and bolted out of the store. Naz hurried behind her, but by the time he reached the door, he couldn't see her anymore.

Yuri

Yuri stuffed the positive pregnancy test to the bottom of the garbage and then she poured sour milk on it. It was Britt's thirty-second birthday, and she didn't want to ruin it. Besides, she wasn't so sure what she wanted to do. The relationship with him was a mess. He made a better side niggah or best friend than a main man. All the sweetness had turned sour and his perfect representative had long since left the building. Now she was stuck nursing a broken heart while not being able to accept that her season with Britt had ended.

For the past month he would come home for a few hours to shower and change and then head back out. Lately, the only time she ever saw him was when he was between her legs, either kissing her pussy or nuttin' up in it.

Yuri set the table with shrimp scampi, chilled sparkling cider and a birthday cake. Then she propped up the pillows behind her back and lay on the couch dressed in a leather bra, matching thong and stilettos.

She prayed practically every five minutes that he would hold true to his word and come home early tonight, especially since he was already an hour late.

In the midst of waiting Yuri drifted to sleep and by the time she awoke the sun was creeping into the sky. She couldn't believe it, somehow this had to be a nightmare. She looked at the clock for confirmation that it was a new day and it read seven A.M. Still not convinced this was real, she looked at the table she'd set, only to see the cake was uncut, her sparkling cider was hot and her shrimp scampi was cold. She sat up on the couch, her stomach feeling like a volcano had erupted, and she began to cry like a distressed baby. Her life was in shambles. And here she sat, all by herself, with nobody to talk to except God, and even He'd fallen asleep.

As Yuri rose from the couch to shower and change (after all, it was a workday) the doorbell rang.

"Britt, you forgot your keys again?" A sigh of relief came over her as she wrapped a robe around herself. She didn't want to go off right away for fear of his becoming pissed and storming back out. "One day I'm not gon' be here," she said as she opened the door, "and then what you gon' do?"

"I'll move in." Troi smiled.

"What the fuck are you doing here?!" Yuri spat. She never expected to see Troi standing here, not in a million years.

"Excuse you, is that how they say good morning in the school of rudeness? Anyway, I thought Britt woulda been here." She handed Yuri his wallet. "Tell him he left this at my house last night and I found it after he left this morning."

"What?" Yuri stood in shock; suddenly she felt like a zombie.

"What's the problem?" Troi placed her hands on her hips. "How about this, because I don't have all morning, you need to understand that I'm not leaving Britt alone. And I'm not stopping at him being back in my bed, I want him back in my life as my man. As my husband. He loves me and you know it. So don't envision me leaving anytime soon, 'cause I'ma be the worst fuckin' bitch you've ever seen. Do us all a favor: Save yourself some heartache and disappear."

There wasn't much to say outside of a "bitch" here and a "ho" there; especially since, at the end of the day, it all added up to be the same. Britt loved Troi and he would never stop loving her. Yuri just hated that she built so many damn dreams on the two of them being in love. She treasured the day he would one day call her his woman or his wife. But now here she stood face-to-face with her worst nightmare. "Kiss . . ." Yuri spoke slowly, "my ass!" And she slammed the door in Troi's face.

Yuri held on to the knob until the cold metal felt clammy. She was too hurt to cry and too emotionless to scream. Here she'd been waiting for him all night and he was out fucking Troi. The same bitch that he swore he had nothing with.

Yuri went in the bathroom, showered and changed. By the time she grabbed her purse and hospital overcoat it was a quarter after eight and she was fifteen minutes late for work.

Once she got to work, she was silent most of the day. She worked in the geriatrics unit and usually the old people, who reminded her of her grandparents, would make her smile, but today she was depressed.

"Smile, chile," one of her patients said. "I'm the one death's looking for."

By the time her day ended she wanted to crawl under a rock. She opened the door to Britt's loft and there he was, lying in the bed. "Wassup?"

"Where's your wallet, Britt?" Yuri tried not to sound anxious.

"Why, you need some money?" He picked his pants up off the floor and searched his back pockets. "Damn." He sucked his teeth. "I must've left it."

"Left it where?"

"I left the shit . . . in the car—at the studio—shit, what the hell are you asking me all these questions for?"

"That's all I needed to know." Yuri went in the closet, pulled out her suitcases and started packing them.

"Where you going?" He sat up.

"Did you forget that I waited for your birthday yesterday?" She turned to him, tears rolling down her face and her eyes turning fire red. "I waited here all fuckin' night for you. Do you remember you told me you were coming home early?! But instead you were fucking Troi!"

"Oh, here you fuckin' go!"

"The bitch came here!" She threw his wallet at him and everything in it scattered to the floor like drops of rain. "And she told me you were fucking her! You left your wallet at her house! I really can't fuckin' believe this. Here I thought it was me, that I was imagining shit, that I was this and I was that, and all along it wouldn't have mattered what I did, because you woulda still been fulla shit. I been holding on to air. You love Troi? You love Troi, then guess what? Troi can fuckin' have yo' ass, cause Yuri is through. It's over and I'm the fuck outta here. You don't ever have to worry about my ass again!"

"Yuri, please." He waved his hand. "I'm tired and you shootin' a buncha shit that I don't wanna fuckin' hear! If you think I'm fuckin' her, then hell, maybe I am, maybe I should be. Then you can be right for once."

Yuri stood and gave Britt a crooked grin. The salty tears running from her eyes slid into the corners of her mouth. "Now I know you're really lying because that's the same shit I said to Jeff when I was cheating on him with you. Oh my God, Britt, you're really fucking Troi—" Yuri felt like her body was closing in on itself. "What am I doing?" she said as if she were in a daze. "What the fuck am I really doing?"

"How about this?" He shook his head. "Maybe you need to step, and we need to end this. You don't trust me, you believe any fuckin' thing, you nag me, you don't understand me and I'm tired of it. For real, I am. It's a wrap for this bullshit. Change your fuckin' position and be out!"

Yuri was convinced there would never be enough words in the English language to describe how she felt or how her heart ached. The feeling of your feet slipping from beneath you was something that could never be put into words.

Her bottom lip trembled as if she were freezing cold. Britt sat on the edge of the bed, shaking his head. "Yo," he said calmly. "Sit down. I'm sorry, I ain't mean that."

Yuri started to pack her clothes. Although she was unsure of where she would go, she knew for a fact she had to leave.

Maybe she would stay with Nae-Nae long enough to give her job two weeks notice and then go to Chicago, move in with her mother and plan her life from there.

As Britt's words screamed in her mind, Yuri's head throbbed. She turned and looked at him. He was sitting on the edge of the bed, his eyes pleading with her to calm down.

She swallowed and walked over to him slowly. She wasn't sure if her feet were moving; all she knew was that she was getting closer to him. She stood before him and tears clouded her eyes, yet she could see a blurred vision of his face. She sniffed as she squinted, bit down on her bottom lip, and then proceeded to smack the shit out of him. Immediately after she slapped him she began fighting him as if she'd been waiting on this tussle all of her life. As if she was warring against life, love, and everything fucked up in the world.

"Yuri." Britt held her by both arms so that she would stop punching him. "Hold it." He swayed back. "Listen to me." He shook her. "Listen to me! Stop fucking hitting me and listen! I'm sorry!"

Yuri was able to free one of her hands and smack him again. She looked at him and screamed in his face. The type of scream that translated to mean you'd been in pain for years. The type of scream that asked why a thousand times over and over again.

Britt gained control of Yuri's free hand and squeezed her tighter.

She hated that she couldn't move; now along with her soul her body was paralyzed. Tears poured like a river down her face and snot clogged and oozed from her nose at the same time. "I kept asking you if you wanted me to leave." Her voice ached, her body ached, and her head ached. "I told you I wanted to leave. I would've been okay had you agreed that I leave then . . . back then . . . at that time . . . when I wasn't so caught up, when I had control over my life . . . I woulda been okay . . . but now—now, I'ma mess." Tears poured from her eyes. "I don't know what to do. I don't know who I am. I'm lost. Where"—tears were now blinding her—"where do I go from here? What do I do now?"

"I love you—I love you—I love you—I'm sorry—I'm sorry—I'm sorry—I love you—I love you—I love you—I'm sorry—I'm sorry—I'm sorry . . ." Britt said it over and over again. He said it so much, he began to sound like a scratched CD stuck on repeat. He knew he'd more than fucked up this time. This time he'd gone too far. He didn't know what to say, he didn't know what to do, all he knew was that he wasn't letting Yuri leave because if she did he knew she wasn't coming back. "You ain't going no fuckin' where, Yuri. We gon' work through this. I don't know what she said but I promise you I ain't fuck her. And I don't love her. I don't love nobody but you. I never loved nobody like I love you. I'm here and I want you. Please don't leave, baby, what I'ma do if you go? I'm so, so sorry."

"Well sometimes, Britt"—Yuri relaxed her shoulders, as he released her from his embrace—"sorry ain't good enough."

"You ain't leaving." He pulled up a chair and blocked the path. "I don't give a damn you say, nah. You mad right now, but you gon' chill the fuck out. This is about us, me and you. We'll camp out in this motherfucker until you get it together. So you may as well sit down." He reached over to the stand that sat next to his entranceway and lit a cigar.

Yuri stood there for a moment and looked at Britt. Confusion started to set in and then she remembered that she was pregnant and maybe she needed to see if they had anything left worth saving. But then she thought about how tired she was and how she just couldn't do it anymore. She needed some time. Some time away from this. All of this was simply too much. She sat down on the edge of the bed and looked straight ahead out the window at the moonlight.

Britt stared at Yuri and studied her beauty. And he studied why he'd fucked up. What in the hell possessed him to kick it, even in the slightest fashion, to Troi? He didn't love her and he knew Yuri would never believe that, especially after the way he acted and the way he spat knives at her from deep in his throat. Damn, he meant to slice her jugular but he didn't mean for the shit to twirl and enter her heart.

He wanted to scream, but he couldn't; all he could do was sit there in the chair blocking the way to an inevitable good-bye, with his legs gapped open, his arms locked behind his neck, and his dreads swaying over his shoulders.

What was he thinking, to fuck up like this? He knew he loved Yuri. He loved everything about her, her smile, the way one cheek sat slightly higher than the other when something was really funny to her. The way her lips folded into her mouth when she was surprised, and the way her mouth curled just a little on the right side when she was about to cry. And she was so pretty, and yeah she had the bomb pussy but now when he fucked her, he didn't just fuck her because her body turned him on, he made love to her because of how she made him feel. Like he was king of the fuckin' world. He knew that she was the type of chick that even if he lived in the projects she would make it feel like a mansion and here he'd ruined it all, in one sweep, one silly-ass night where he stayed out, lay next to Troi with all the intentions in the world to do her, only for her to take her clothes off and for he and his soft dick to realize that he didn't want anybody but Yuri.

Britt walked over to Yuri and stood between her legs. He could look in her eyes and tell she still loved him. The only thing missing from her glare was a second chance. He didn't want to say anything because he knew his words weren't having any effect, so he figured he would try this: running his hands through her hair, kissing her, caressing her and holding her tightly. He knew his hold was too unyielding but he needed her to understand how much he loved her and that he was never letting her go.

Yuri knew he was trying to tell her he loved her by the way he was kissing her. His tongue was speaking a language all its own as it licked a trail down her neck, over her breast and to her sweetness. He pulled her pants off. "I love you so fuckin' much," he said as he spread her legs, "I can't let you leave. Because then what I'ma do?" He sucked her pussy soft and slow and then fast and hard. With every thought he had he stroked his tongue and the faster he moved the wetter she became and the more he said I love you.

Yuri didn't even fight off the urge to scream. She simply let it all out, especially since this would be the last time they made love so intensely.

After she came Britt took off her blouse and nursed her swollen nipples.

Yuri wrapped her arms around his neck as she looked in his face. His eyes were filled with tears, but he never let one slip. Her mind combed through the thousand memories they shared, from the first time they made love, to the last time he made her laugh. She thought of all the good times and the bad all while feeling his dick cry out to her.

As Britt made love to Yuri he didn't know if he wanted to go fast or slow or both. So he rotated the movement. Yet his strokes were always long and deep. Intense and with precision. Neither one of them had ever felt like this. His body was begging her to stay and hers was fighting to go.

"Don't go, baby," he whispered in her ear. They were both rocking and she was crying. As each tear fell he kissed it off her face. "I won't be able to breathe if you leave me." His voice was extremely low, yet firm as he spoke. "I need you Yuri. I need you to breathe." He held her with such intensity that he was sure his fingers made bruises on her back.

Yuri attempted to push him over so she could ride him, but he held her down. "Stay here."

Their bodies made the most engaging music either of them had ever heard; it was better than Miles Davis, Duke Ellington, Billie Holiday and Nina Simone all put together. The sound of their bodies tussling with one another, him entering her over and over again. And the sound of her cumming all over his dick. The sound was so magical that anyone listening would swear they'd captured the essence of love.

As Britt felt his nut about to rush and Yuri felt her pelvis begin to contract they held each other and they both came while he pressed his face against hers, causing her tears to slide against his cheeks as he whispered her name.

Britt rolled to the back of Yuri where he kissed her from her shoulder to her tailbone. He held her tightly to his chest and buried his nose into her hair, as they both lay and eventually fell asleep.

Hours later the radio was playing Toni Braxton's "Another Sad Love Song" as Yuri crept out of the bed. She stepped quietly to the floor, slipped on a pair of jeans and grabbed one of his tee shirts and put it on. His smell lingered in it, but it was okay, besides she was pregnant so his smell wasn't all that she would be taking.

She grabbed her suitcase, slipped her shoes on and headed toward the door. "So that's it, huh?" poured over her shoulder, as she turned the knob. She could hear him breathing from across the room.

She refused to turn around. Turning around would've made her stay, his eyes would've persuaded her and that's not what she wanted; she needed this, she needed to leave.

"Yo' my man, I love you. And I don't want you to go. Don't go, baby, please don't go."

Yuri turned the doorknob an inch more, the lock slowly folding back. She opened the door slightly and placed her hand in the crack.

"Yo' my man, you leaving me?"

Yuri didn't say a word, instead she opened the door and walked out.

Drae

The scent of jasmine and the sensual beats of Apollonia welcomed Drae to the home she once shared with Hassan. This was the first time she'd been here and realized it was a stage. A movie of sorts, an impromptu blue script that unfolded over and over again. Some takes better than others, but nevertheless the film kept rolling: from her showers to the secret times she played with her pussy and rode the retractable pole she thought was for her husband's eyes only. All the times she sucked her cream off his dick . . . and the auditions. The auditions. The auditions were the worst; everyone knew but her. The actors . . . Hassan . . . everyone knew and here she thought they were secretly being freaky.

The shock of being a famous porn star had given

Drae a headache. All she could hear was Naz saying, I thought *you knew*— How didn't you know? I thought *you knew*— How didn't you know? *I thought you knew!* It was like a broken record, an echo that pumped in and out of her mind. As soon as she thought she'd forgotten about it, it came back with a vengeance, *I thought you knew*. Wretched whore, stupid bitch, dumb-ass slut. Everything she could think of, she was. A porn star. A fuckin' porn star named Sunshine. With a pussy that people came from miles and miles to get up in. She'd become the Beyoncé of the underground world, a rising staple. She didn't even know, until she saw the jacket for her latest DVD, that she was this year's XRCO, AVN, and Eroticline awards winner for best oral performer, best rider, best actress and most creative techniques. And no one even cared that she didn't show up for the ceremony, it just added to the mystery of it all.

It was like walking into someone else's life. She thought she'd traded places with an impersonator. It was all too much in one day. And now here she stood, not knowing who she was or what she was doing. Was she being taped now? There were recessed lights all around, and she didn't know which ones contained cameras. Her life was over, she just didn't know if she should surrender her soul at this moment or after she sliced Hassan's throat.

For the first time since they'd moved here, Drae noticed that the wooden floors creaked. So she did what she could to quietly tiptoe through the house.

As she walked through the dining room, she saw two plates of half-eaten salmon and salad, a basket of bread, two candles that were burned almost to the last of their wick and an empty bottle of wine. Confirming for her that not only was Hassan here, but his bitch was too. It had crossed her mind to say "To hell with it," walk out the door and never come back. But how could she do that? She'd given everything to this man and he had to pay for what he'd done. She grabbed the butcher knife and was prepared to go to work on Hassan's ass. If there was a price to pay for chopping him up, she'd have to worry about it later, but for now all she wanted was to see blood.

As Drae approached the bedroom, she could hear moans and the bed squeaking. She took a deep breath and kicked the door open. "You motherfucker!" she screamed, as Hassan lay on his back with a woman—Crystal—galloping backward on his dick with her extremely large titties flopping in the air.

Immediately the woman's eyes popped open and she looked at Drae.

"Drae!!!" Hassan yelled as she ran toward the bed waving the butcher knife in the air as if she were flying a kite. Yet before she could bring the knife down on Hassan, the girl attacked her, knocking her to the floor and causing the knife to slide across the room.

Drae started defending herself with everything she had. Punching, kicking, biting and swinging as if she'd been professionally trained. "It's over, Hassan!" She pounded the woman on the head. "I don't believe this shit!" she screamed.

"Get offa her!" Hassan yanked the woman who'd been riding his dick away from Drae, and threw her into the wall.

"You fuckin' crazy!" the woman screamed.

As Drae stood up straight, breathing as if her lungs were being snatched out, she looked up at the woman, who was pressed against the wall. And as if Drae's eyes were controlled by a fast-forward button, they darted from Hassan to this chick, over and over again. She couldn't stop, something was wrong. Something had to be wrong. Why did this chick pinned against the wall have a dick? A dick. Slowly Drae's vision went blurry and, like a slithering snake, she withered to the floor and passed out. When she came to, the chick was gone and Hassan was standing there with a gun pointed in her face.

"What the fuck you doing here, Drae?" He kicked her in the side. "You gon' embarrass me in front of my friends?! Do you know how that felt?!"

"Your friends?!" Drae screamed. "You were fucking a niggah! A man! He was riding your dick with his ass! Oh my God, you been fucking men all this time?!"

He kicked her in the side. "You don't know what I've been doing! 'Cause you left me! Left me all alone, knowing you owed me. Knowing that you were supposed to stay with me no matter what!" He continued to kick her.

"Stop kicking me, you fucking faggot!" she spat. "I can't believe you're a fuckin' faggot!"

Hassan started kicking Drae over and over again, and she could feel her skin burst open. "Aww!" she cried, her voice filled with pain. "Get off me!" she screamed. Hassan took his foot and kicked her again. She could feel blood dripping, but didn't know from where.

"Apologize, bitch!" He waved the gun.

"I'm not apologizing for shit! You ruined my life. How did you think I wouldn't find out, Hassan?! Huh? How did you think I wouldn't find out that you've been selling porn tapes of me! You made me a fuckin' porn star, some bitch named Sunshine; you didn't care shit about me. I wasn't shit to you but a high-class piece of pussy! A porn star, Hassan . . . Oh . . . my . . . God!"

Hassan looked stunned for a moment, and then he snatched her off the floor by her hair. "What you need to be doing is thanking me, bitch! So you found out," he chuckled. "Well then, good, you can be about your fuckin' business and I won't have to keep cartin' these motherfuckers in here as if it's nothing. I made somethin' outta you. You wasn't shit, do you know that? You were nothing, and if it weren't for me you still wouldn't be shit!"

Tears poured down Drae's face as she gave a hard snort and gathered what felt like an abundance of spit, hauled off and skeeted it directly into Hassan's face.

"You spit on me, bitch?!" He wiped it off his face with the back of his hand. He cocked his gun and pointed it to her head. "I got one bullet in this motherfucker and you 'bout to be buried with it!" He pulled the trigger, the gun went off and, although she felt like she was bound to die, she was still alive. There was no bullet in that shot.

Within an instant Drae started throwing up. "Please stop!" she cried and gagged at the same time. "I can't believe this is happening to me. I have to get away from you!"

"You ain't going nowhere, bitch!" He cocked the gun again. "You gon' leave me, Drae?"

The room was practically silent and the only sound that could be heard besides Hassan's heavy breathing was the vomit thrusting between Drae's lips onto the floor. "Talk, bitch!" He yanked her head back, her vomit pouring down the front of her clothing. "You leaving me?!"

Silence.

"Answer me!"

"No—" she screamed.

"No, what?!"

"I'm not—I'm not leaving you."

"I didn't think so!" He kissed her roughly on the cheek. "Now apologize, bitch!"

"I'm sorry," she mumbled.

"Say it louder!"

"I'm sorry."

"I know you are." He started pushing her head down toward his crotch.

"No, Hassan," she cried.

"Bitch, don't tell me no!" He pointed the gun at her head. "Now suck this dick! Eat that niggah ass and apologize while you at it!"

As he held the gun in one hand while unzipping his pants and taking out his dick with the other, he rubbed Drae's face in his crotch, before smacking her across the face with his dick. "Think you so fuckin' stand-up? Huh, bitch? Think you leaving me? Think you ain't doing no more fuckin' pornos? You owe me, bitch." He tried to smack her in the face again with his dick but she turned away.

"Oh you tryna get away?" Hassan, still holding the gun in his hand took his dick, aimed and pissed all over Drae. The pee ran like water down her face, over her body and onto the floor. "The next time I tell you"—he picked her up by the hair—"to suck this dick, you better be on your job, bitch!" As he thrust her face onto his shaft, she hauled off and bit him so hard that the splitting skin around his pubic bone left blood on her lips.

Instantly the gun went off and Hassan tumbled to the floor inches away from falling on top of her.

Drae was moving so fast she didn't know she'd been shot. All she could see and feel was the flowing blood pouring from her shoulder and the burning sensation racing through her arm.

Since standing up would've taken too much time she crawled toward the door, and fled down the stairs.

Once she reached the bottom, she ran into the kitchen and looked around. She wanted to run toward the front door, then she saw the patio doors and the lanai lights from the neighbor's house shining through. As she started to run she felt Hassan grabbing her into a choke hold; instantly she started to gag. "Jesus! Please, Jesus! Please stop!" The more she yelled stop, the tighter his hold became.

"I'ma kill you!" As she started to think of how she could whither away and die, she felt strands of hair falling like snow over her face; that's when she heard the sound of the scissors. "Oh my God!" She held her hands up to feel the crown of her head, and as she did, the scissors chopped pieces of skin from across her left knuckles. "Argh!" she pulled her hands down and blood splashed onto the floor. "My hair! Hassan, please stop! Hassan, please! Don't cut my hair!"

"Shut up!" Hassan screamed. "You leaving me, Drae?! Huh? You leaving me?! If I can't have you, nobody will!"

The neighbor's lights, which continued to sparkle, created red, green and yellow hues across the room and illuminated an empty bottle of Hennessy on the kitchen counter. Instantly Drae reached back, grabbed it and hit Hassan with it. She didn't quite know where it landed, but she was thankful for any damage it was able to do.

"Aw shit!" Hassan screamed as the glass bottle exploded.

He flung Drae against the patio doors, causing the glass to shatter and shower over her body like a sheet of crumbling hail.

"Sunshine!" Crystal screamed as Drae's body fell in slow motion to the ground. "I'm sorry, Sunshine! I didn't believe him when he said you didn't know." As she cried, the police bolted into the house. "I'm so, so sorry."

Drae

Drae lifted the white hospital sheet wrapped around her thighs. She wiped the crust from the sides of her mouth and looked around her hospital room. She'd been here for a week and today, for the first time since she'd been here, she awakened all alone. None of her friends were there, and Naz had long since gone home.

She tried to sit up but the I.V. in her right hand prevented her from moving far. *I'm fucked up,* she thought, now looking at her left hand and noticing how the stitches ran across her knuckles like railroad tracks.

Tears flooded her eyes. She flung her head back and looked at the ceiling. She thought about praying, but quickly changed her mind because she couldn't think of what to say. *Am I supposed to say thank you?* she thought.

But thank you for what? Hell, maybe I should just start off with Amen. How about that? Yeah that's it. Amen.

Drae fluffed the pillows under her head as best she could. For a moment, she thought about going to a million different places to live. She figured she would stay with Nae-Nae until she decided where she would go.

"Wassup, ma'?" Naz walked in the room, kissed her on the forehead and sat on the bed. "You look so pretty."

"Stop lying," she laughed. "I look ridiculous."

"So what you been thinking about?" he asked her, stroking her cheek.

"Why couldn't we meet under different circumstances?"

"Wasn't meant to be that way."

"But I care about you so much," she cried.

"It's good, ma', I care about you too."

"You don't understand, Naz."

"What's to understand?" He wiped her tears away.

"I can't see you anymore. You know I have to get away."

"I'm a big boy, baby, I can handle it. We talked about this already, remember?"

"I don't really wanna leave you."

"You gon' come back." He smiled. "And come back sexy-ass shit, don't go off nowhere and be all fat, unrecognizable and shit."

Drae laughed. "I just need to get away, for me, my sake. And I have to let anything that I have from this life go."

"It's cool, ma'." He kissed her on the forehead again. "Naz understands." He rose from the bed. "Look, I'm not gon' keep you too long. It was real while it lasted."

After she watched him leave, Drae turned to the side and cried out what felt like every ounce of her soul. Just as she wiped her eyes and wondered if she should change her mind, she heard footsteps entering her room. "Andrea?"

She turned over and saw it was the transvestite that saved her life. "Please don't be scared."

"You saved my life, I could never be scared of you."

"I've been thinking about you for the last week, and I think I have something that belongs to you."

"What's that?"

"Everything. Hassan told me everything. You need to know that Sunshine is not just a porn name, but it's an overseas empire. It goes beyond movies: there are dildos, erotic mouths, wax pussy imprints, blow-up dolls . . . and then there's the lingerie, the leather, chains, whips, candy, chocolate and crotchless underwear, lotions, jellies and condoms called 'Exclusively for Sunshine's Pussy.' It's a multimillion-dollar industry. Here is all the paperwork you'll need. Get you an attorney and take him for everything he's got."

"Why are you doing all of this?"

"Because it could be me lying there in that bed, and I feel I owe it to you. Besides," he smiled, "I have his three-million-dollar stash, so I'm okay."

"Thank you, Crystal. Thank you."

Drae

"Good morning!" The Wake Up Club belted through the radio as Drae turned over in her bed. It'd been a week since she was released from the hospital and had returned to the scene where she'd been robbed of herself. She sat straight up in bed and decided today was the day she would choose for it to all end. All the pain, the crying, the suffering and the never-ending questioning why: Why didn't she see? Why didn't she know? Why didn't she leave a thousand times before? Why? Why? Why? Well, fuck why! Why hadn't done shit for her but cause her a bunch of grief. So here she was, looking around a multi-million-dollar pornographic Broadway wondering when it would be okay to not give a fuck anymore.

Drae opened up a new bar of Lever soap and stepped

into the shower. After ten minutes of bathing her skin, she was out and dressed in a new pair of formfitting Norma Kamali jeans, a sleeveless cow-neck sweater and navy stilettos. She grabbed her hobo Coach bag, picked up the keys to the brand-new white Mustang convertible she'd purchased the day before and walked out the door.

She threw her purse and a suitcase she'd packed in the Mustang's backseat and slipped into the front. The early-morning sun was gleaming as she put the top down and started the engine running. She stared at the house that she became a star in before blowing it a kiss and yelling, "Take that and kiss my ass with it, Sunshine!" Finally the fat lady had sung, and it was time to take a bow.

Watching everything get smaller behind her, Drae took off and headed west. She had no particular destination in mind, other than a place to get away to. Somewhere she could breathe and cry and scream, and no one would know why . . . and no one would care to know why. Somewhere she could rock her new honey-colored bob like a fierce top model and no one would ever know she worked it because her husband had cut all her hair off. And she could lie and say that the railroad tracks, running across her knuckles, were from botched stitches she got as a kid, and no one would ever think they were from her getting her ass kicked.

Everything was official and it was time to let it go. There was no Hassan, there was no Sunshine, there was simply Andrea Shaw, ex-porn star, and now was the time to take charge of her life.

Drae slid her round-eyed Gucci shades on, leaned back, gripped the wheel and raced up the highway headed for the sunset. . . .

Britt

Britt couldn't believe what he was seeing: Billboard had his self-entitled CD at the top of the charts, and the acclaimed dancehall artist, Lady Saw, who he was able to sign on his imprint, was climbing the charts right behind him. *Rolling Stone* had contacted him for an interview, one of the first of this kind. He was scheduled to be on the cover of every major magazine, and his agent had him booked on BET, MTV VH1 Soul, and a zillion other cable shows. He was even booked for *Good Morning America, The View,* the *Late Show with David Letterman.* Finally he was taking off, and he couldn't wait to go home and celebrate. He had a special bag of weed for this occasion and along with that, he had a four hundred dollar bottle of vintage wine. There was only one person in the world who would feel what he felt about his success and he couldn't wait to bust through his front door and bellow out that he'd finally made it. Finally, after all this time, he'd arrived.

Once he parked his truck in the garage he practically fell, skipping the elevator and rushing up the stairs, taking them two at a time, all while singing his favorite cut from his CD.

When he stepped to the door, he noticed how quiet everything was on the inside, but he quickly dismissed it. He turned the knob and the door flew open, "Yuri!" he yelled, "Yo, my man . . ." his words began to fade. He walked around his loft, looking for absolutely nothing. He remembered that Yuri wasn't there. She was gone and there was nothing left for him to do other than deal with it. And he did, at least until today. He dealt with her not being there by keeping himself busy, by recording enough tracks and writing enough songs to fill a thousand CDs. He'd even written songs for other artists and not just reggae or soca; he'd written R&B and jazz tunes and even recorded a song with Jay-Z where he laid the hook. But now, today, at this very moment there was nothing left to do but face what he was: alone and in pain. He missed his lover, his best friend and his soul mate. His everything. He sat down on his piano bench, lifted the cover to the keys and began playing a song. Any song, some song, he didn't know what it was until he realized he'd been playing "The Sweetest Taboo" . . . "*Sometimes,*" he sang in a whisper, "*I think you're just too good for me . . .*" As the tears filled his throat he started banging his fingers on the keys, each key crying out in a loud thud sound. Britt held his head down and for the first time since Yuri left, he cried, and he cried, until he couldn't cry anymore. He cried until all he could do was get up from the piano, turn on Sade's CD and set "The Sweetest Taboo" on repeat. Then he lay back on his bed, lit a blunt and sang the song so low it was almost incoherent. "*There's a quiet storm and it never felt this hot before* . . ." Britt sang, cried, and got high until all he could do was close his eyes and eventually fall asleep.

When he awoke hours later his doorbell was ringing. He hopped out of bed, praying that it was Yuri but somehow knowing in his heart of hearts that it wasn't. As he approached the door, the bell rang again.

He opened the door and Troi was standing there with the Billboard list in her hand and a bottle of champagne. Britt looked down at his watch; it read ten P.M.

"Britt!" Troi screamed, "I can't believe it! Congratulations! I'm so proud of you!" She jumped up and hugged him around the neck.

He pushed her off of him, "If you don't step the fuck away from me, I swear to God I'ma fuckin' hurt you!"

"Britt," Troi said in disbelief, "are you"—she sniffed—"high?"

"Nah. This is the clearest I've ever been, because right now at this moment I get it. I really fuckin' get it. I fucked up my life for nothing. I didn't love you."

"Excuse me? You came back for me."

"Nah," he said as if a lightbulb had just gone off, "I didn't. I didn't love you. I didn't want you. I was just scared, scared to love somebody the way that I loved Yuri and now I get it. I have to find her."

"You love Yuri?"

"Yes"—he smiled—"I do and I gotta find her. I gotta go and get her." He went back inside and grabbed his keys and then returned to the door.

Troi's mouth was dropped open. "Oh now you think you love Yuri. You always did like to dream."

"Yo for real, keep her name outcha mouth. She too fuckin' good for you to even call. You too fuckin' grimy and I know you tried to make her think we slept together, when we didn't. But it's cool, 'cause the only way for me to really show you is not to cuss you out, but it's to let you watch me lock my fuckin' door and go get my wife."

"I don't believe this."

"And by the way," he said as he turned to leave, "don't ever again say shit to me." Then he hit her with the peace sign and walked out the door.

Hassan

Hassan sat in his isolated jail cell in what appeared to be complete and utter silence. His eyes danced across the room and his dick constantly rested in his hands. But inside everything was screaming. There was too much noise, which is why he couldn't speak. People were always talking to him, telling him what to do, how to act, and that he needed to kill Drae. That if he ever got from between these cement walls, he needed to slice her throat and then kill himself. It would be classic and everyone would understand that if he couldn't have her no one could. And who would care that he liked men, because he loved her and there was no way he could let her go.

He lay back on his bunk and stared at the ceiling. He

was due to be sentenced today, yet in his mind he'd served his time. He knew the judge refused to give him bail and that he'd been charged with two crimes, but attempted murder was the only one he could remember.

All of his assets were frozen, because his lawyer told him that Drae was suing him for divorce and wanted all of his money. And that was the only day anyone in the prison other than the people locked in his brain heard him speak: "I'ma . . . kill . . . that . . . bitch!" After that he said nothing and neither did they. They all sat in silence looking at him, wondering if he even knew what the fuck was going on.

Three guards dressed in riot gear came to get Hassan from his cell. They made him stand against the bars for handcuffs and shackles. One of the guards, who wore white rubber gloves, shoved his dick back in his orange jumpsuit. And Hassan's face lit up as he imagined the guard who'd just tucked his dick away fucking Drae.

Once they were at the court and Hassan stood before the judge, he had intentions of speaking, but the judge interrupted him. "Mr. Shaw, please stand. Do you have anything you wish to say to the court?"

Hassan stood as best he could given his hands were still cuffed behind his back and his feet were shackled together. "Wassup?" he said inside his head, but no one on the outside heard him.

"Mr. Shaw," the judge repeated, "Do you have anything to say?"

"Check this"—no one could hear Hassan but himself—"this bitch who was nothing when I saved her, fucked me over and now I'm in here. So peep this, I'm paid as hell so, I'ma hit you off with some dough, you let me out and then I can kill this bitch. You know what I'm saying?"

The judge stared at Hassan, whose eyes danced all over the court room. His facial expressions changed but nothing came out of his mouth. It was obvious that he was off in another world someplace where nobody else wanted to be.

"On the charge," the judge began to speak, "of attempted murder I sentence you to twenty years. No possibility of parole. On the charge of exploitation I sentence you to ten years. No possibility of parole. Both sentences must run concurrently and based on the prison's psychiatric reports and evaluation your time will be served at Fishkill Correctional Facility." And he slammed his gavel.

"I was still talking motherfucker!" Hassan screamed but nobody heard him. He started banging his head on the table, over and over again, until his skin burst open and there was blood everywhere. It took about five guards to take him out and all the way to the hospital for treatment as he screamed in silence.

later

Is It a Crime Loving
You the Way that I Do?

Drae

The heels of Drae's stilettos clapped against the concrete as she walked through midtown, headed for the courthouse. Drae was so fierce that her flawless beauty rocked the autumn breeze and cut through the morning air like a .350 Magnum. As she passed by a mirrored high-rise she checked her reflection and prepared herself for the last time she would have to see Hassan.

It'd been a little over a year since she left New York and headed for someplace, anyplace, to start her life all over again: Chicago, L.A., Phoenix, Atlanta, Charlotte, Seattle, Columbia, Charleston and Prince George's County, Maryland. She felt like a runaway slave going from state to state aiming for the great escape, only to get up north and realize there was no promised land. It was simply dressed-up shit and no matter where she went, there was no place she could outrun herself. And now it was time she dealt with who she was: Andrea Shaw—former porn star.

"Drae," Nae-Nae called as he and Raphael met her on the stairs of the courthouse. Finally, they had worked their problems out and shared custody of the twins with Freeda. They greeted one another with kisses on each cheek before going inside. Today was the day the judge would render his decision on Drae's divorce settlement.

As they sat in the court's vestibule, waiting for her case to be called, Nae-Nae said, "How much you think we gon' get for your pussy today?"

"What?"

"Well . . . don't get offended, homegirl, this is business. I got a vision."

"What, Nae-Nae?"

"Check it out: You could open a brothel and turn all these motherfuckers out!"

"I will smack the shit outta you!"

Before Nae-Nae could go on, Drae's attorney motioned for them to come inside.

Hassan was handcuffed and shackled to the chair and his attorney stood next to him. He'd been sentenced to twenty years in prison for attempted murder and, although this was a divorce hearing, it was a requirement of the psychiatric prison he was in that he not be allowed to get up.

"All rise," the bailiff said as the judge took the bench.

"It has taken well over a year," the judge began to speak, "since this motion was first filed and the defendant has fought this divorce tooth and nail. However, it is the judgment of the court to grant Ms. Shaw the petition of divorce. I am giving her ownership of the name *Sunshine* and its empire. The DVDs are to be removed from the shelves and destroyed immediately. All four of the houses have been granted to Ms. Shaw, the joint accounts, the CDs and twenty million dollars in stocks and bonds. The divorce has hereby been granted under the previously stated conditions. Court dismissed." The judge banged his gavel.

Drae couldn't believe it. Her knees were so weak that all she could do was hold her head down and cry. Finally her nightmare was over and she was free to start again.

"Stop crying." Nae-Nae walked over to her.

Before Drae could answer she had one last thing she wanted to do. She walked over toward Hassan.

"Yes?" the officer asked.

"Can I say something to him?"

"Go ahead," the officer said, "but don't get too close."

"At first I thought I would hate you. I wanted to. I wanted to hate you because of what you did to me. But after spending months and months running from myself, I realized that you did the best thing for me, which was help me to free myself. I didn't need you or anybody else to secure me and make my life happy for me. All I needed was me. Ain't that some shit? I needed me. And I was here all the time. And the money, the unwanted fame and fortune is simply . . . a sweet taboo."

Hassan sat still and stared at Drae. He thought about spitting on her, but then he changed his mind and looked her up and down, wondering why he hadn't killed her when he had the chance. He looked at the officer. "I'm ready to go." The officers stood him up and his shackles dragged across the floor as he headed toward the back of the court.

"Fuck that niggah!" Nae-Nae spat. "We rich now, where us gon' live?!"

"Excuse me," an unfamiliar voice poured in their direction. When Drae looked up, she saw it was Crystal.

"I'm not here for no trouble," she said, almost in a whisper. "I just wanted to see Hassan get his just due."

Drae walked over to her. "Thank you. Thank you so much for caring enough to tell me the truth."

After they hugged, Drae said, "I want to give you some money. Please give me your number so I can come see you. You really didn't have to do this."

"Don't you give me anything, you hear me? The pain he has caused you, this money will never be enough. You, worry about you, 'cause believe me, Crystal is hooked up." She winked at Nae-Nae and walked away.

Drae looked at Nae-Nae. It was a good thing Raphael had stepped away to go to the bathroom, "I will kick yo' fuckin' ass!"

"I didn't do nothin'. Somebody wink they fuckin' eye and all of a sudden Nae-Nae fuckin' him. Shit, it's more to my life than dick."

"Really?" Raphael walked up and placed his hand on his hip. "Don't start no shit, Nae-Nae."

Drae could do nothing but smile. "I need to call Yuri." Drae called Yuri from her cell phone. "It's almost over." She cried tears of joy. "It's almost over."

"What do you mean it's almost over?" Yuri asked.

" 'Cause I got one more thing I need to do . . ."

"What?"

"Aren't you nosy? Just know that I do." She hung up. "Look," she said to Raphael and Nae-Nae. "Go pick out a house or something and call me with the price. I got somebody I need to see."

"Oh shit, she buying houses. I did tell you, you were the twins' godmother, right? I'll call Yuri and tell her I changed my mind about her, she too goddamn broke. I'm swinging with you. Can I get me a mansion next to 50 Cent?"

"Raphael, make sure he doesn't get carried away." Drae laughed.

"You got it, girl."

"I swear pussies is always hatin' on Nae-Nae. And see I'm 'bout to hook you up."

"With what?" Drae asked.

"Check it out. Homeboy," he said as they headed out of the courthouse, "who you're looking for is not at Fantasy Island anymore."

"How do you know?"

" 'Cause he came to my house to hook up a phone, and now I got ten lines in my house."

"You a mess, Nae-Nae."

"Go to the office, someone should be able to tell you what route he's on."

• • •

Drae took Nae-Nae's advice and went to the Verizon office. The receptionist knew she wasn't suppose to tell but once Drae slipped her two hundred dollars, she all but told how much money he made.

As soon as she pulled up on the corner of Morningside she spotted him. "Somebody told me," Drae said, as she pulled alongside of a Verizon truck, "that this fine niggah named Nasty Naz worked here and I just wanted to know if you'd seen him."

"Naw, not since I left the strip club have I seen that niggah, but I have seen a Nasir."

"Really and where is he?"

"You lookin' at the one and only. You know what?" He stood staring at her with his worn jeans, sagging just right, his tight, fitted Verizon tee clinging to him, and his tool belt hanging to the side. "You look just like this chick named Sunshine."

"Well I'm sorry to disappoint you but Sunshine doesn't exist anymore. All I know is Drae."

"Uhmmm," he looked her up and down. "Well shit, Drae, you kinda fly and since you standing here and neither one of us seems to have found the people we use' to know, why don't we try and get to know each other?"

She blushed and held her hand out. "I'm Andrea, but everyone calls me Drae."

"And I'm Nasir." He pulled her close by the waist.

"Nice to meet you." Drae smiled.

"Well look. It's almost time for my lunch. Are you hungry?"

"I sure am."

He pressed his lips against hers. "Then let's go get something to eat."

"Yeah, let's do that," she said as she responded to his kiss, "let's do that."

Yuri

It was the middle of fall and the Windy City was living up to its name. Yuri stood on a busy corner of Michigan Avenue waiting for the light to change. Her rust-colored trench coat blew open, revealing the Similac stain running down her chocolate-brown Lauren dress pants. She tapped the heels of her stilettos and quickly wondered why she didn't stop long enough to change into her running Nikes. Her mother had warned her about picking up the baby and not making herself comfortable on the commute home, and now it seemed she was paying for not listening. She'd already missed the bus headed toward her duplex and now she either had to wait twenty minutes for the next one or catch a cab—and the fact that she had to pee real bad didn't help her situation any. This was one time she wished she'd driven her car instead of leaving it at home.

Pushing her baby bag to one shoulder, she decided catching a cab was the quickest way to get home. She held the baby on one hip and proceeded to run across the street, hoping to hail the cab she saw coming.

"Goodness," Yuri sighed as she reached her destination. She was breathing as if she'd been in a marathon. "Little girl," she said, looking at her ten-month-old daughter. "You are soooooo heavy."

The baby, who wore two curly ponytails and was the spitting image of her father, smiled and started to coo.

"Where to?" the cabdriver asked Yuri as she opened the door and quickly slid the baby onto the backseat. "Seven seventy-seven Grandview Court." As she placed her bags on the taxi's floor, a familiar voice poured over her shoulder.

"Yo, my man."

Immediately tears she thought she'd learned to live without beat against the back of her eyes like a drum. Her heart sank to the bottom of her stomach in never-ending pieces and her hands began to shake. She bit her lip, closed her eyes and fought off the desire to turn around. After taking deep breaths and praying to keep her composure, she opened her eyes and decided she would ease into the backseat and somehow shut the door without ever looking up and confirming that it was actually Britt somehow standing there.

"I get it now," he began to speak again, her back still turned to him. "I understand how bad I fucked up."

She stood silent, holding the cab's door open and looking at the baby coo, while sucking the side of her fist.

"I've spent over a year begging Nae-Nae to please tell me

where you were and he wouldn't. Not until I came to his house every night for a month straight, sat on his couch and refused to move, did Raphael give me the address. He thought me and Nae-Nae were trying to have an affair. Man, you shoulda been there, Nae-Nae lit our asses up. He said child support was causing him enough damn problems and he didn't need my beggin' ass adding to 'em. Then he turned around and told Raphael he was sick of pussies always hatin'. I know you wanna laugh, ma'.'" She could hear a lump trembling in his voice. "Ya boy was on his knees like please—please—please. Who woulda ever thought I would beg? Here I am gettin' nonstop radio play, selling CDs like crazy and I'm begging. And I didn't give a fuck either, pride didn't mean shit. I wanted you, I needed you and I was gon' find you even if it was the last thing I did. I didn't even bring no change of clothes, I didn't pack no bag, nothing. I didn't even book a hotel room. All I brought was a one-way ticket, a broken heart and a chance. I called your mother this afternoon. . . . And I could tell by the sound of her voice that moms was not feeling my ass, *humph* . . . but I can't blame her. But she did tell me we needed to see beyond ourselves and how we feel because there were some things we needed to talk about."

Yuri's face was completely covered in tears. The cabdriver sat waiting as the meter continued to run. "Miss, are we going anywhere?"

"One minute, please," Yuri said to the driver.

"Yo, my man, I'ma mess," Britt went on. "I ain't never felt no shit like this in my life. I thought I knew what love was, but when you left and I realized that you weren't coming back, I got it. I fuckin' got it. And that's when I knew what love was. I ain't never loved nobody else. Ever. What I had for Troi wasn't even love. Love is you. You are love and I need you. Please, I can't get over you and I don't want to.

"For a few months, I was onstage and every night I was out there I was looking for you in the crowd, backstage, everywhere.... I was looking for you ... and looking for you ... and then it clicked I lost you. And I wondered what the fuck was I gon' do without you? Do you know how many times I came home wanting to tell you something funny, wanting to sing to you or hear you sing to me? Do you know how many times I wanted to make love to you? It was like for a while when I came home, I could still smell you and then, when the scent faded, I cried. Yo, my man, it was crazy.

"Yuri, please look at me, I'm out in the street. Ole dude looking like I'm 'bout to pay a hundred dollars for this cab. I'm in the middle of the fuckin' street in rush hour doing my damnedest to tell you I love you and this time I ain't letting you go."

"What?" Yuri turned around, her face flooded with tears. "You have sooooo much fuckin' nerve, you know that?"

"I know—but I love you,"

"You don't know how to love me!"

"Teach me."

"It was always about you, Britt. Always. Do you know how many nights I cried and cried and cried? You were my world, my best fuckin' friend! So you were hurt for a year and a half? I spent my entire life loving you, only for it to be reduced to shit. You were a better fantasy than reality, so do me a favor and go the fuck back where you came from."

"You don't mean that." Britt walked closer to the cab.

"Britt—" Yuri tried to block his path, but he politely stepped around her. "Thanks ... for ... waiting ... but ...

she'll . . . be . . . leaving . . ." He spoke slowly, his words sounding mechanical as he turned toward the backseat and spotted the baby. Staring at her was like looking at himself in a smaller package, with ponytails and diamond-stud earrings. For the first time in his life he felt motionless. Stunned. As if someone had stuck a pin in him and let all the air out of his lungs. He started counting the time and before he could guess how old the baby was, the day he asked Yuri if she was pregnant flashed across his mind.

He stood straight up and looked at Yuri. She knew he'd spotted the baby. Now she felt she had no choice but to deal with what she'd been running from.

"How old is she?" He took a step back.

"Why? How is that any of your fuckin' business?"

"Don't play with me, Yuri. I'm not in the goddamn mood. I haven't had a good night's sleep for the last year and a half. I been kissing Nae-Nae's ass trying to get to you, been accused by Raphael of being on the down low. I had a nightmare about you fucking another niggah. Your mother gave me her ass to kiss, yet she told me where to find you. I'm hungry, I'm pissed off, I'm out here with no clean clothes, no socks and not even a clean pair of drawers. And I'm standing here looking at my reflection, cooing at me, and you talking shit. Now I'ma ask you again, 'cause I'ma 'bout two seconds off yo' ass. Now, how old . . . is she and is that me?"

"You do the math, motherfucker, and quite frankly I really don't see why you would give a fuck." She slid into the cab. "Last time we spoke, Troi was in your bed and I was on your nerves—"

"This go-round I never slept with her, Yuri. I swear to God. I know you don't believe me, but I don't have a reason to lie. The only person I slept with was you." Britt's voice pleaded with her to know he was telling the truth. "I swear to God, I didn't."

"That doesn't mean shit to me."

"I love you, Yuri."

"Then love shoulda brought yo' ass home every night." Yuri attempted to close the door. As she grabbed the handle to pull the door, Britt jumped in the cab next to her. "I'm telling you the fuckin' truth! And I don't care if I have to beat in your damn head, you will believe me. Yes, I shoulda come home, but I didn't touch her ass. I promise you I didn't." He slid the cabdriver a hundred-dollar bill, and closed the door. "We cool. You can drive."

The driver looked in the rearview mirror at Yuri.

"Tell this niggah we cool."

"It's all right," Yuri assured the driver.

"Why didn't you tell me, Yuri? Damn," he said answering his own question. "I was that bad? You couldn't even talk to me? You were my best friend, man. Didn't you know that?"

"Was that before or after you told me to step?"

"I can't believe this. . . ." He paused. "Where did we get lost? We got a baby together. I don't care what you say, I know that's my baby," he said as he looked in the baby's face. He studied her eyes, which were round like full moons, her skin was like the sweetest chocolate anyone could ever have and her smile made his heart full. He leaned over and touched her curly ponytails as if he were checking to see if they were real. He wiped the drool from the sides of her mouth and kissed her.

"This is my baby?" he said, more as an amazed statement than a question.

"Yes," Yuri said quietly, "she is. . . ."

"Can I hold her?"

Yuri handed the baby to Britt.

"What's her name?" he asked.

"Bree . . ." Yuri started to cry uncontrollably. "Bree . . . Sanaa . . . Lake."

"You gave her my name? Little Miss Lake . . . Bree . . . Sanaa . . . Lake," he said as if he'd won a prize. He turned and looked at Yuri. "How you think I'm 'spose to stop loving you now?"

"I'm not going back to New York and I'm not taking my heart back to where it was . . ." As Yuri continued to speak her words turned into inaudible tears.

"Stop, Yuri," Britt said, taking the baby's hand and wiping Yuri's tears away. But Yuri couldn't help herself, she needed for him to understand how she felt.

"Shhh, stop." Britt brushed her with a kiss. "Can you give me another chance? Can you love me again?"

"But I'm scared," she said with her tears spilling onto his lips.

"Please don't be scared." He kissed her again. "I got you. . . . Now you have to show me how to do this."

"Do what?"

"Change a Pamper and move to Chicago."

"What you moving to Chicago for? You can be her father in New York."

"Yeah, but I don't wanna leave you. I wanna 'nother chance."

"I don't know about that."

"Why, Yuri?"

She didn't answer; instead, she picked up her things as the

cab pulled in front of her duplex. She took the baby out of his arms. "I'm not looking back." She hopped out of the cab and as rain started to pour she ran up on her stoop, opened her front door and slammed it.

Yuri stood at her front window and pulled the curtain back just enough to see him. She watched him step out of the cab and lean against it. She could tell he was trying to compose himself as he looked up and down the street. He tapped the back passenger door, said something to the cabby and, as the driver pulled off, Britt walked down the street. The raindrops seemed to get lost in the beauty of his dreads and the heartbreak of his walk. With every step he took, Yuri felt like forever had finally left and all that remained was the here and now.

As Britt faded into the elements, Yuri placed Bree in her high chair and fed her. Afterward, she looked out her front window and all she could see were the raindrops as they slid down the windowpane.

In between giving the baby a bath and laying her down, Yuri continued to look out the window. She knew the shit was crazy, especially since she'd run him away.

The more time went on, the more her heart hurt. Maybe she should've listened to him, maybe she should've given him a chance. Maybe he'd changed, maybe she'd changed. After all, she wasn't perfect, she also contributed to their breakup. Perhaps she should've trusted him more, listened more and maybe complained and accused less.

Didn't she owe it to herself, owe it to him, owe it to their daughter to see what could be?

While she lay in bed staring into the night, her stomach tossed and turned as her heart begged with her to check out the window once more. Anxiously she got out of bed and walked swiftly through her house, her bare feet slapping against the cold wood floor. She took a deep breath before pulling the curtain back. As she ran her hands across the glass, in between the raindrops she saw Britt sitting there. Instantly her heart stopped. She couldn't believe it, there he was, soaking wet and sitting on her stoop.

She stepped away from the window and opened the door. "What are you doing out here?"

"What *you* doing out here?"

"I forgot something."

"What?" He stood up. "What'd you forget?"

"You . . . I forgot you . . ." She walked onto the stoop and stepped into his embrace. The rain fell heavily from the sky, causing the curls in her hair to melt and stick to her head like silk. He brushed her hair away from her face and they began kissing each other on the lips repeatedly as Britt told her he loved her at least a thousand times before engaging in a passionate kiss. "I wanna marry you. I wanna be with you forever. I wanna call you my wife, my woman. Please, baby, please. I'm never leaving you."

Basking in his scent she asked, "You think this can last forever?"

Bending down on his right knee and taking her left hand, he said, "Shhhh . . . this is forever."

Acknowledgments

To My Father and Savior Jesus Christ: I thank you so much for continuing to bless me, for seeing beyond my faults and fulfilling my needs. This year has truly been a test and I thank You for never leaving my side. I will forever give all thanks and praises to You, as without You, neither I, nor any of my books would've been written!

To my children: Mommy loves you!

To my husband: thanks for taking the baby and letting me write. You are truly an inspiration to me.

To my parents who are always in my corner: I couldn't ask for more!

To my editor, Melody Guy, for being simply wonderful. I hope to make you proud! And to the One World/Ballantine staff and family, thank you for believing in me!

To my wonderful and loving family, who call me on the phone and say "Guess what I saw somebody reading?!" (LOL). Thank you for your never-ending support.

To my church family: thank you for your support!

To my friends: I purposely didn't name names this go round because there is always someone who feels left out, but to all of those who I am very close to, whether we speak often or not, know that I love and appreciate you, for your realness and for always being there. I will always be indebted to you.

Oh, wait. There is one name that I must call (sorry y'all). To my cousin Kaareem who came to my house and asked me every day if there was a way he could write four lines and still get paid. Here, fill these in,

_____

_____

_____! (LOL)

To the readers, fans, bookstores, and book clubs: I saved the best for last. Thank you for your undying support, for your e-mails, and for your encouragement! Please email me at risque215@aol.com and let me know your thoughts! You can also visit me at myspace/ risquetheauthor.

To everyone who understood when Sade sang: *There's a quiet storm and it never felt like this before,* I wrote this for you!

Love y'all
Risqué

About the Author

RISQUÉ is the erotic pseudonym of an *Essence* bestselling author. She lives in New Jersey where she is working on her next novel. Visit her online at www.myspace.com/risquetheauthor.